DON'T LOOK FOR ME

Also by Wendy Walker

The Night Before
Emma in the Night
All Is Not Forgotten

DON'T LOOK FOR ME

WENDY WALKER

ORION

First published in Great Britain in 2020 by Orion Fiction
an imprint of The Orion Publishing Group Ltd
Carmelite House, 50 Victoria Embankment
London EC4Y 0DZ

An Hachette UK Company

1 3 5 7 9 10 8 6 4 2

A CIP catalogue record for this book is
available from the British Library.

ISBN (Trade Paperback) 978 1 4091 9006 6
ISBN (eBook) 978 1 4091 9008 0

Printed in Great Britain by Clays Ltd, Elcograf S.p.A

www.orionbooks.co.uk

For my mother,
Terrilynne Kempf Boling

Day one

The sky grows dark as I drive.

I tell myself to concentrate, to focus on the two narrow lanes of smooth, black asphalt and the double yellow lines that divide them.

The road feels like a tunnel, carved between walls of brown cornfields which flank the road on both sides and go on as far as the eye can see. Darkness now hovers above and below, and from side to side. It's everywhere.

I hear the woman on the radio talk of the storm, but she is muted by thoughts that will not relent as the events of this terrible day unravel in my mind.

This stretch of Route 7 passes through an endless chain of small New England towns—not the quaint villages farther south, but the old industrial hubs that have been left to decay.

Neglected farmland, dilapidated houses, abandoned factories— they stand like tombstones. I wonder where people live. Where they buy groceries. Where they work and go out to dinner. Why they don't leave.

The unease causes my shoulders to rise and my back to straighten. It's the same every time I pass through. These towns will haunt me well into the night.

There's a gas station up ahead. The Gas n' Go. It sits at the intersection of Route 7 and an eerie road that leads to the heart of one of these towns. I have never been down that road, and I don't ever intend to. Still, this seems to be the spot where outsiders find themselves in need of gas as they journey from southern Connecticut into western Massachusetts. There must be half a dozen boarding schools and small colleges which are accessed from Route 7. Sometimes I recognize cars, even faces, when I have to stop.

And I will have to stop today. The gas light has been on for miles now.

After the Gas n' Go, it's two hours to my home at the southern end of the state. I have already passed the green welcome sign. *Welcome to Connecticut.*

Home.

It will be just after nine. My husband, John, will likely be out. At the gym. At work. Having drinks with a friend. My daughter, Nicole, will also be out somewhere. Anywhere that's not near me. She just turned twenty-one so she has options now. Options that keep me up at night, watching the clock. Listening for the door.

The dogs will bark and jump on my coat. They'll only want food. They save their affection for my husband. He was the one who brought them home after Annie died, so they've been his dogs more than mine.

The house will smell like Fantastik and lavender dryer sheets because it's Thursday, and on Thursday the cleaners come. I wonder if they'll remember to clear the ashes from the fireplace in our bedroom. It's late October and cold enough for a fire. John likes to sit in bed with the fire burning while he watches television.

He had one going last night. He was asleep by the time I made it up the stairs, though now I remember that the fire had a fresh log. Conclusions are quick to follow and one hand now covers my gaping mouth.

Am I too sensitive? Am I just being too me, too *Molly*? I hear these thoughts with John's voice. *Stop being so Molly.* He has come to use my name as an adjective that allows him to dismiss me. But, no—I'm not wrong about the log on the fire. He was pretending to be asleep.

The day unravels and I can't stop my thoughts.

My son, Evan, attends one of the boarding schools off this road. He was recruited as a freshman to play football. He's a junior now, and a starting lineman this season. I make this trip every other Thursday to watch his home games. The season is half over and they are leading the ranks. They may win the entire league this year.

The drive is four hours each way. John tells me I'm crazy to make the trip twice a month. He tells me Evan doesn't care. Nicole has harsher words for me. She tells me Evan doesn't want me there. That I embarrass him by going. That he's not a little boy anymore and *he doesn't need his mommy watching him play.*

He has changed. She's right about that. He knows the power he has on the field. I hadn't seen it before today. It was in his stance, his walk. It was in his eyes.

And it was in his cruelty. I wonder when that began. If it's new. Or only new that I can see it.

I waited for him outside the field house where the team enters the locker room. I picture him now, as the day plays out again, slowly, painfully.

How he walked with his friends, the enormous bag hanging over his shoulder, high-tops unlaced, baseball hat turned backward, and a mischievous smile that probably had something to do with talk about a girl.

In that moment, before his eyes caught sight of me and his face changed, I felt my heart fill with pride.

These thoughts come, and like the log on the fire, they don't go. My boy, my sweet Evan, the easy middle child, walking like he owned the world. A smile pulled clear across my face as I waited for his eyes to turn and see me at the door.

And they did turn. And they did see.

And then they widened and looked away. He grew closer, and still, they did not return to me. He positioned himself between two of his friends and passed through the door, leaving me in awe of his dismissiveness.

It is just now, one hundred and eleven miles later, that I feel the bite of it.

My vision blurs. I wipe away tears. *Christ*, I hear John. *Stop being so Molly! He's a teenager.*

But the thought won't leave, this image of his back turned as he walked into the building.

I look up at the dark clouds stirring in the sky and see the sign for the Gas n' Go sitting atop a giant pole. The storm is a hurricane. I am driving right into its path.

John said this was another reason I shouldn't make the trip today. The school could cancel the game if the storm got too close, and even if they didn't, I would surely run into it on the way home.

The storm, Evan not caring.

And Annie. He stopped short of saying it, but the words lingered between us.

Today is the anniversary of her death. Five years ago, on this day, we lost our youngest child. She was nine years old.

No. I will not think of Annie. I will not go backward. I will go forward.

Put one foot in front of the other.

I learned this in grief counseling. I used to be a middle school science teacher, where the focus is on learning to analyze problems by breaking them down into pieces and forming hypotheses—so I studied the grief this way. Objectively. Clinically. We are not wired to witness the death of a child. To endure it. To survive it. But like every other human defect, we have used science to outsmart our own biology. We can take a brain that is shredded ear to ear and we can put it back together with mantras like this one. Mantras that have been tested in clinical trials. Vetted in peer articles and TED Talks and now appear in self-help books.

You just put one foot in front of the other, Molly. Every day, just one more step.

Had I not had other children to care for, I would not have been able to take these steps. I would have died. Let myself die. Found a way to die. The pain was not survivable. And yet I survived.

Forward.

But the day continues to unravel, back now, to the morning.

Nicole was just coming in from one of her nights. I don't know where she slept. Her skin has gone pale, her hair long and unruly. She's become lean from running. She runs for miles and miles. She runs until she is numb, head to toe. Inside and out. Then she sleeps all day. Stays out all night. She is a lean, fierce, unruly warrior. And yet the pain still gets inside her.

Where have you been all night? I asked. The usual exchange followed, about how this was none of my business . . . *but* it was my business because she's living in my house and what about her GED class and trying to dig herself out of this hole . . . *but* it's my fault she's in the hole; she's in the hole because of Annie and her grief and because not everyone can just get over it . . . *but* when is she going to stop using her sister's death as an excuse for getting expelled from her private school senior year, never going back?

She shrugged, looked me straight in the eye. When did she become like this? This soldier, ready to fight off anyone who comes too close?

What about you? When are you going back to work? she asked.

She likes to remind me that I, too, stopped living—breathing, yes, but not *really* living.

I had no response to my daughter this morning. I had no response to my son this afternoon.

I didn't even see Evan after the game. I waited by the door but he must have gone out a different way. I almost marched straight to his dorm to tell him what I thought of his behavior. To do what a mother does when she knows she's right and when her child needs to learn a lesson.

The sign for the Gas n' Go grows closer, the clouds darker as these thoughts come. I didn't find him. I didn't do what I now think a mother should have done. A good mother.

Suddenly, I know why.

The car slows. I step on the gas, but it doesn't respond.

I am not a good mother.

I can't hold them back now, the thoughts of my dead child. *Annie.* Not that they ever really leave me. They are always lurking, hiding, wearing disguises so I don't see them as they sneak up.

I steer to the shoulder. The wheel is stiff. The car is dead. When it stops, I try the ignition, but it won't turn over.

I see the message on the dashboard. I have run out of gas.

How long has the light been on? I have been preoccupied by

this day. By these thoughts. John was right. I should not have made this trip. Not today.

I look down Route 7 and see the entrance for the station. It can't be more than thirty feet. The wind whips hard, rocking the car. I can see the rain coming on an army of clouds. A blanket closing over the sky. I can't tell how far away they are. How much time I have.

Thoughts exploding. Heart pounding. What have I done?

Now comes the thought about the fire last night. We have four fireplaces in our house, all of them wood burning. I have been making fires and stoking fires since we moved there twelve years ago. I know what a log looks like when it's just been placed on top of the flames.

I have no umbrella, just a flimsy jacket. I put it on anyway. I reach for my purse and tuck it inside. It's only thirty feet.

I open the door, get out, close it behind me. And I run, clutching the purse. I run into the wind which is more powerful than I imagined.

I run and think about that log which had just been put there—last night—on the fire. John wasn't asleep. John was pretending to be asleep so he wouldn't have to see me, even just long enough to say good night.

It's not the first time.

Flashes of the fight with Nicole break free as my body pushes through the wind. We fight every day now.

Open your eyes!

The fight had been so fast and furious, I had not processed each word. But I do now.

They are open. I see you clear as day, Nicole.

Not to me. To your own husband!

I can't see what's right in front of me. He never comes home for dinner. He pretends to be asleep when I come into our bedroom.

My husband doesn't love me anymore. My husband loves someone else.

This thought feels old, like a jagged stone I've been carrying in my coat pocket, trying to rub it smooth. But no matter how much I dig my fingers in, the edges never soften.

And then, the words I had not heard before, but had felt many times. Still, hearing them from my own daughter twisted the knife.

I hate you!

Tears fall as I run.

Annie. Wispy blond hair resting on delicate shoulders. Big, round eyes and long lashes. I can still feel her in my arms. Her life just beginning. *Annie.*

Annie!

And now I know why the thoughts have all come. They have been leading me to this one, last thought. This naked admission.

I am not a good mother because I did not drive four hours to watch my son play football so that he would feel loved. I drove four hours so that I could feel loved.

The log in that fireplace. My daughter's words. *I hate you.*

Evan was all that was left. I had to see his face, see him thriving, so I could validate my life.

Gasps of breath. The wind is strong and the air cold. My lungs are on fire.

Maybe Evan knew. Maybe he could sense it seeping from my skin. The need I wanted him to fill which must have felt like poison. A mother shouldn't need things from her child.

I caused Nicole's demise. She is certain of it and it now feels real, though disorienting. I went to my son under false pretenses, caused him pain. Caused him to lash out with cruelty. My husband pretends to sleep so he won't have to look at me.

Yes, I think as the grief spins violently in my head. *I am a bad mother.* This is an objective fact. There's no way around it.

I let a child die.

I am at the entrance to the Gas n' Go. I look up and see there are no cars. No lights on inside the store. Orange cones stand in front of the pumps.

The rain comes suddenly. The blanket covering the sky is now a broken dam. It's dark but I can still see the writing on a cardboard sign. *Closed for storm!*

I stop and let the rain wash over me as I stare at these words.

Evan, Nicole, John. I am a burden to them now because they don't love me. Because they can't love me.

It's been five years to this very day that they stopped.

Five years since Annie died.

Five years since she ran into the road.

Five years since I struck her with my car. Since I killed her.

Tears, rain, wind. I walk a few paces to the intersection, to the road, Hastings Pass, that leads to the town. There is nothing but pavement and dirt riding over hills, and the dead cornstalks in fields that go on and on. Not another car in sight.

The hurricane is a category four. That's what they said on the radio. I remember the voices now. I remember the name of this town. *Hastings.* I have driven into the eye of the storm. I hear the mantra in my head. *Don't give up.* I feel the weight of my guilt like a rock I hold above my head. How I fight to keep it from falling. I think now that maybe it's time. Maybe I can just let it fall.

Maybe I can just walk away.

These words bring a sudden, jarring euphoria.

Walk away. Just walk away.

The road with the brown cornfields, darkened by the angry storm, is now a thing of beauty. An oasis. An escape. My legs begin to move, pulling my body. My mind is in a trance. Sedated by these words and the promises they offer.

You can leave all of this behind.

You can start again.

You can put down the rock, the burden you carry.

I walk along this road until I am part of the storm. Numb to the wet. Numb to the cold. Numb to the truth about the promises. And for the first time since I killed my child I am at peace.

Please let me go. Let me walk away. I feel the words in my head like a prayer.

Please, they whisper. *Don't look for me.*

I don't know how long I walk, or how far, when I see light coming from behind. I turn to find headlights moving slowly toward me. They're high and bright. It's a truck of some kind. Tall but also long. And in spite of the trance I am in and the peace it has brought, I feel both of my arms rise above my head and wave wildly, the purse still clutched in one hand.

The truck pulls in front of me and comes to a stop.

I walk closer until I am inches beside the passenger window. There are two figures inside.

I make a shield with my hand, just above my eyes to keep the rain from my face. I lean in closer and see the window come down a few inches.

"The storm's coming, you know—you shouldn't be out here." It's a man's voice. Friendly. But also urgent. "Do you want a ride to town?"

Another voice calls from the truck. The window comes down a few more inches.

The voice of a little girl. The face of an angel.

"Well? Do you or don't you?" she asks.

I stare at her, at her blond hair and bright eyes, and beyond her to the man.

I stare at her, this young girl, and, God help me, for a split second I see my dead child.

And then I see this road for what it truly is. A mirage. An illusion. And the words that caused my legs to carry me away from my life—liars. Their promises nothing more than cheap deceptions.

The guilt will never leave me. I will never leave my family.

"Yes," I say.

The passenger window of the truck closes and the girl disappears. But now I hear the click of the locks opening. I reach for the handle of the door to the second row, desperate to be out of the storm. Desperate to get back to my family. To forget what I have almost done. This storm might have killed me. The wind and the cold. Then the guilt would be theirs to carry. John, Nicole, Evan. How could I be that selfish after everything I've already done to them? I will never think of it again.

I climb inside, close the door. Relief fighting with despair.

And before I can clear the rain from my eyes and see what's really before me, I hear the click again. The doors locking.

Locking shut.

2

Day thirteen

The phone rang. Stopped. Rang again.

Nicole Clarke awoke, felt a body beside her. It didn't stir.

The ringing was loud. The daylight bright, even through closed eyes. Remorse crept in as her hand reached toward the sound.

She pulled the phone to her ear, eyes pinching tightly together, then moved herself closer to the edge of the bed so she was no longer touching the stranger she'd brought home.

She managed a *hello*. Her voice was hoarse.

"Nicole Clarke?" a woman asked. She seemed nervous. "I'm calling about the disappearance of a woman in Hastings."

The name of that town. Adrenaline, nausea. Nic didn't answer.

Then came the flashes from the night before.

Vodka shots . . . the man at the end of the bar . . . now in her bed.

She'd told him to leave in the early morning hours. Or maybe she'd passed out before she could.

The woman continued.

"My name is Edith Moore. I hope this is the right thing to do, but I may have something . . . I may know something about that woman—your mother, right?"

The man groaned, draped a heavy arm over her chest. Nic pushed it aside.

There had been a moment last night when his arms couldn't hold her tight enough. Now they repulsed her. It was always the same.

She rolled onto her side and pulled her knees to her stomach. "Hold on," she said, waiting for the nausea to recede.

The calls about her mother had begun to slow. Most of the crazies had moved on to other things. Other ways to feed their appetite for attention. The psychologist had explained it to them, why people feel drawn to these stories, to other people's grief, and why they seek ways to get involved even if they muddy the search for the truth with their lies. Their made-up stories. Their bullshit.

There was also the reward money. A million dollars for her mother's safe return. Five hundred thousand for tips leading to her "whereabouts." Nothing brought out a liar like cash. Her father had hired an investigator to manage the tips.

The woman continued.

"I live in Schenectady, which is two hours from Hastings—over the border into New York. I was on my way home from a trip to Manhattan. I met some girlfriends there. That's why I was on the road."

Nic began with the questions that would likely end the conversation. *What day? What time? What road?*

The callers never did their homework. They usually got the town right. Sometimes the make and model of her mother's car—an Audi Q5, light blue. Stopped just before the gas station.

Edith Moore rattled off the answers. It was the last one that made Nic pay closer attention.

Hastings Pass.

Most people said they'd seen Molly Clarke on Route 7. That was where her car was found. That was the road that led to the casino where her credit card was used. It was always the best guess for the crazies. And the liars.

This was something new.

"What were you doing on Hastings Pass?" Nic asked. Her tone was harsh. "It's completely out of the way if you were heading to Schenectady from Manhattan."

Nic knew every inch of that town. *Hastings.* She knew every road, every field, every abandoned well her mother might have fallen down as she sought cover from the hurricane.

"I was trying to stop for the night because of the storm. There's a place there, the Hastings . . ."

"Hastings Inn." Nic was sitting up now.

"Yes—the Hastings Inn. I got to the inn around seven, but it was already boarded up. I knew I had to get out of the storm path, so I turned around, back toward Route 7. I was on Hastings Pass and I think I drove right past your mother."

Now came another voice. The man in her bed who'd overstayed his welcome. *Who's on the phone?*

Nobody . . . you need to go.

Nic waved at him, then toward the door, then to his clothes littered across the carpet of her bedroom. When he looked at her with confusion, she made it clearer.

"Please—just get out." But then, "I'm sorry."

She said it again. *I'm sorry, I'm sorry,* until he started to move.

And she was sorry. For last night and the nights before and the nights to come. She was sorry for so many nights since Annie died.

Back to the woman on the phone.

"Why didn't you come forward sooner? It's been two weeks."

"Like I said, I don't live in the area. And I don't really follow the news. But then a few days ago, I was catching up with one of the friends I met in the city and she asked me if I got caught in the storm, and then she mentioned a woman who went missing."

Nic listened carefully as she watched the man move about the room, grabbing a shirt, pants, underwear. These nights had to stop.

She knew they wouldn't.

Edith Moore continued, her voice trembling with excitement. "I looked up the story on the Internet and I just knew it was her! I saw her on that road. Hastings Pass—not Route 7. She was about a mile down the road. The rain had begun. She was soaking wet."

Nic rested her head in one hand as the facts from the case flooded out.

The car abandoned just before the gas station.

Out of gas.

Nothing inside but her cell phone, attached to the charger.

Every field, every home, everywhere searched and searched.

Then, two days later, her credit card used at a nearby casino resort.

And her clothes, still wet, found in the hotel room—along with the note.

The note which explained everything—and nothing.

"And you didn't stop? You didn't help her?" Nic asked.

The woman rambled on about how she slowed to a crawl, but then a truck came from the other direction.

"A truck?"

"Yes. It was a pickup truck. Dark color. It stopped and she got in."

Nic was on her feet, then quickly buckled over.

"I read everything I could find," the woman said. "About the car found the next morning and the gas station closed and then the winds and blackout. Oh, and how the town searched for her everywhere until they found that gut-wrenching note in a hotel room. Your poor mother and everything she'd been through. And then the case was closed, or reclassified, I think it said. They were calling it a 'walk away' in the press."

That was exactly how things had gone down.

Nic and her father had been there with the search parties. Four days in Hastings that had become a blur of images. Rough sketches of cold air and stiff cornstalks, stale bitter coffee on folding tables brought by the local residents. The bar across from the inn. Vodka. Tequila. A stranger in the back hallway—the bartender. It had not been pretty.

Then came the slow reveal of the family's bad behavior on the day of the disappearance.

Nic's cruel words in the kitchen overheard by the cleaners. Evan's shunning of his mother's visit witnessed by the kids on his team. And Molly Clarke's husband, John, who didn't even notice that his wife hadn't come home because he'd fallen asleep.

And why would that be? He had a million excuses. It took everything inside Nic not to give them the real one—that he didn't love his wife anymore. That he was having an affair. Nic had seen his car in town when he said he was at the office. She'd seen the way he avoided looking at her but then was suddenly polite and considerate, covering his tracks. There were so many changes, and they were recent. They were new, subtle changes. Except for the one that screamed out to be noticed. For the first time since his wife killed his daughter, he seemed happy.

All of this bad behavior had come on the anniversary of Annie's death five years before.

It was against this ugly and unforgivable backdrop that her mother's note was interpreted. Chicken-scratch words on a page from the hotel notepad found in the room. Words Nic had read just once, though she could still close her eyes and see the shape of each letter.

My beloved family, I am so very sorry. I couldn't make it home, and then I thought maybe you are better off without me. I pray you don't look for me. I pray for your happiness.

She signed it with her full name. *Molly Clarke.* The police said she had probably done that to make sure it found its way back to them—so the hotel would know who'd left it.

But she'd paid for the room with her credit card. It was in her name. And the words, the phrases—they didn't sound like her mother.

The note was sent to a handwriting expert. It matched the samples they'd provided. It matched the writing of Molly Clarke.

Still, she had fought against them. The local police. The state troopers. Even her father. They'd given her the statistics which supported the walk-away theory. Most adult women who disappear were trying to leave their lives behind. They came home when, if, they were ready.

What did she have to fight with? Remnants from the past, fragments of memories about a devoted mother who could never cause her children to suffer by leaving them? The truth was, Nic had no idea what was in her mother's head, what was even in her heart, or what narrative had been taking shape inside her—that she was a burden to them and they would be better off without her.

Nic had said as much to her face the morning before she left them.

The belief in her mother's betrayal had come as a shock, but then settled in quietly, burrowing into the hollow spaces alongside the grief and the guilt that Annie's death had carved. They were amorphous, covering every inch of her, living in every cell. And they had an insatiable yearning to be filled. The men and the alcohol were barely touching them anymore.

Evan had fared better. There'd been tears, but then his quick return to school. Her father had done his duty by wearing a somber face and taking care of his wife's elderly parents. They lived in a home and were already in the throes of dementia. Nic envied them. Now, nearly two weeks later, friends had stopped bringing casseroles. Everyone was returning to normal life because it was unbearable to remain in a state of grief and loss. Evan at school. Her father back to work and his after-work activities. And Nic, back to her nights.

Only they'd been getting worse.

Now the woman again. "The driver of that truck may know where she went."

Yes, Nic thought. *The driver might know why she left us.*

"Is there anything else you can tell me? Any details about her that you noticed? I have to ask."

"Yes, of course," Edith Moore said. "Let me think . . . well— there was something she did, and I don't know if it helps . . ."

"What?" Nic asked, suddenly desperate to have this be real. "What did she do?"

"When she waved at the truck—she used both arms, over her head, crossing back and forth. She had her purse in one of her hands, so it was odd, you know? That she didn't just wave at the truck with one hand. I remember thinking that it was strange."

Nic closed her eyes and saw her mother from years ago. At a cross country meet, standing at the finish line. Waving just like that—two arms overhead. She did it at Evan's games too. And when she was trying to get their attention at a pickup, or when they ignored her walking through the kitchen and she asked them how their day was.

They had all poked fun at her. And yet, they had all found it endearing.

Years ago—when there was still room for endearment.

"What about the purse?" Nic asked.

"It was orange. Very bright—oh, and there were letters on it. NEA. At the time, I assumed it was a monogram, but after I read about your mother and saw her name, I thought maybe it was the name of the designer."

"They're our names," Nic said. "The names of her children."

Her mother had ordered the purse herself. No one else would have been that morbid. And that's exactly what it was. A bright, bold, daily reminder that she had three children. *Nicole. Evan. Annie.* Three children, not two. And that one was dead. The giant gold "A" to punch her in the gut as she went about her day. That purse followed her everywhere.

Nic opened her eyes and let the truth find her.

This is real. This woman saw my mother.

"Why don't you come and meet me?" Edith Moore asked. "I can show you exactly where she was when the truck picked her up."

The thought was unbearable. *Hastings . . .*

"Maybe you can meet with the local police," Nic offered.

But the woman insisted. "I don't think that will go anywhere now, given what they believe."

Silence then. Nic closed her eyes and tried to chase away the sickness in her gut.

Hastings . . .

"The thing is," the woman said next, "no one is going to care about that poor woman on the road as much as her family."

Ten minutes later, Nic was throwing clothes in a duffel bag. Jeans, shirts, sweaters, sneakers. What else? Pajamas, underwear.

She went to the bathroom for her toothbrush, shampoo.

A voice crept in, whispering, *Is this just more running away?*

The grief counselor had her theories about Nic's behavior.

Don't run from the pain. You have to feel it before it will get better.

But she did feel it. And it never did get better.

There were things she'd said that morning to her mother that she hadn't told anyone. She couldn't even think them. Things about Annie.

She'd wanted to see misery on her mother's face instead of love. And she had succeeded. Now she had the image in her mind, placed there by Edith Moore—her mother standing in the rain, soaking wet. In the storm. A storm Nic had put her in with those horrible words.

And now, too, there was someone out there who knew where she'd gone. Someone who owned a truck. Someone who could help her get to her mother and tell her she didn't hate her, and *God*, take back the other things she'd said that morning. She chased the voices away. The good advice. The well-meaning guidance she knew would be coming. *She doesn't want to be found. Take care of yourself, Nicole.* But Nic knew things they didn't, things she'd said to drive her mother away.

This was her fault and now she had to make it right. She had to find her mother.

3

Day one

The girl wears a mask. She pulls it up after I enter the truck. It's some kind of medical mask which I can see now only in the reflection from the side mirror. The man wears a wool hat, pulled down low.

We drive through sheets of rain. A violent wind pushes against the truck.

"Thank you for stopping," I say. "I ran out of gas."

The girl turns around.

"That wasn't very smart," she says. Her voice is perky, like she's just stating the obvious and not rendering a judgment. Still, it is odd for a child her age not to know that she's done just that.

"You're right," I say.

The man smiles. "No harm done. The town's not far."

I notice his eyes dart up into the mirror so he can see me. He quickly looks away and glances at his daughter.

Daughter . . . I wonder now. I am making assumptions.

The girl keeps talking.

"I'm allergic to everything so I have to wear a mask when I'm outside the house. Does it make my voice sound funny?"

Her words pass through me. I look out the window wondering where we are, exactly how far from town. I can see nothing but the small pieces of road where the headlights strike the pavement. The sky is a canvas of black.

I smell gasoline and notice three plastic cans on the floor beside me. Otherwise, the truck is clean but old. The leather on the seats is cracked, worn all the way through in places.

"Hey!" the girl says, annoyed with me now. "Answer my question!"

My concern shifts quickly from the road and the black sky and the gas cans to the girl with the mask who has just admonished me for not paying attention and answering her question. I somehow pull the question from my immediate memory. *Something about the mask and her voice* . . . I take an educated guess.

"It sounds just fine to me," I say. She looks at me through the side mirror with folded eyes and I imagine her whole face is in a scowl.

So I smile. A big, warm smile through lips that tremble from the cold and now, also, from the realization that I am locked inside a truck with strangers.

"What's your name?" I ask. I try to be friendly. I just need a ride to town.

The girl looks at the man before answering. He nods and says, "Go ahead! Don't be shy," which is strange because she seems anything but shy to me.

She spins all the way around this time, smiling so wide I can see the creases of her cheeks poking out from the sides of the mask.

"Alice!" she says. I take a moment because the name sounds out something else in my mind. She says *Alice* but I hear *Annie*. And my heart skips just one long beat.

Alice again turns back to face the road, this time with a little bounce and the man tousles her hair. It's playful but awkward, like he doesn't do this often.

The truck slows.

I look through the windshield to where the headlights are shining and see storefronts with boarded windows. As we pass, they fade back into the darkness.

The truck rolls down the street. The man keeps his eyes ahead.

"Is that the town?" I ask.

We pass a building that looks like a diner from the shape of the gray silhouette and the large sheets of plywood that cover a row of windows. Beside it I see a sign on a lawn. It's merely a flash as our lights pass. It says *The Hastings Inn.*

"Maybe there—at the inn. You could just drop me . . ."

The man looks carefully out the window, scanning the street.

"Looks like it's closed. Everything's boarded up . . . and gosh—looks like the whole town's lost power."

My voice cracks as I ask the next question. "Can we go back to my car? Maybe I can use some of the gas you have here? Even just a gallon. There's another station about half an hour away—at the casino, right? I saw a sign for it on Route 7 . . ."

Please, please, please! Let us go back to my car and then my life two hours from here, no matter what's become of it. I crave it now and I don't even know why. I crave my irreverent daughter who hates me and my cruel son who dismisses me. I miss my husband who pretends to be asleep when I come into our bedroom to be with him and I miss the dogs who want nothing but food. God help me, but I even miss the pain that never leaves.

It comes from a hidden place. A primal instinct. This missing of things.

The truck makes a turn and picks up speed.

"They're empty," he says now. "We were on our way to get them filled but the station was already closed."

I look at the gas cans. I swear I can hear liquid splashing inside them but maybe I'm mistaken. Or maybe what I hear is nothing more than a few drops left at the bottom.

Why would he lie? The gas station was closed.

"What can we do?" I ask now.

"Road's blocked. Tree just came down. Didn't you hear it on the radio? Only one way to go now."

I didn't hear anything. I can't hear a radio over the sound of the engine. And how was it reported so quickly?

The girl seems to know where we're headed.

I open my purse to grab my phone. I have to tell them what's happened, John and Nicole. I dig through the contents—wallet, brush, mints, tissues. I take them out and place them in my lap until the purse is empty.

Now I remember—the phone was in the charger, out of the purse, sitting on the seat.

I have no phone. A new kind of fear rises.

I ask now—

"Do you have a cell phone I could use? My family is probably very worried."

Alice looks at her folded hands which sit in her lap.

And the man shakes his head.

"No. Sorry. I left it at the house. Don't worry. We'll be there soon. You can make your call and we'll see what can be done about getting you home."

"Or you could just stay with us tonight!" Alice says. Again, turning back. Again, with exuberance.

The man is smiling now.

"One thing at a time," he says.

And so we drive. We make turns. Left turns. Right turns. Deeper into the woods.

I can't bear the silence. I can't bear not knowing what this is. So I do what I think would be normal if my mind weren't running in circles.

"I'm Molly, by the way. Molly Clarke. I really appreciate your help."

Alice giggles nervously. The man stares ahead.

I try to catch his eyes in the rearview mirror.

"Can I ask your name as well?"

He looks at Alice. Alice stares back at him and pokes his shoulder with her finger.

He shrugs, his attention returning to the road. His face is amused.

It's Alice who answers.

"His name is Mickey Mouse!" she says. Then she laughs.

The man smiles and I realize this is a little game they play. Alice gets to make up his name for strangers.

I play along, though I feel ill.

"Should I call you Mickey or Mr. Mouse?"

He laughs out loud but doesn't answer.

The truck moves slowly through the storm. The storm moves quickly around us. Time and distance lose their calibration.

I cannot see beyond the headlights. The wind is powerful, rain blowing sideways. Falling hard. Turns and turns, avoiding fallen trees, the man tells me, though I can't see them from the second row.

He does not make conversation. He does not ask the obvious questions, like who I am or where I'm from. I think then that he is just nervous about the storm, about getting Alice home safely.

I taste the blood on my lip from where I have bitten down too hard. I am warm now but I can't stop shaking.

The truck slows again and this time stops fully. Alice perks up. She looks out and sees what I see—a tall metal fence. There is a gate with a lock and we are stopped in front of a dirt driveway.

The man gets out. Alice doesn't ask why. He pulls up the hood of his jacket but it does little to keep him from getting drenched. He runs up to the gate and stops at a large chain that winds between two of the fence posts. It looks as though he's turning a manual lock. One hand holds steady. The other twists, then pulls hard. He unwinds the chain and a section of the fence swings open.

I look at the lock on the car door which brushes against my right arm. It did not release when he left the truck, but still, I slide my hand to the handle and pull as softly as I can. It does not click open. A child lock must be on. I see through the console and wonder if my body will fit between the seats—if I can climb over into the driver's side and make an escape through that door. Alice is too small to stop me. But loud enough to call to the man and, surely, he would catch me in fewer than a dozen strides.

Then I stop myself. We are at a house. A family lives here. Maybe there's a wife, more children. Alice and her father were just out to get the gas in the cans which sit on the floor beside me. And some bottles of water. I see them in the front seat by Alice's legs. They happened upon me. They offered me a ride.

Stop being so Molly, I tell myself. But *Molly* killed her child. *Molly* knows that unthinkable things can happen and now she has thoughts that are sometimes not realistic, that are *hyperbolic*, as John would say. Still, she thinks them. Because one time, they were real. And they did happen.

Molly.

I think about the log in the fireplace last night and wonder if that was a crazy, senseless thought. And Evan with his cruelty . . . and Nicole—does she really hate me?

Alice speaks now.

"We're home!" She sounds victorious.

The man runs back. He gets in and closes the door.

"Wow! That's some storm!" he says, shaking off the rain.

He pulls the drive shaft down and the truck moves through the open gate. On the other side, he stops again. Gets out. Runs to the fence to put back the chains. And locks us here, inside this property on this dirt driveway.

He gets back in and we drive. I pay close attention this time. I watch the speedometer hover at twenty-eight miles per hour. I count the seconds in my head. I count them like a school girl. *One Mississippi . . . two Mississippi . . .*

I count to twenty. That's maybe a sixth of a mile—a sixth of a mile to get from the road to the house.

I try to store this information somewhere inside my scrambled mind. I try to picture what it means for this property and the house that I can see now in front of the truck when it comes to a stop.

The man shuts off the engine and removes the keys.

He gets out and runs to the passenger side. He opens my door, then Alice's, and he scoops her up. She wraps her arms around his neck and squeals when the rain hits her face and her body. She presses herself against him the way a child does in the arms of her father, and a wave of relief takes me by surprise.

Alice loves this man and he loves her. Where there is love, there cannot be danger.

"Come on!" he calls to me now. I get out and follow behind them. I feel myself pull my inadequate but fashionable rain jacket up over my head as far as it will go and I laugh because I am overwhelmed now, with this relief. The laughter brings tears, which I stifle before I catch up to my rescuers.

I see little as we walk. Just the shadow of a large porch with posts and wide steps with no rail. I watch my feet as I climb. *One, two, three, four . . .*

Six steps bring us to the porch floor. Three steps bring us to the door, which opens without a key. A waft of dry air emerges, smelling of must and wood.

When the door closes again, we are all three inside, immersed in the darkness. The rain pounds on the roof but it is quieted by the walls which absorb the sound. The man sets Alice down and walks to a side table. The darkness is suddenly broken by the bright light of an electric lantern.

"I'm gonna try to start the generator," he says. "I think there's enough gas in there to last the night. Alice, why don't you show Molly to the guest room. Get her a towel from the closet."

He says my name so casually, like we're old friends.

Towels and guest rooms and lanterns. There are no other family members here, but this will do. *Yes,* I think. *This will do—until I can make the call.*

He hands me the lantern and goes back outside. Alice takes off her mask. It's a white medical mask, the kind you can buy at the drug store. I've used them before when painting a room, though that was years ago, when John and I were just starting out. When we used to do things ourselves because we had more time than money.

The thought of my husband steals my breath as the feeling rushes in. I still love him. Even if he has stopped loving me.

Alice has bright blue eyes and soft blond hair and skin like snow. It never sees the sun. Still, she is not gaunt. Her cheeks are rosy from the cold. And all of these colors—the blue and yellow and white and red, they are stunning. The colors of youth. The colors of a little girl. It fills my heart, then empties through the hole I made five years ago.

I carry the lantern and follow closely behind her through a living room and past a door to a kitchen on the right. Then down a hallway where we stop. She opens a closet which holds towels and blankets and sheets. Normal things. *Normal.*

She pulls out a worn white bath towel and hands it to me. I take it with one hand and wipe my face dry.

"Come on!" she says cheerfully.

I look down the hallway but don't get my bearings. There are doors which are all closed.

I want to be dry. I want to be warm. I want the man to return so I can use the phone and call my family. These things all feel close now and so I want them with greater urgency.

We enter the first room on the left. It has a bed and a dresser and an oval mirror which hangs on the wall. The bed is neatly made with a quilt and two pillows. It has a private bathroom which I can see through an open door. The one window has been boarded with plywood. *For the storm,* I tell myself. Like the diner back in town.

"This is the guest room. You can sleep here tonight," Alice says. "I sleep right next door."

I smile at her. She smiles back. But I have no intention of sleeping in this house.

John will come for me—even in the storm. Even if he doesn't love me.

"Can I wait with you?" she asks.

"Sure," I say. The house is dark. I understand. But then we both hear footsteps moving about. Stopping, shifting, moving again. A new light comes down the hall and suddenly the man is there in the doorway.

"Go get ready for bed," he says to Alice. He holds two lanterns and he gives one to her. She obeys, leaving us alone.

Then he speaks to me.

"I turned on the generator. It'll run the heat. Use the lantern to get around tonight. There are some clothes in the dresser. You can wear those if you want."

I stare at the man now, the towel pressed to my face all the way up to my eyes.

"I need to make that call—I'm sure my husband will find a way to get me home."

Even as I ask, I already know the answer. I know because he hasn't offered me a phone and that is strange. *Not Molly strange*, I think. *Truly strange.*

And then the answer comes.

"The thing is—we don't get cell reception out here and the landlines are down. I just checked the phone in the kitchen."

I nod and manage a polite smile. I don't know why I do this. A habit from living where I live, in a culture of emotional suppression.

"Can we try, at least? Maybe a different part of the house, or outside? Or I can borrow the truck and call from the road, farther down?" And then I continue, rambling now. "Because my husband and daughter are going to be very worried. I was supposed to be home over an hour ago and I left my car on the side of the road. I'm sure people are already wondering whose it is. I imagine the police will be looking for me and I would feel terrible using up their resources like that."

I ramble and stare at his face, searching for acknowledgment or surprise or anything resembling a human response. But he just watches me, watches my lips move, and smiles sympathetically.

"We can go in the morning—as soon as the sun is up," he says when I stop talking. He places his hand on my shoulder and gives it a gentle squeeze. "I know it's strange to be in someone else's house. I would feel the same. But we're not in the suburbs here. You could have gotten hurt out there—that wind would have knocked you right off your feet. And the cold—it's going down below thirty degrees tonight."

He looks at me. I look at him, frozen until he takes his hand off my shoulder.

"You okay?" he asks.

Again, I nod politely, as I wonder why he mentioned the suburbs. How does he know where I live?

He leaves me alone then. I stare at the space where he stood and I let his words sink in. I let the words find reason inside my unreasonable head.

I am the very embodiment of suburbia. Surely he just put pieces together. He must see people like me driving through here every day, on their way to the schools, stopping to get gas.

And there is a dangerous storm outside. Wind. Rain. Cold. Roads are likely blocked. Lines are down—power, phone. Everything on a wire is dead. And there's no cell phone reception. All of those are facts that I either know to be true or are likely true.

Stop being so Molly! I command myself.

I close the door to the bedroom. I look in the dresser and find clothing. Women's clothing. I find pajama bottoms and a sweatshirt. They are dry. And they smell of laundry detergent.

They are freshly washed. And I wonder if this means they are freshly worn.

Where is their owner?

I go to the bathroom and close the door. I take off my wet clothes, put on the dry clothes of a strange woman. Back in the bedroom, I hang my wet clothes on everything I can find. A chair. A radiator. A dresser. A bedpost.

I climb beneath the quilt and sheets. I curl myself into a ball.

The tiniest ball I can make myself into. I leave the lantern on at the foot of the bed because I am not quite ready to be in the dark.

I let the fear show its face and then I tell it exactly what it is. Just like my unreasonable thoughts are remnants from the past, this fear is just guilt. That's all. Just guilt. I did something stupid and now my family will worry and the police will come looking. But I will make it right in the morning. Like the man said. *As soon as the sun is up.*

Facts are facts and the facts add up. Fear is just guilt finding a way in. Finding a way to masquerade because I don't want to face it.

It folds around me like another blanket. A familiar blanket.

This blanket of guilt.

4

Day thirteen

astings Pass.

Nic hated this road. She hated the way it fell off at the shoulder into dirt and gravel and how the dirt hung in the air long after being kicked up. She hated the thick, brown cornfields that stood high on either side like a scene out of a Stephen King novel. She hated how it was straight as an arrow, but rose and fell over the small hills so she could never pass a car that was driving too slow.

Hastings Pass intersected Route 7 at the Gas n' Go. It was a left-hand turn coming from the south. A right-hand turn coming from the north.

Her mother had been coming from the north. The car parked just under thirty feet from the station. Parked on the shoulder and abandoned.

The call had come the day after the storm. Friday. Midmorning, before they'd even noticed that she hadn't returned home. Nic had been sleeping off one of her nights. Her father had gone to the office like it was any other day. Never thought about the meat thawed on the counter, or the dry cleaning hanging on the door, or the dogs not fed, or the coffee not made. He said he assumed she'd gotten in late and was asleep in the guest room. *How considerate she was not to wake him.* He didn't check for her car. Didn't think to. Didn't notice. His mind had been preoccupied with relief, Nic imagined. It must be hard to look at your wife after being with another woman.

She wanted to hate him for that. But there was no road map for what their family had been through. Molly Clarke reminded her husband of his dead child. Molly Clarke reminded Nic of the way Annie died, and the role she'd played in the series of events that led to her death. And wrapped up in the horrible memories of that horrible day were the sweet memories of sweet moments, and there was no way to untangle them.

Strong arms holding her. Soft hands brushing her hair. The smell of homemade bread and bubble bath. A loud voice cheering on the sidelines. A soft voice whispering in the dark. *It's okay, I'm here.* So many sweet, sweet memories that were now too twisted with grief to be remembered.

Molly Clarke's voice and face and smell could provoke feelings that were at war inside her. Agony and bliss. Rage and love. Nic had avoided her, just like her father had. It was painful to be with her.

Two miles down Hastings Pass was the police station. Past the inn and the diner. Past the bar, the auto body shop.

After the downtown were strips of houses on small lots of land—ranches, capes, colonials, in various states of disrepair. A scarce few seemed cared for, but in a way that evoked desperation, a last, futile breath. Flower baskets hanging on a broken porch.

Then came the station and town hall. After that, Hastings Pass continued to the river, with dirt roads on either side leading into the woods where there would be bleaker dwellings, deeper poverty.

The gray sky added to the grimness, an exclamation point on the despair. Nic remembered now, how it crept inside.

They had never gone down Hastings Pass before the disappearance. Her mother said it made her uneasy. The few times Nic had gone with her to visit Evan, they had not even stopped at the gas station.

And now Nic knew everything about this town they had always driven past. Hastings was built to support a chemical company in the 1950s. The company used the river to dispose of its waste. No one knew any better. Or no one gave a shit. A pharmaceutical manufacturer eventually took its place and sustained the town until the recession pulled it under. And then the dominoes fell.

Towns like this were littered all the way up the Housatonic River, into New York State, up to the Canadian border—left abandoned like a jilted first wife, trying to take care of its children with whatever resources it could find. Farming, mostly. And then unemployment and government jobs. Cops, clerks, construction workers.

Nic pulled into the small gravel lot at the police station and parked her mother's car. She looked in the rearview mirror out of nothing more than habit, really. Her hair was in a ponytail and she'd stopped wearing makeup years ago. There wasn't much to see, or to check, or to fix.

Not that she would bother if there was.

She closed the mirror, irritated with this relic from her former life.

She left the car and walked inside.

The department consisted of four people—a secretary, a chief, and two uniformed officers. The state provided troopers when additional resources were required, like the night of the storm. Like her mother's disappearance.

Inside, the secretary, Mrs. Urbansky, was at a desk behind a tall counter.

"Nicole!"

She got up and lumbered her large girth around the metal corners. She reached her hands over the counter and grabbed Nic by the shoulders.

"Nicole," she said again, her face contorting with sympathy. "How are you? How was the drive?"

Mrs. Urbansky had been nothing but kind to her during the search for her mother. It hadn't been easy to let it in then. And it wasn't now.

"Fine," Nic answered.

Mrs. Urbansky let up on her hold and crossed her elbows on the counter. The soft flesh of her arms bulged out from the creases as she rested her chin on her knuckles.

"So, you think you have a new lead?"

Nic shrugged. "We'll find out tomorrow."

"So odd after all that searching, and the reward money . . ." Mrs. Urbansky said, apprehension in her voice.

She wasn't wrong—the search parties had been thorough. They had begun at the edge of the dense fields that lined Hastings Pass and Route 7, and moved through the tall, sharp stalks until they ended. Some of the property bled right into other fields. Some was divided up by split-rail fencing. Others were met with lawns belonging to old farmhouses. When all was said and done, Nic, her father, the police, and volunteers, had covered thirty-two square miles of land. Which was a lot of land.

Houses were checked as well. Five miles in every direction from where the car was found. No one had seen Molly Clarke the night of the storm.

It all played on a loop now, a recurring bad dream.

Hastings. She'd spent much of those four days swinging between panic and sedation. She'd spent much of it in that bar. She could see the acknowledgment on Mrs. Urbanskys's face.

"But you never know, right?" the woman said, smiling now. "Come around, sweetheart. I'll take you back to see the chief."

Chief of police Charles Watkins. Most people just called him "the chief." Average height. Full head of hair. Nic remembered him better than the others because he had been in charge of things, or at least that was how it seemed.

Mrs. Urbansky had made a point to tell her about his dead wife—*Died of heart disease, and at such a young age!* She'd said it as though Nic might be interested, as a single woman herself. Never mind that Nic was just twenty-one and Watkins was old enough to have a dead wife, even if that wife had been relatively young when it came to dying.

She'd said it after the note was found, when the mood had lifted off the town just like the cloud cover from the storm. Hearing Mrs. Urbansky's voice now brought it back—the feeling as everyone began to believe that this was not a tragic accident but instead a scandal. A fun story to tell at the bar, the wealthy woman from the southern part of the state, the richer part, the enviable part. *Unhappy Housewife Leaves It All Behind; Walks Away from Kids and Husband . . .* And with the fun story, relief that their misery hadn't ensnared an outsider. A sign that their plight wasn't as dreadful as it seemed.

But, *yes, it was, Hastings*. It was every bit as dreadful.

Chief Watkins was in his office. The smell was the same—carpet cleaner and printer ink. A hint of mildew from the dying leaves outside.

He got up, nodded in her direction. After the time they had spent together, they were somewhere between a hug and a handshake. The nod served the situation.

"Sit," Watkins said.

Nic took a seat on a hard metal chair across from his desk.

"I'll leave you two." Mrs. Urbansky left, still smiling.

Watkins wore a beige uniform with short sleeves and a blue tie. There were patches sewn on the chest. A badge was pinned there as well. She had thought it then and she thought it again now, how he looked like a Boy Scout leader.

He leaned back and stretched his arms into the air, clasping his hands behind his head.

"Is this about the call?" he asked. "From the woman who says she saw your mother?"

"Yeah," Nic answered. She went on then to explain about the truck and the letters on the orange purse, and about Edith Moore and how she'd been driving from town that night.

Watkins nodded as though taking in the information.

"Okay," he said. "I get it. Why you came back. I would do the same if it was my family. Gotta sleep at night, right?"

"Something like that."

"So how can we help?" Watkins asked. His tone was patronizing.

She rambled off the list she'd made, things about the DMV and dark pickup trucks in the area, and finding their owners and asking where they were the night of the storm, driving their trucks.

Watkins groaned, but he humored her, listening, nodding. Then he leaned forward, clasped his hands in front of him on the desk. He had the authority moves down to a nice little dance. This was something else she now remembered, how he had provoked her with the comfort he seemed to find in his position of power.

"You should have someone with you," Watkins said then. "She could be after that money. It was too much for around here. That kind of money—makes people a little crazy."

"I'm meeting her tomorrow at ten—at the Gas n' Go."

Watkins nodded, palms now pressed into piles of papers. "I'll get Reyes to meet you. Remember him? Officer Reyes?"

"Yes," Nic said. But not exactly. She remembered a lot of cops—the two local policemen and the state troopers. Their names, faces, had all melded together behind the uniforms.

"Are you staying at the inn?"

"I guess so."

"All right. Meet Reyes at the diner next door—nine thirty? If she seems legit, we can run the registrations for dark-colored trucks."

"Thanks," Nic said. She stood to leave. Watkins stood as well, something clearly weighing on his mind.

"Hey," he said, stopping her at the door. "Is this because of the handwriting analysis? Because, you know, an inconclusive report is not the same as a negative report."

Nic had no idea what he was saying, and her face gave her away.

Watkins turned suddenly, finding a box in the back corner of his office. He sifted through it. Pulled out a thin bundle of papers stapled together.

"This," he said, handing the papers to Nic. "It's the handwriting analysis."

Nic stared at the report, scanning each page quickly, reading things about slants of letters and spacing of words, turning them until she got to the end—and the word "*inconclusive*."

"I thought it was confirmed—the note? That it was my mother's handwriting?"

Watkins was at a loss.

"And my father knew about this?" she asked.

"Jeez, listen. I had no idea," Watkins said now. "I assumed he told you. It came in a few days after you left."

Nic sat back down, stunned by these new facts, but also her father's lie. She knew why he'd done it—he wanted her to move on the way he had. The way he'd forced Evan to do by sending him back to school. He'd said as much on the phone when he'd gotten her text earlier that morning, saying she was coming back to Hastings to follow a lead. *This is absurd . . . I'm having my PI look into this woman, what's her name? Why would you do this? Do you need me to come?* He was in Chicago for a sales conference. *I'll be on the next flight.* And then, after he'd relented, *When you get back we are going to have a long talk about your life.*

They'd been having this part of the conversation for days. With her mother gone, he'd suddenly taken up parenting as a new hobby, insisting she get on with her life. Stop her *bad behavior.* His favorite new expression—*you're not your mother.*

She tried to explain this to Watkins. "My father thinks what you think—that this new lead is a scam. And that even if it's not, my mother doesn't want to be found. He wants me to come home."

"I see," Watkins said. "Well, I can't argue with him. Everything supports that conclusion."

"Is that why the case wasn't reopened—after this report came in?"

Watkins shrugged. "The facts haven't changed, that's why. Look—the report is inconclusive. It's not negative. The note was found in the hotel room she paid for. It was on paper from the notepad in the room. She was upset, nervous. Maybe her hands were shaky." Then he said it again—"It wasn't *negative.*"

Nic felt irritated now, and skeptical of everything she'd been told, or had assumed.

"What else should I know?" Nic asked. "Any more charges to her credit cards? Any communications on her cell phone account? And what about the casino? Are you still looking at the security cameras? It can't be that hard to find someone there."

The Laguna casino and resort was nothing more than a small cluster of businesses built on tribal land—exempt from the state's gambling prohibitions. It wasn't exactly a hotbed of tourism— more like an escape for locals looking to exercise their right to throw their money away in slot machines. Connecticut already had Foxwoods and Mohegan Sun. Laguna was their ugly stepsibling. A hotel. A gas station. A Jiffy bus stop with a ticket machine and a covered bench.

Molly Clarke had made one charge paying for two nights. No one recalled seeing her, but the place had been a zoo—people without power seeking refuge. The security cameras were set up high, looking down at heads, facilitating the identification of petty theft more than faces. They'd been through all of it, going back to the night of the storm—looking for her, her beige coat and jeans. Blond hair. A woman alone.

Watkins shook his head eagerly. "No, no. There's nothing. And we have everyone on alert at Laguna. But, again, the absence of new evidence suggests she covered her tracks. That she doesn't want us to find her. And, hard as this is to hear, that she doesn't want *you* to find her."

Nic let his words settle in place. She had no reason to doubt him. Or at least to doubt that he believed what he was saying. There was no point arguing until she met Edith Moore.

"Okay," she said, finally. "Thank you for everything you've done. So—Officer Reyes? At the diner? I'll be there by nine thirty."

Watkins stood up. Nic did the same.

"I take it this means you're not going home?"

Nic looked at him now, with surprise. She knew how all of this seemed. To her father. To Chief Watkins. To everyone. She didn't care. It had never seemed right to her, even when she'd tried to force it down, and now this—the inconclusive handwriting report.

"No," she said. "I'm not going home."

She left the station with a pounding head and churning stomach. As she got in her mother's car, still smelling of her perfume, she could hear the voices screaming out from the hollow spaces—begging for some kind of relief. For a drink. For her "friends" at the bar back home. For some loser who might stumble in.

And she told them what she'd just told Chief Watkins. She wasn't going home. Not this time. Whatever anger she'd felt for her mother for what happened to Annie, the love was deeper, and it was in her bones. With her mother's absence had come a powerful longing to reclaim those sweet moments that had been lost.

She could see the paths this new information would lead her down—conclusions of what may have happened if her mother hadn't written that note. If she hadn't walked away on her own. Two weeks had passed—none of the conclusions were good.

But for now, for right now, as she drove away, there was just one thought.

I'm not going home.

Not without my mother.

5

Day two

awake startled. A body lies with me.

Nestled into the curve of my abdomen, head woven under one arm and resting on top of the other as I lie on my side in fetal position.

A little girl in my arms.

She doesn't move even after my body jolts. Even after I lift my head to see her face.

"Are you surprised?" she asks. She asks this as though I've just opened a gift she's presented to me.

Breath heaves in and out. The room is light. The bed is warm, but the air is cold against my face. Strange bed. Strange clothes. Strange house. It all floods back in.

And a dream lingers. A dream that I was holding Annie. The dream had lulled me into a state of bliss which now breeds despair.

I force myself to remain still.

"Yes!" I say. I don't want to hurt her feelings, but I want to jump from this bed. I want to put on my clothes and run.

From where my head rests, I can see most of the room. And

I can see that my clothes are gone from the places where I hung them to dry last night. And my purse—did I bring it into the house? Where did I leave it?

I give Alice a little squeeze but then I slide my arm out from under her head and sit up.

"I need to get some water from the kitchen," I say.

She lets me go and I climb out from beneath the covers.

The lantern on the floor is off, or dead. My clothes are gone from every place. Every single place.

"How did you get under the covers without waking me?" I ask this with a playful tone because I don't want her to sense the panic that grows.

She giggles and shrugs. "I'm good at sneaking," she says.

Another smile and I make my exit. I close the door to the bedroom and walk down the hall to the kitchen. The house is dark. I try a switch but it's dead. And that's how the house feels with no power. Dead. I feel my heart beating in my throat. I hear my footsteps along the hard wood.

The kitchen is empty. I look farther down the hall into the living room. The part I can see is also empty. But through a window to the outside, I see the back of the truck. And blue sky.

The storm has cleared.

I step into the kitchen and search for a phone. It hangs on the wall near the stove and I go to it quickly and lift the receiver. I hear only silence.

Please.

I press down on the button again and again, but still, there is just silence. I place the receiver back on the wall mount.

A man's voice stuns me. Stops me cold.

"I told you last night. The phones are out." I turn quickly, instinctively. I do it before I have time to hide what is surely on my face.

The man stands in the doorway. He's dressed in fresh clothing, but otherwise they're the same. Jeans and a flannel shirt. He has a slight beard—thicker than last night—which tells me he doesn't wear a beard. That he is just unshaven.

Beside him, clinging to his waist, is Alice.

She looks up at him. Tugs on his shirt.

"She told me she was going to get water," she says. Then she looks at me like I'm the child and she's the mother. And I've been naughty.

"I thought I would check the phone first," I say. It's normal, wanting to make a call. To call my family. Why do I feel defensive?

I see his eyes run up and down my body, and I remember that I'm wearing the clothes of another woman. A woman who used to live here. Or does live here. I have to stop making assumptions.

"I hope it's okay," I say, looking down at the clothes. "They were in the dresser, like you said."

"They belong to my wife," he tells me. "But it's fine. I'm glad they fit you."

"Oh . . . well, I hope she won't mind. I can change if you tell me where my clothes went." I have a cheery voice now because I feel hopeful and because I want things to be okay in this room. In this house. In this family. I feel hopeful that there is a family now. He said *my wife*.

"They're in the laundry room. Hanging on a rack," he says.

I smile. "Oh! Okay. I'll go see if they're dry. Should I leave these clothes in the washer for your wife when she gets back?"

Alice buries her face in his side as though she's watching a scary scene in a movie. A scene she knows is coming. Maybe because she's seen this movie before.

"My wife is dead," the man says. His tone is neutral. Maybe he's been instructed on how to speak about this in front of Alice.

Maybe I feel better now. At least there was a wife. A dead wife, a dead mother and her death would explain some of the behavior.

"I'm so sorry," I say. But I don't ask questions. Alice peeks out from where she's buried her face. "I'll just leave the clothes in the laundry room."

I walk toward the door slowly, thinking they will clear a path. But they hold their position. They hold me in place with their bodies, trapped in this room.

"They're still a little wet," the man says. "Give it a few hours. You'll be more comfortable staying in dry clothes. Sorry if it feels strange—the house, the clothes."

Again, he apologizes. I pause long enough to think.

"I suppose I can wear these to town," I say.

He looks at me now, curious. "Town?"

"To make the call on your cell phone. We talked about that last night—about driving to town where there's a signal. I need to call my family. I need to let the police know that I'm safe—I left my car . . . and my phone . . ."

"Oh, right," he says. But he does not say yes. He does not move toward the door and the truck and the road that will take us to town.

I feel apprehension now. I won't call it fear. I can't.

"Can we go, then? To town?"

My voice is firm. He can't keep me here. He can't make me stay one second longer. He can't just take my clothes, and she can't just crawl into my bed while I'm sleeping. They can't . . .

"I can go to town," he says now. "But I really need you to stay here with Alice. It's not safe without the phone working or the power. Lots of trees still weak. Some are close to the house."

No, I think. *I am going to town! I am going home!*

I shake now, head to toe. It's in my cheeks and on my tongue as I try to shape words in my mouth.

"We can bring Alice with us. Like last night . . ."

"She has allergies, remember?" He says this like I should feel ashamed. Like I have been inconsiderate of this poor little girl. "She gets sick when she goes outside. I had to bring her last night because no one was here to be with her and I needed to fill the tanks and get the water. There's no need to take the risk today."

I struggle with this information. It comes at me fast. I cannot get my clothes. I cannot leave this house. I cannot call my family. Disbelief bleeds into acceptance and acceptance triggers fight or flight, adrenaline. I feel my skin flush and burn. My vision is unclear, muddled now with floating white circles. I breathe.

I breathe.

He turns to leave and Alice steps into me, clinging to my waist. She looks up at me with that smile and those wide eyes.

"You can make me breakfast!" she says cheerfully.

My hand reaches out before I can stop it and grabs the man's shirt. I look at him, pleading.

He pulls away and walks to the dead phone. There's a notepad next to it, and a pen on the counter. He grabs them both and brings them to me.

"Here," he says. His tone is now cheerful, just like Alice's.

"Write down the names and numbers of everyone you want me to call."

Yes!

I write furiously—names and numbers. John. Nicole. Evan. A few close friends from my grief support group. I rip the paper from the pad and give it back to him.

He looks it over. "Can you write your name?"

"It's just Molly," I say. "They'll know."

"Write it anyway," he insists. "Just in case. I forget things sometimes."

I write my full name. *Molly Clarke*. I hand back the paper.

"Can you call them as soon as you get a signal? Tell them where to come get me? That I'm safe?"

The man's face softens. It melts into a smile that is friendly and warm.

"Of course! It's going to be just fine. I promise."

I feel like crying now.

"And maybe you can check on my car? Let the police know?"

I think about my phone in the car, how it must be sending out a signal. How John will know how to find it online. We share an account.

Maybe they are already on the way!

Something about this thought feels strange. I don't want it to feel strange and I fight against it.

They will come, won't they?

Oh God . . . how it feels strange, a sudden alarm as I wonder about the log on the fire, and Nicole's words and Evan's behavior.

The man folds the paper carefully into the pocket of his flannel shirt.

"Sure thing!" he says with enthusiasm.

I feel relief, though it rests on shaky ground.

I talk myself through it. The man will go to town and call my family. He will check on my car and tell the police where I am. Maybe later today when he feels better about the trees we can leave Alice and he will drive me to town to get my car and fill it with gas from his tanks. Maybe I can drive home myself.

Alice pulls a chair up to a cupboard.

"Do you like tea?" she asks me.

It takes me a moment to process her question. I am still adjusting to this new situation—not going to town. Not calling my family.

"Yes," I say, finally.

"Look at all the kinds we have!" she says, opening the cupboard to reveal several canisters of loose leaf tea.

"Come here and pick one!" she demands.

And I obey.

"You can heat the water with the stove. The generator should have it working," the man says.

I smell coffee so it must be his dead wife who liked tea. He wants me to have some now. Maybe he wants to put my mind at ease—because there is no need to worry. He will contact my family. They will come for me.

As he turns to leave the kitchen, a thought rushes in and I call after him.

"My purse!" I say. "Is it with my clothes?"

He shrugs. Ponders.

"I think you left it in the truck. I didn't see it last night in the house."

I can't remember either, but it's unlike me to leave my purse. I carried it with me into the storm.

"Can you bring it inside? Before you go?"

"Sure thing," he says.

He leaves the room. Alice and I make tea. I listen for the door, for the man to return with my purse.

But the next sound I hear is the truck driving away.

6

Day thirteen

Roger Booth owned the Hastings Inn, the diner next door, and the fifty acres of land that sat behind them. The businesses shared a parking lot of cracked, potted asphalt. The painted white lines had all but faded. A parking free-for-all.

The inn was rarely occupied, as Nic had learned the last time she'd been here. It was mostly the diner that kept the business afloat. Booth lived in an apartment on the first floor.

He owned it all free and clear, a parting gift from his father who had been an executive at the pharmaceutical company before it closed. Booth Senior had managed to get out before the crash, retiring to Florida with his wife of thirty-two years. There was a sister, as well, though she had married and moved to Buffalo. Booth was left with the family's properties and was the unofficial mayor of Hastings because of it.

None of this was information Nic had intended to gather. But one of the waitresses liked to talk. So did the bartender across the street. *The Booth family are the Kennedys of Hastings.* That depiction had been dead on.

Nic parked in front of the entrance to the inn. It was a pristine, fabricated white farmhouse with a wraparound porch, one of the few with that style of architecture that sat along the road. Most of the original farmhouses lined Route 7. The Booths' inn was sadly out of place.

The diner, however, was true to form—a rectangle with a silver roof. Black smoke billowing from a chimney. Big windows. Neon sign.

The two structures sat side by side, a small row of shrubs and about twenty feet between them.

Nic reached for the car door, opened it, but then pulled it shut. She stared at the inn with its white porch and red shutters. Four days she'd spent here with her father. Four days that had just been the start of the dismantling of the life they'd hobbled together after Annie died. The cornerstone of that new, disfigured life was her mother soaking up whatever abuse they handed out. She could see that now. Nic had been cruel to her. She'd paraded her bad behavior with fantastic fanfare, and massacred any attempts her mother made to help with harsh vulgarities.

You're not your mother, her father had texted. You don't owe your life to Annie's death.

But he had no idea. He hadn't been there the day Annie died. He didn't know what Nic owed her death. Owed to her.

He wasn't the one who'd seen Annie running away from the house, hair flying around her face. Then looking back with a mischievous smile. Running. Smiling. Reaching the end of the driveway. He hadn't been the first to see the car. To know what was about to happen. *Annie!*

Her mother had been racing home from work because Nic hadn't answered the phone. She'd been in charge of them, Annie and Evan. And at sixteen, she'd had things to do—serious things back then when she still cared about her life. It wasn't as though they were babies. But Annie was so precocious. She never listened.

She'd wanted ice cream. She'd heard the truck. And she'd run.

Her father hadn't been there. He hadn't heard Nic screaming for her to stop. Too far away to reach her. The screeching tires on the asphalt. Annie lying in a pool of blood. Lying dead in the road. And her mother behind the wheel, driving the car that had struck her. There were no words to describe it.

Maybe Nic wasn't her mother. But they were bound together by their actions that day, the bow and stern of a sinking ship.

She let Annie recede back into her place of hiding. Hair flying. Smile pulled clear across her face.

She grabbed her duffel, then made her way up the steps to the front door.

Inside, the air smelled stagnant as it had before. Nic walked to the reception desk, and set her mother's key down on the lace runner which lay unevenly across the counter. There were small bowls with soft mints, toothpicks, business cards, a guest register where people could write things about their stay before leaving. And a silver bell, which Nic rang.

Footsteps, creaking wood, a door closing. Booth emerged from his apartment in the back, startled.

"Miss Clarke?" He said her name like it was a question, like he couldn't believe she was here again.

"One and the same," Nic said.

Booth looked sleepy, as though she'd disturbed him from an afternoon nap, but he was also freshly groomed. She could smell the aftershave. She remembered that about him now, the way he wore his part in this town, gave it reverence with his appearance.

Khaki pants. Button-down shirt. Clean shave. He was fit, though slender. He'd mentioned something about cycling. He was lean like a cycler. And his hair was short. Neat.

That was how she'd come to think of him. Neat. Tidy. And completely unaware that his royalty status ended at the crossing of Route 7.

He walked behind the counter.

"What brings you back here?"

Nic took a moment to consider how much to tell him.

"Following up on some things. A new lead. Probably nothing, but I have to be sure."

Booth nodded. Thinking. But, oddly, he didn't ask for details.

"You here alone?" he asked instead. He sounded concerned. Or maybe curious. Either way, his face lit up a little.

"For now," she said. "Can I get a room for the night?"

He busied himself then, looking at a handwritten ledger, finding a key—an actual key on a large wooden ring.

"You want 2A again?"

"Sure."

She threw a credit card on the counter. He handed her the key on the wooden ring, the number *2A* carved into it and painted gold.

Booth slid the card across a manual imprint machine, then gave her the slip to sign.

"Have you been doing okay?" he asked.

Nic signed. Handed back the slip.

"Sure, you know. Given everything."

The wheels were turning now. She could see it on his face, the way he scrunched his eyes and cocked his head to the side, slightly askew.

"No word from her?"

"No. Nothing."

He shrugged, held his palm up to the sky. "Strangest thing. How easy it is to disappear in this day and age."

Only it wasn't, Nic thought. It wasn't easy at all. A person needed money and a place to stay and food. All of those things forced a person out into the open, into systems of data that could be traced.

What was strange was how easy it was for everyone to believe Molly Clarke had just left. Just disappeared. Including herself.

A response was on her tongue, but she said nothing. Booth seemed like a decent man. Well meaning. He'd told them before that he hadn't seen Molly Clarke the night of the storm. He'd boarded up both places, the inn and diner, well before she could have made it to town from Evan's school. Said he was in his apartment, in the back, all night. Reading with a lantern. Having some tea. Listening to the radio until the storm had passed. And then trying to get to sleep with the wind still roaring and the worry that the plywood wouldn't hold.

"Well, I'm happy to help any way I can."

He winked at her then, and Nic smiled in response.

"I need to rest if you don't mind," she said.

Booth waved toward the stairs.

"Of course."

The room was the same. Old. Frilly, as though that's what guests at a quaint Connecticut inn would expect. Grandma décor. And Booth kept the heat running—she remembered this all too well. The crackling radiator, the hot, dry air. It was stifling.

She tossed her phone on the nightstand, her bag on the small chair in the corner by the window. She pulled the shades and drew the curtains. It was nearly six, dusk, gray skies.

She ran water in the scalloped sink, splashed her face.

Back to the bed. She changed into pajama pants and a T-shirt, pulled up the covers and climbed beneath them. The sheets were stiff, but cool. She lay her head on the pillow.

It offered little comfort. The mattress had hardened unevenly over time. The pillow turned soft. Blood rushed into her head, making it pound harder, right into her eardrums. It wanted a drink.

She reached for her phone on the nightstand. There was a text from her brother.

WTF? Hastings?

She started to text back, but the phone rang in her hand.

"Finally!" her father said when she picked up. "What's going on there? What's happening?"

Nic winced. Everything felt worse now, lying down. She got up and walked to the window, opening it a crack to let in the cool air. The grounds behind the inn were nothing but bare, scattered trees with stubborn patches of dead leaves clinging to the branches.

"Nicole!" Her father was in a panic.

"I'm fine," she said. "I'm at the inn. I got a room."

He let out a moan.

"It's not like last time."

"I don't like any of this. I should come back."

It occurred to her then—how he would have insisted on coming if he thought there was any real danger. From Edith Moore or someone in this town. Or the town itself. He still believed that his wife had walked away on her own, even after seeing the handwriting analysis.

"No, Dad," Nic said. "One of the cops is coming with me

tomorrow to meet Edith Moore. I won't leave the inn until then. Maybe to the diner next door, but that's all."

Now a sigh and another moan.

"She just wants a chance at the money, Nicole. She waited almost two weeks to come forward and that doesn't make any sense. How did she even get your number? You can't hold on to false hope that this is more than what it is."

Words flew from her mouth before she could stop them.

"Is that why you lied to me—about the note?"

"Oh, Nic . . ."

She hung her head, the phone still pressed to her ear. "I remember, you know. That last day of the search, when they found it."

"So do I."

"We went to the diner to talk about it and you ordered a sandwich, Dad. And fries and a soda and you . . . you ate it . . . all of it!"

He knew what she was implying. She could tell from the silence. For the first three days, neither of them had been able to get down any real food. They'd gotten by on coffee and a few bites of toast, crackers. Walking through cornfields with strangers, hoping to find her mother, then hoping not to as the hours turned to days, making it more likely that if she was found, she would be found dead.

The credit card charge had come through on day four—taking two days to post. The note and clothing were found next. And her father's appetite suddenly returned, like magic. Fear had transformed into resignation. And then acceptance.

"I have to find her, Dad. Even if she wrote that note and doesn't want to be found. Even if that note was forged and . . ."

"Stop! I know what you're thinking. That's why I didn't tell you about the report. I knew you'd go down that road and it's wrong, Nic. Think about what the note said. How would anyone know those things about her? She wasn't herself, Nicole. She was upset and nervous, but the words—that was how she felt. Only she could know that."

"Then I'll find her safe and sound and make her come home. Maybe the truck . . ."

He wouldn't let her finish.

"I just can't stop thinking about how you used to be. When you were a little girl, full of spitfire, and then a big girl and then a young woman with everything in front of her . . ."

Nic felt tears coming. *Not now.*

"Dad—stop!"

But he didn't stop. "And you loved your life. You loved school and running and your friends . . ." He was crying and laughing now, at the same time. "I used to get so worried about all you girls, meeting up with boys at the mall, and now . . . Oh God, Nic . . . now I would give anything to be worried about you having fun with your friends. I would give anything to see you go to college, or just to see you smile again, not back in Hastings chasing after dead ends."

He was full-on now, crying into the phone, making her cry.

"Dad . . ." She didn't know what to say to him. How to make this better for him. It was hard enough to get through each day herself. She couldn't carry her father's anguish as well.

"I know I'm not supposed to say these things to you," he said, catching his breath. "They told me not to, that it would make you feel worse. I'm sorry, sweetheart. I just need you to know that even if you don't remember what it felt like when you were happy, that I do. I do! And I will hold those memories until you're ready to take them back. Until you're done running away—and that's all this is, looking for your mother when she doesn't want to be found."

The therapy speak was unbearable. She recognized every

theme—the holding of memories, the holding of feelings, the running away. Each of them was another layer of mental sedation, wrapped around her and Evan and their father, keeping them from crashing into one another. Keeping them cocooned and preserved, until—what, exactly?

"I'm not running away . . ."

"Your mother wasn't happy." He said this like it was some kind of revelation.

"I know that."

"Do you? Do you know how unhappy she was? She was in agony. Unrelenting agony."

I know.

"I know, Dad."

"And that agony was spreading into all of us. Into you, especially. It was so hard to watch . . ."

"Dad—stop!" What was he even saying right now? He kept going.

"And I know you blame yourself for that day, for not bringing your sister to her playdate and not answering your phone—but it was your mother behind the wheel . . ."

Nic closed her eyes, listening carefully to words that somehow had a harsher tone this time.

". . . it was your mother who was left to wonder about how fast she hit the brakes and turned the wheel, and whether she was driving as slow as she could have, knowing you kids were home alone and hearing the ice cream truck . . . You were a teenager, Nic. A busy teenager and it wasn't your job to babysit your sister. That's how she saw it. And she knew what other people thought about her."

"Is that what you thought?" Nic asked him now. It sounded as though he was rendering a judgment. A guilty verdict. Is this what her own father thought about her mother? And if it was, how much of this toxic waste had seeped into conversations meant to provide comfort and support the way a husband should?

"Nic?"

"I'm here," Nic answered. She wanted to say more, ask more. But she didn't know where to begin. She was too tired, head on fire now after the tears, stomach still churning.

Was this how she also felt about her mother? Did she blame her more than she even blamed herself? Did it feel good to blame her, so she could be let off the hook?

Maybe that's what people did when something like this happened. A child run over in the driveway. A child drowned in the pool outside. A child who'd choked on a toy. *That could never happen to me, to my child, because I would never be so careless the way she was. That's why it happened.* If there was fault, then there could also be prevention, the illusion of control to make life bearable.

Yes, Nic thought. It felt good to think that about her mother. That's where the rage was coming from. Blaming her mother was the only thing that eased her own guilt, and the hatred she held for herself.

Then there were the facts. The driveway sat on a blind corner. Her mother had been slowing down to make the turn. Estimated miles per hour, under ten. Skid marks from the tires suggested they were employed immediately. The wheel turned as far as it could go—away from Annie. Her phone tucked in a briefcase. She'd come home the way she did every day. Safely, responsibly, even though her head had been full of worry.

Responsible was how she'd lived her entire life.

Until the night of the storm.

"Did we do this?" Nic asked now. "Did we secretly blame her

and did she know? Could she feel it even though we said it wasn't her fault?"

Her father took a moment to answer. Then, "I don't know, sweetheart. I honestly don't. I know it could have been me behind that wheel. It could have been anyone coming around that corner. But it wasn't. It was her. And nothing we do can change that."

Nic pressed a palm into her forehead and turned it slowly, back and forth.

Her father and his mind-numbing therapy.

Her head resumed its screaming. She had to end this call. He had to understand why she was here and let her do what she needed to do.

"I have to find her, Dad."

He sighed again, long and hard.

"It's not as though I've stopped looking. The PI is working on this every day, all day—monitoring her credit cards, social security number, passport—he's going state by state contacting train and bus stations, airlines."

And yet, Nic thought, *he ordered that sandwich*. Then he went home. Went back to work. He walked the dogs and went to the gym and fucked his mistress and then came home to watch TV in the same bed he had shared with his wife for twenty-four years.

"You want me to get over Annie and get over Mom and go to college, and now I want you to get over me looking for her. I guess that's a draw."

He said nothing for a long moment.

And then, finally, just, "I love you, Nicole."

When all else failed, there was always this last mantra in the box. Even if he meant it.

"I love you too, Dad." Then she hung up.

Nic went back to the bed, under the covers. Her father's words lying right there beside her.

She unlocked her phone again and sent a reply to Evan.

> I'm fine. Don't be worried.
> Where r u?
> At the Inn.

And then, something strange.

> The one with the fence?
> What fence?

Nic got up and walked back to the window. She couldn't see a fence.

> Dad said he saw it when he was out searching for Mom. He
> said it was creepy. He said they had to stop when they got to it.
> IDK.

Nic stared at the woods. They went on forever.

> U ok?
> I guess.

She wondered then what he really thought about their mother. Was it easier for him to believe she'd left them? Was he relieved that she was gone? They had never talked about it. They texted, mostly, about everyday things. Nic asked him about football. She'd promised to make it to watch the playoffs, though being there without their mother was an emotional hurdle she wasn't sure she could clear.

Dad wants me to come home.

The reply came quickly, and without a hint of the banter that was normally part of their conversation.

No. You have to find her.

And there was the answer to her question. She wasn't alone. She replied, Promise.

7

Day two

stand with Alice by the window in the living room. She doesn't understand why I've run to watch the man drive away.

Drive away with my purse inside.

The truck kicks up dirt from the driveway. It's dented in the back. A taillight is broken.

"Do you know what happened to his truck?" Alice asks me.

I don't care about the truck. I am thinking about my purse, and now the fence—the one that attaches to the gate at the end of the driveway. The gate that is chained shut. The fence with the coils of barbed wire.

"No," I say. My voice is perky as though I can't wait to find out.

Alice takes my hand and pulls me until I am looking at her with all of my attention.

"Well," she begins, and anxiety fills me head to toe.

But she continues. "Someone was following him too close. You're not supposed to do that. You're supposed to stay far away from the car in front of you. Then he slammed on his brakes, and the car behind him crashed right into the back of him! And it was one of those really little cars so it got all dented. And then the driver of that stupid little car said she was going to call the police, but then he told her that when you hit someone from behind, it's always your fault. *Always*."

My heart pounds as she rambles on. I try to be patient. I don't want to agitate her. But I am finding it difficult.

Alice keeps rambling.

"And then she gave him a lot of money so he wouldn't go to the police or the insurance people—and you know what else?" She giggles then. "He gets to keep all the money when that happens."

I open my mouth, am about to ask her what she means by this and how she knows. Is he filled with rage? Is he proud of making people crash their cars?

But I don't ask. I don't care. I need to get outside to that fence and see where it leads, see where we are in relation to the town. The sky is clear. The air is warm enough to go out in these clothes. At least while it's daylight.

I don't know if I can trust this instinct, but it is strong. And it tells me to leave this house.

"Come on!" Alice says. "Do you want to see where I was born?"

Alice takes me back down the hall, past the bedroom on the left where I slept. Past another bedroom on the left, then a bathroom on the right and a third bedroom after that. This is a strange house—I have not seen any stairs. It's laid out like a long ranch, but has the facade of a farm house, with the porch and the gable roof.

Next to the last bedroom is a smaller room. It's dark and windowless and has a sink and hookup for a washer. The floor is not wood like the other rooms and the hallway. It has hard ceramic tile. There is some kind of toilet in the corner.

"Here!" she says. "Right here! My mother didn't like hospitals."

I look at her and wonder if she knows how strange that sounds.

Her mother had a home birth in a cold, dark laundry room. Alice rarely leaves the house herself. But I come from a different world. Maybe they couldn't afford the cost of the hospital. Maybe they didn't trust the government to educate their child. Maybe they didn't trust anyone.

And then—wait. He said my clothes were drying in the laundry room. There are no machines in this room. No drying rack. No clothes.

"Alice," I ask. "Is there another place where you do the laundry?"

Alice shrugs. She has no idea and she doesn't care.

"Now it's time to play!" she says. She takes my hand and we walk.

We sit on the floor of a small room at the front of the house. There are shelves on the walls, filled with children's books and toys—and dust. There is so much dust it makes me wonder if anyone ever cleans this house. And it is then that the small memories come flooding in—memories from last night and this morning. Walking up the porch with loose steps. Paint peeling from the shingles. Even in the storm and darkness I could see the patches of brown. The floorboards of my room, and the hallway, are caked with a thick line of dirt—the dust that has condensed and slowly crept to the sides as air flows through the rooms. And the kitchen, the one with the phone that is dead—its floor is yellowing. White linoleum turning color from age and neglect.

Maybe I was wrong to think the man's wife just died. No woman has kept this house for a long time. Years perhaps. And yet the clothes are freshly laundered. Maybe she was sick for a while.

Maybe she was young and didn't know how to clean a house.

I have to find my clothes. I have to get outside.

"You be this girl," Alice orders me. She hands me a small plastic figurine with chestnut hair. "Her name is Suzannah."

I take the little doll and smile. "Okay," I say.

"I'll be Hannah. She has blond hair like me. It's better to have blond hair. Did you know that? Is that why you make your brown hair blond? I can see your roots, you know."

I want to tell her there's a nicer way to ask a personal question like that, to be a parent to her because she needs one and it's unthinkable that she lives this way, never leaving this filthy house, never seeing another child. But she is not my child, even though she slept in my arms and made me dream about Annie.

She is not your child. You'll be leaving soon.

"What are you allergic to?" I ask her.

I think now about gathering information. Maybe it will help me leave here.

"Everything that's outside the house," she says.

"Like what?" I ask.

"All the trees and the grass and the sky and the air. All the animals. All of it. I can't ever leave. Except with the mask and only if it's an emergency."

She says this without emotion. She says this without longing because she doesn't know any other way of life. She must have been living this way since she's had memories.

I make some mental notes and pretend that they are important so that I don't jump out of my skin playing with dolls when I want to run.

First, she has been here since age four or perhaps even earlier. She has no memory of any other life.

Second, she never calls the man by a name. She uses only the pronouns *he, him, his.*

Third, he has lied to her to keep her here. If she had such severe allergies, the dust in this house would have killed her by now.

Fourth, this man who won't say his name is angry and impulsive. I picture him slamming on his brakes, causing a car to crash into him. He may also be violent.

"Suzannah!" Alice yells.

I am pulled back into the moment where I am playing with dolls.

I hold mine up. "Yes, Hannah?" I say in a different voice than my own.

Now Alice throws hers down. "She doesn't talk like that!"

"I'm sorry," I say. "How does she talk? I will try to be just like her."

Alice calms and picks up her doll. "Just normal. In your regular voice."

"Okay," I say. "What, Hannah?" I try again.

Her face lights up. It's night and day. Dark and light. The emotions that flow through this child.

We talk then, Hannah and Suzannah. We talk about childish things. We talk about our pets. Suzannah has a little puppy named Oscar and Hannah has a cat named Whiskers. At every turn, I am redirected with my answers. This is a game Alice plays the same way each time, and I imagine before today, she played both parts. Hannah and Suzannah.

When she tires of the game, I begin again with my inquiries.

"Who else gets to play Suzannah?" I ask. "Your father?"

She turns away in a huff.

I've hit a nerve so I push harder. "Your mother?"

"Stop asking dumb questions!" she says.

She walks to the wall of shelves and pulls out a board game. Candyland. It's old, the box broken and taped back together.

She doesn't say a word as she sets it up on the floor.

We draw cards. We take turns. I wait. And then I resume.

"Well," I say. "I sure am glad you found me last night. I haven't gotten to play Candyland in years. Not since my children were younger."

She ignores me and moves her player five squares. I draw. I move. I pass her and it makes her angry.

"No fair!" she yells. "You're cheating!"

"Don't worry," I say. "You'll catch me on the next turn. Just draw a card—you'll see! And either way, win or lose, we're having fun, right?" I am doing it again. Parenting.

She is not your child.

She draws another card. She passes me and smiles.

I smile back. I spot an old-looking doll on the shelf. She has a porcelain face with chipped paint around one cheek. The rest of her is soft so she is propped up between books.

"Who is that?" I ask. "On the shelf."

I point to the doll. Alice looks up at her. The smile on her face changes to something mischievous.

"That's Dolly," she says.

"Is she yours?" I ask. "She looks very old. Did she belong to your mother?"

This causes her mood to shift darker. The smile leaves and she changes the subject to me.

"How many children do you have?" she asks.

"Three." The answer will always be *three*.

"How old are they?" she asks.

"Twenty-one and sixteen."

She looks at me now and I can see that she is smart. Or perhaps clever.

"You said you had three children," she says.

I consider my answer carefully. I do not want to disclose anything to this girl, but I don't want to lie and get caught in it. I need her to trust me.

I take a leap.

"One of my children died. When she was a little girl."

Alice stares at me. "How did she die?" she asks.

"She was hit by a car. She ran into the street."

I say the words but don't allow myself to hear them. I have to move out of this conversation quickly before she breaks me.

But then she is in my lap, climbing right over the Candyland board, arms squeezing me tight. She begins to cry.

"That is so sad," she says. But her tears, her arms around me, they do not seem real. They do not pull me in. I do not feel like crying, not even with this memory being dragged out before me. My dead child. Lying dead in the street.

Instead, I am stiff as a board. I cannot even close my arms around this child, this new child, who clings to my body.

"I'm okay," I lie. "It's really okay. It was a long time ago."

Alice heaves in and out. The tears stop and she turns her body so her back is nestled against my chest. She takes my forearm and pulls it across her. She strokes my skin like she's petting me.

"I'm nine too," she says. "That's why we picked you up."

What? I think I must have heard her wrong. So I ask—

"What do you mean?"

She turns her head to gaze up at me. Wide eyes. Angelic. Haunting.

"We were waiting for you. We had to wait a long time."

I let the words sink in. Each one is a bolt of lightning. Each one shocks me into disbelief.

"Waiting for me?" I ask now. "How did you know I would be there?"

My heart is wild in my chest and I pray that she can't feel it as she pets my skin. I need to find out what she's saying.

"We knew lots of things. We knew you were coming. And we

knew about your daughter. I didn't think you'd tell me but you did. You're a very honest person."

She leans her head into my chest. The hairs stand up on every inch of my skin as she continues to stroke my arms. To pet me like an animal.

"Oh!" I say. My voice trembles. "And here I thought you just happened to run into me."

She giggles. "I know. That was just a little secret we kept. We waited for you, silly. We saw you running to the gas station and then stop and look around like you were confused and sad. And then you started to walk to town. Then I said 'is that her?' and he said 'yes' and I asked if we still had to run the truck into you, and he said 'no' and then we followed behind you with the lights off for a while, then we pulled up close and then we got you!"

I am standing. She is lying on the floor, stunned. I don't know what happened in this instant, except that I could not stand to have her in my arms after those words left her mouth.

"What are you doing?" she asks as I walk out of the room. I hear her follow me, little feet running.

"I just have to get something," I say. "From the kitchen. Some water . . ."

My voice shakes as I walk. She is right behind me. I have to get away from her. Away from this house.

They followed me. They took me. They knew I was coming.

I search the drawers.

"What are you looking for?" Alice asks.

I don't answer. I find a pair of scissors. I take them, and a knife, from a butcher block. I fold them into a dish towel and then set them aside, hoping she doesn't notice as I get a glass of water and drink it down. My throat is tight. My mouth bone dry as I try to swallow.

I look at her and focus now. I can do this. I can outsmart a nine-year-old girl.

"You know how you have allergies to the outside?" I ask.

She nods.

"Well, I have something similar. I have allergies to the insides of houses. I have to go outside every day for a few minutes or I start to get sick."

She looks at me, curiously. "Really?" she asks.

"Yes. I am feeling sick now. It happened suddenly when we were playing. I'm sorry if I scared you. The water helped. But I need to get outside. Can I go for a little walk?"

She shrugs. "I guess. I think there's a lot of woods. What if you get lost?"

"I won't go far. Maybe just to the end of the driveway and then right back. I can't get lost doing that."

She nods. "That might work. When you come back, maybe you should wear the mask."

"Oh! That would be wonderful," I say. "Can I borrow it?"

"Sure!" Alice is thrilled to help me.

"Do you know where it is?" I ask.

She nods.

"Can you get it for me and we'll meet by the front door? That way I'll have it as soon as I come back."

She smiles and bounces out of the room. I hear her skipping down the hall. I move quickly, grabbing the towel with the scissors and the knife, rushing to the living room. I open the front door and place them outside. I close the door just in time.

Alice is there now, the mask in one hand. In the other hand, she carries a pair of rain boots.

"You can't go outside in bare feet, silly," she says.

I look at my feet. They are bare. My shoes disappeared along with my clothes last night while I slept. I would walk with bare feet across broken glass to get out of here but I shake my head and feign self-deprecation.

"Oh, my! I am silly, aren't I?"

I take the boots. I can't tell if they belong to a man or woman. They are big and my feet swim inside them. But I can walk and that's all that matters.

I smile at Alice. I force myself to pull her close to me. She nuzzles her face into my chest.

"Thank you, Alice. You are a very sweet girl."

I release her now.

"I'll be back really soon and I'm sure I'll feel better. Will you be all right for a few minutes?"

She nods. "I stay here alone all the time."

"Okay." I kiss her forehead and open the door. She steps back from it so she doesn't have to breathe the air from the outside.

My heart dances with the hope of freedom. It is near euphoric.

As I step outside, I hear Alice call after me.

"Be careful," she says. "Don't get lost in the woods."

I look back. And she tells me, "That's how my first mommy died."

8

Day fourteen

An hour passed. Then another, and another, until Nic stopped watching the time—until a mild form of unconsciousness had shut down her mind, mercifully.

She came to in the middle of the night. Head still pounding, sheets tangled around her body. Wondering how late it was, and if the bar across the street would still be open.

Where was it coming from, this craving? She scanned her body, looking for the culprit. Her head was the obvious suspect, but that was just a red herring. A clever misdirection.

She thought back to the first time she'd had a drink and felt the relief. It was the fall of her senior year—two years after Annie died. She'd managed the fallout with punishment. Schoolwork and running. She'd gotten a job at a local clothing store to fill the bits and pieces of spare time. She'd lost fifteen pounds because she'd deprived herself of every indulgence.

It was Columbus Day weekend. Three days off from school. No cross-country meets or tests to study for. Her parents had both been gone—her father to a conference and her mother to visit

Evan. Saturday she'd woken up and run ten miles. She'd worked her shift at the store, then come home to an empty house. A quiet house. She'd tried to read but her mind had been tired and refusing to cooperate. She'd turned on the television but nothing had been able to pull her in.

That was the first time she'd felt them—the hollow spaces. The emptiness that would not fill up. Not with anything.

She'd gone for another run, at night, until her body had shut down and she'd been able to sleep. But then morning had come and her legs wouldn't move and her mind wouldn't focus. The store was closed. She'd run out of distractions.

She would come to understand that the hollow spaces had been carved out by the grief, and the guilt, and the self-hatred—the fallout from Annie's death. But on that Sunday, they had felt like a wild beast writhing with hunger. For the first time in her life, she'd understood why people jumped from bridges, and when she'd found herself thinking about the bridge over the river downtown, she'd gone to the liquor cabinet and poured a glass of vodka.

Within minutes, she was crying. And then laughing. And then bingeing some inane show on her laptop. She'd woken up Monday morning still in her clothes, the laptop dead beside her.

And she'd thought—thank you, God. Thank you for vodka.

By the end of senior year, she'd been caught four times with alcohol at school. Expelled. Her college acceptance revoked.

And still, she thought—thank you, God. Thank you for vodka.

As she lay in the bed now with her pounding head, she muscled back the craving, the hunger of the hollow spaces, and let herself go down the path that she had to consider. If her mother hadn't walked away, and two weeks had now passed, she was likely dead. Dead in a field that they didn't search. Or dead at the hand of a stranger.

Maybe that's why her father was so eager to believe the note was real. Maybe he couldn't bear to lose her this other way. It would be hard to hold another woman with this thought in his head.

Vodka . . . the bar across the street . . .

Nic grabbed her phone to check the time. *Shit*. It was just past four. The bar closed at two.

There was a red dot above her email. A message from her father. She sat down on the edge of the bed.

The email had an attachment, a document that included clips of things her mother had written in her correspondence. He had been the one to read through them when she first disappeared. Her password was stored on the key chain of a computer they shared.

The message now said only *FYI—thought you should know.*

A new hour followed, then another, reading her mother's words, but then going into the account herself and reading them firsthand and for the first time. Every word her mother had written going back in time, month by month.

Most of it was insubstantial. Small talk, planning for lunch dates and holiday gatherings. But some of it was more than that. Like after the days she had sessions with her shrink or meetings with her grief support group. Those people had a way of teasing things out of her, keeping her immersed in her self-analysis. Lost in the past. Drowning in it.

You have to feel it all before it goes away. They said this repeatedly— Nic knew firsthand because her counselor had said it to her.

But does it? Does it ever go away? her mother had asked. One of them had given an honest reply. *It goes away enough.*

She wrote things about Annie, and the depth of her grief. The depth of her torturous guilt. Then about her husband and the extent of her love but also her inability to embrace that love. She felt unworthy. *I killed his child, our child. I can't stand for him to hold me . . . I would sooner he punch me in the face.*

Nic had to read that twice.

Then there were things about Nic and her behavior. They had all given it a name—*survivor's guilt*, they called it. *She can't enjoy her life because it feels wrong.* Her mother was terrified about the path she was on.

Sound advice was given. *Maybe your husband is right, tell her she has to leave if she doesn't go to college . . . cut off the money . . . tough love . . . but what if it pushes her too far?*

Fuck them. Fuck all of them and their therapy shit.

Nic didn't feel guilty about being alive. She felt guilty about the role she'd played in Annie being dead. Some things just were what they were.

At the end of that particular exchange was the summation of her mother's terror.

I can't lose another child.

She would never be able to unsee those words.

Those words were never going to leave her head.

Officer Jared Reyes was waiting for her in the diner at nine-thirty—as promised. He looked at her with familiarity, like an old friend, though Nic hardly recognized him.

"Hey!" he said with a smile.

"Hi," she said back. She was too exhausted to wonder if she knew him better than she was remembering. Those four days had been brutal.

"Thanks for meeting me."

He touched her shoulder, gave it a squeeze. It felt good. Good enough to make her worry.

"Yeah, no problem. Want to grab a coffee?"

"Do I look like I need one?"

He smiled again and Nic found herself smiling back. It was a reflex with attractive men, and Reyes was attractive. She couldn't decide what it was about him, but it was there. His face was average. Height, average. Not overweight. Some muscle tone, or just bulk, filling out the uniform in all the right places. No ring.

There was something between him and the waitress, a past maybe. Or anticipation about a future. She seemed irritated when Nic walked in and drew his attention.

Nic got a coffee to go. Reyes waited.

Outside, the officer stopped as they walked to the squad car—his eyes catching the blue Audi parked by the inn.

"I'm driving it now," Nic said. "It's nicer than mine." But that was not the reason she'd been driving her mother's car, which still smelled of her mother's perfume and held her mother's lipstick in the console.

Reyes nodded as though he got it—her need to be near any small part of her mother.

They turned right out of the diner and drove along Hastings Pass toward Route 7 and the Gas n' Go. Reyes studied the fields on both sides. Brow furrowed. Eyes pensive.

"I've been up and down this road," he said, glancing at the cornfields. "Must be a hundred times since your mother went missing. Every time, thinking about what we might have missed."

Nic was surprised.

"I thought the investigation was closed."

Reyes shrugged. "A woman is missing. Gone. I never met her. I barely know you or your family. But, I mean, what the hell? If a woman vanishes and it's your job to find her—how does that not keep you up at night? Make you want to do something the next day? She can still be found, even if she doesn't want to be. Those four days, everyone running around like chickens with their heads cut off—how can it hurt to slow down and do a more methodical search? She has to be somewhere. And just because we don't know where that is doesn't make it unknowable."

Reyes shifted in his seat, like he had felt a sudden wave of something uncomfortable inside him. Something he wanted to get out because it was hard to sit with. It shot through the air like electricity, and Nic suspected this was the very thing that drew people to him. The waitress. An old couple in the diner whose eyes followed him out the door. Even the car they passed back in town, a woman driving, waving at him. Big smile that she was hoping he would see.

Nic had come to know men, the things they found to lure women. There were those who didn't have to try. Who couldn't stop it if they wanted to. That was the attraction of Officer Jared Reyes.

Men like Reyes were almost as good as vodka.

They drove to the Gas n' Go. Reyes pulled the car over and turned off the ignition.

"Is that her?" he asked.

A small white sedan was parked on the other side.

"I don't know."

"It's got New York plates," Reyes said. "Come on."

They walked to meet Edith Moore as she stepped outside her car. She was in her late thirties, it seemed. Slacks, sweater, loafers. Short brown hair. Glasses. Her face wore the appropriate expression of empathy and eagerness.

"You must be Nicole," she said, extending her hand. "Edith Moore. Nice to meet you."

Her eyes moved quickly to Officer Reyes. Her expression changing. Nic hadn't told her she was coming with the police.

"Jared Reyes," he said with a nod. "Hastings PD."

Edith Moore nodded as well. "I'm glad you came. I hope I can be helpful."

"Well, let's see," Reyes said. "Take us through it. The night of the storm."

They drove in the Chevy. Reyes in the front with Edith Moore. Nic in the back, dead center and leaning forward as far as she could to see through the windshield. They drove toward town on Hastings Pass for a mile and a quarter, then made a U-turn, driving slowly toward the intersection.

"This is about how fast I was going. It was all I could manage with the rain. I couldn't see a thing beyond the headlights."

"But you saw Molly Clarke somehow," Reyes said.

"My lights caught her. The road is narrow. I could see both sides of it."

When they were just before the mile marker Edith thought she remembered seeing, she pulled the car to the side. "It was right about here that I saw her, and then the truck coming from the other direction, heading into town."

Nic went through the rest of it with her. The things she'd already said on the phone, about her mother and how she'd waved them down. And the purse with the three letters. Nothing they asked now brought forth any more detail—not about the truck or the driver.

"Can you be any more specific? The color, license plate, symbols, bumper stickers—anything?" Reyes asked.

Edith thought carefully. "It was dark in color, like I said. It might have been black, a very dark gray. Charcoal. But not a light gray . . . maybe dark brown, I can't remember much else about it. The rain was coming so hard . . ."

But then another thought seemed to come over her as she was trying to recall the truck.

"You know," she said. "Now that I'm here—there is something else. But I can't be sure."

Nic looked at her with urgency. "What is it?"

She paused, squinted her eyes, lifted her arm and pointed at the road.

"When I saw it drive off with your mother and it passed me, I looked at it through my rearview mirror. I'm not sure I saw two taillights. I think one might have been out. At the time I thought it was just a distortion from the rain. It was so heavy it was like looking through a pool of water. So I thought the two lights had just looked like one."

Reyes studied her face. "And now?"

"Now," she said. "I think it's possible there was just one tail-light."

"Which one was out?"

Edith Moore shook her head. She didn't know. "I'm so sorry that I didn't get the plate number or the make and model. It wasn't on my mind that I would need those things."

Reyes was uncomfortably silent as he stared at Edith Moore. He seemed irritated, shifting into a more hostile stance.

"Let me ask you something else," he said.

"Okay."

"Are you sure you were coming back from New York City?"

There was a long pause.

"Yes. Of course I'm sure."

"I see you have an E-ZPass. Did you leave on the east side or the west side? The east side would take you over the Triborough Bridge. There's a toll scanner on that bridge."

Edith Moore's eyes lit up. "No—I definitely didn't go that way. I went on the west side."

Something wasn't right about her answer. Nic could hear it in her voice and see it in the creases of Officer Reyes's eyes. A little smile.

"The thing is," Reyes said, going in for the kill, "your E-ZPass has no record of you entering or leaving New York City in the past sixty days. You can't get into the city on the west side without passing under a scanner."

Shit.

If she was lying about this, what else was she lying about?

"Well, maybe I was wrong. Maybe I went on the east side. Maybe that other bridge without a toll. On Willis Avenue."

Reyes let this bone go. But he moved on quickly to other parts of her story. And her life. She was a nurse practitioner in Schenectady. Lived with her boyfriend. No kids. She had three cats. *No*, she was not in any financial trouble, and *why are you asking me that?* The reward money, of course. *That wasn't why I came forward.*

Where did she go when she left the scene, left Molly Clarke to disappear on Hastings Pass? Did anyone see her when she got home? Did she stop along the way? What time did she go to work the next morning? And, the last question—*are you sure you weren't with someone in Hastings and not New York City?*

What was he saying? That she was conspiring with someone in the town to fabricate a story about her mother?

"No!" she said defensively. "Why would you ask me that?"

Reyes backed off then.

"Just dotting my i's and crossing my t's."

They drove back to the Gas n' Go, got out of the car and stood in an awkward silence. But Reyes wasn't through.

"Do you have time to come to the station—maybe look at models of trucks? It would help to narrow things down. You'd be surprised how different they can be," he said.

Edith was flustered. "I don't really have time for all that—I have to make my shift at the hospital."

"Then we can send you photos. Do we have your email address?"

She handed Reyes a business card. "You can use the one on here," she said.

Reyes paused, let the discomfort ease in. "I think that's everything."

Nic touched her arm softly. "Thank you for coming all this way."

"Well, you know how to reach me—if you have any questions. Or if this helps you find your mother. I didn't come forward because of the money, but I'm sure you'll let me know if this information turns out to be useful."

Of course, Nic thought. There was nothing pure in this world.

Reyes answered. "We'll let you know."

They started to turn away from one another, but then Nic remembered the question her father had asked her.

"Hey—one last thing."

Edith smiled, but she seemed nervous as she glanced between Nic and Reyes.

"How did you get my number?"

She shrugged, again looking between the two of them. It was an easy question. The answer should have rolled off her tongue.

It was Reyes who answered. "Was it Mrs. Urbansky?"

"Is that the woman at the police department?"

"Yes," Nic said.

"Right. That's it. Sorry. That's not an easy name to remember."

They said their goodbyes. Edith Moore left. Nic and Reyes got back in his car.

"What was that about?" Nic asked. "The way you grilled her."

Reyes drove back onto Hastings Pass, heading into town.

"She's lying. She never went to New York. She was never driving home."

"Maybe she was at the casino. Maybe she didn't want her boyfriend to know. She said she lives with him, right?" Nic threw out scenarios but they sounded unlikely, even to her.

Reyes hit the gas harder.

"Look—I don't want to dick you around like everyone else. This woman is lying. Her E-ZPass records show her on the New York State Thruway the day before the storm, getting off at the exit that leads to Route 7. It's not the fastest way to the casino. Only thing that makes sense is that she was headed right here, to Hastings, coming from the north, not the south. She must have spent the night."

"Then someone in this town knows her."

Reyes continued. "If she's the reason you came back here and started looking again, and if you do find your mother, she'll get the money even if there was no truck. It won't matter—she brought you back."

Nic had considered this. "But then why make up the story about the truck? It would only lead me in a wrong direction, further away from finding my mother. Further away from her getting the money. Why not just say she saw my mother—and I know she did because of what she said—about my mother's purse with the letters."

Reyes considered this. "So maybe there is a truck with a broken taillight."

They were back at the inn. Nic reached for the door handle, then stopped.

"You really think she was in Hastings? That she was with someone here the night before the storm, before she left for home?"

Reyes shrugged. "It's the only thing that makes sense."

Then, a thought that made her gasp.

"What is it?" Reyes asked.

Nic shook her head slowly, putting the pieces in place. "What if she saw my mother because she was involved in her disappearance? Maybe someone from Hastings is involved as well—with her. It could be anything—maybe they helped her get to Laguna but don't want to be implicated. Or maybe something else . . . there's money at stake even if she's not found alive—five hundred thousand dollars. And the note—what if it really is a forgery?"

"Okay, stop right there."

"What if they hurt her?" Nic's voice started to tremble.

Reyes tried to talk her down, off this ledge.

"Listen—there's a reason she doesn't want to come clean about why she was here, but it doesn't have to be something like that. People lie for all kinds of reasons."

Reyes placed his hands squarely on her shoulders. "This is about the money. Nothing else. Edith Moore saw your mother and now she wants to play her lottery ticket. Look, we have new leads now—not just the truck, but the taillight and the reason Edith Moore lied."

"And you'll follow them?"

Reyes shrugged. "I'll do my best. The chief, well, I may have some convincing to do there."

"Then I should stay," Nic said. "Maybe the second I leave is the second the search for Molly Clarke dies a second death."

Another shrug. Then, "That's up to you."

Nic had planned on staying a day at most, just long enough to meet Edith Moore. But Reyes was right. Now there were new leads.

She turned back to the inn and the diner next to it. Something caught her eye in the side-view mirror.

"You should get going," she said. "You probably have work to do." She reached for the door.

Reyes stopped her long enough to hand her his card.

"I'll follow up on the taillight. If you think of anything, call me."

Nic studied the card as the question formed in her head. She didn't want to say it out loud, but she needed to know.

"Do you think she's dead?"

"No," he said. "I don't. Do you really want to know what I think?"

"Of course."

"I think she's somewhere safe trying to get through whatever it is she needs to get through. I've seen it before. The stats support it. Her story supports it. The evidence supports it. But I also think we can find her. And I will help you any way I can."

Reyes reached right into those hollow spaces and filled them up, just a little. A little dose of intoxication.

She waited for him to drive off, taking a few steps toward the diner. When he was gone, she turned and looked across the street.

At the bar.

And the bartender who was opening the door.

9

Day two

Alice watches me from the window as I walk down the driveway. The packed dirt is dry in places from the morning sun, but also littered with potholes that overflow with water from the storm. I scuffle more than walk because the boots slip down when I lift each foot. I make tracks in the dirt. I get stuck in the mud. I move quickly in spite of everything.

The driveway is no longer than a sixth of a mile. I counted the seconds as we drove it last night, the odometer just under thirty miles per hour. I pray I'm right.

The house sits on a sloping hill and when I reach the top and begin to descend, I turn to wave at Alice, to reassure her that I am just out for some air. I see her smile and wave back, and when she finally falls from sight, I take off the boots, holding them against my chest, and start to run.

I run down the driveway until I reach the gate. I pray that he forgot to replace the chain, or that he didn't feel the need to. I tell myself that I am crazy and that he only locks the gate to protect

Alice when she stays here alone. I delude myself just long enough to reach the chains, finding them locked. I pull on them furiously, knowing they won't release. Knowing it's futile.

I have to hold it together now. I have to be methodical. Time is precious.

I inspect the gates and the chain and the lock that holds them. I have scissors and a small kitchen knife. The gate is strong and the lock secure. I remind myself that this is the main point of entry. This is the place least likely to be vulnerable.

I look right and left. On both sides, the fence disappears into a dense tree line. I choose right because I remember turning left into the driveway. Somewhere to the right is the way back to town. This is all I have to work with. It's entirely possible that he drove us in circles and that the town is closer to the left. It is possible we are nowhere near the town. We made so many turns.

Still, I have to decide. I have to move.

I step into the ungroomed woods and am thankful for the boots. I stop long enough to put them back onto my frozen feet. The ground harbors the sharp edges of fallen branches and protruding roots. It is uneven and soaking wet. The water is cold in spite of the sun.

The fence is wire. It is woven in small squares and is about eight feet high. At the top is coiled barbed wire. But that is the least of my concerns. The wire at the top is thin and I think I could cut through it. I can cut the barbed wire at the top, and I can jump to the other side. What I cannot do is climb to the top.

The holes are too small for the boots to fit, and every inch of the wire has barbs. They are smaller, almost invisible. But when I run my finger across a piece of it, my skins catches and starts to bleed. Little, tiny metal barbs embedded in every inch of this fence that goes on for miles it seems. Surrounding this property. This fortress.

Why?

The question has no answer that does not terrify me.

Alice said her first mommy died in these woods.

But now I think her first mommy died trying to escape. I wonder if the same words were in her head. *Just walk away.* I wonder if they led her to her death. And now I wonder where they've led me.

No. I can't wonder. Not about anything. I have work to do.

I can cut the wire, or saw through it. But it is thicker than at the top and will take time. As I walk along, pushing aside the branches of small trees, climbing over the roots of larger ones, my face stings from the ones I miss that snap back and scratch my skin. I think about the least number of cuts I will need to make in the wire to create an opening. Four up, four across. Then I can fold it along the midline, making a triangle flap large enough to slide through. I will put the boots on my hands and use them to push against the wire, to protect myself from the barbs.

Where do I stop? Where do I begin to cut this fence?

My legs want to keep moving. My mind tells me to run. It is instinct but instinct is not always smart. I could run and run and end up right back at the gate, having made a circle and gone nowhere. I fight against the instinct. I will only walk until I see something on the other side of the fence that will help me once I cut my way through.

I don't know how much time passes. I feel tired. My legs ache from pulling the boots that want to fall from my feet. I am cold from air that is damp in the woods. The leaves and bushes are wet from the rain, and they rub against me and soak through these clothes I wear. My cheeks burn from the cold.

As I walk, my mind wanders. I think about John. I think about us years ago when we'd only just met. When we were two young lovers with all of life in front of us. And that's what we were— lovers in every possible way. I loved him like I had never loved any man. I loved the things about him that drove other people crazy. He could be far too serious, too honest, too earnest. He was desperate to be a good man. I loved his desperation. I loved that I could ease it just by lying beside him.

We met at a deli on the campus where we both went to grad- uate school. He was studying business. I was getting my master's degree. He was a customer. I worked behind the counter. I wore a bright blue apron and he told me it was the color of my eyes, which made me blush. He had ordered chicken salad, but I was so flustered by him, the way he'd noticed my eyes, that I gave him tuna. He came back later that day to tell me. But he didn't want a new sandwich. He wanted to take me hiking.

We liked to walk in the woods, just like this. We would hike from March until November, cold, hot—it didn't matter. We would drive up to the mountains. And we would hike until we felt our legs ache and our heads grow dizzy with endorphins. And then we would return to our little room at the bed and breakfast and make love, furiously. Passionately.

I loved him. But that was before.

Now there's a line that divides the before from the after. Before our child died. After our child died. The love doesn't dare try to cross, to try to navigate the new people we have become. Not much of me is left. I wonder how much of John is still there. The earnest- ness I always adored, the man who always wanted to do good and be good, now feels rigid. A man who must live by the strictest rules of behavior. Maybe it keeps him from having to think or feel. He still says *I love you* but that's a lie. Lying is against the rules, isn't it? And what about the other woman he now loves?

Maybe I don't know the new rules. Maybe I don't know John anymore.

The love won't cross the line to find out.

I think about the man in this house with his dead wife and his child. I think about the odd rules they keep. The secrets.

The wondering returns as I walk.

How do they know about me? About my family? That I would be driving on Route 7 last night, in the storm? Or did they? Alice never leaves the house. She plays out her fantasies with her dolls. Maybe that's all this is. A fantasy.

I told her about my family before she said she knew. Maybe she was lying.

She said she was nine. Did I tell her how old Annie was? God, I can't remember!

I walk and walk until I see something on the other side of the fence. It makes me stop. I close my eyes and breathe it in. Fire. Smoke. Burning wood. I open my eyes and see it again—the white plumes rising in the sky. A house or factory, maybe. Someplace with a furnace. Or someone burning brush in the yard, although it seems too wet for that. More likely a furnace or fireplace.

It is, at the very least, a sign of life. A sign of people. People who might help me. A place to run. A place to hide.

I tell myself to stop. I kneel down into the wet debris and take out the scissors. I take out the knife. And I go to work.

More time passes. My fingers are sore from cutting. I have only cut through three wires. The barbs make it hard to hold steady. The scissors slip. The knife won't stay in one groove. I have to saw and cut slowly. Carefully. I can't steady the wire without cutting my fingers. My hands are cold and my tools slip from them. Over and over. They slip out and fall to the ground. I blow on my fingers desperately. I need to warm them up. I need to ease the muscles so they can hold my tools.

Please. One more cut up. Four more to the side . . .

A voice calls out. It tells me to stop. It asks me where I am.

I stand quickly and move away from the fence, leaving my tools in the leaves. Leaving my work behind me. I walk furiously away from the fence, into the woods. Away from the smoke and fire and the people who can help me. I have been picturing them. I have been seeing their faces as they fold me in blankets and call my family. As they call the police and break through the gates of this insanity and discover Alice and the man and put a stop to it, whatever it is. Tears fall as I leave them behind. I will find a place to hide. Somewhere in these woods. And then I will return to my work. To my cutting. I will not stop until I reach my saviors.

I walk carefully, but the dead brush snaps and pops beneath my feet. I get far enough away from the fence that it is out of sight. And then I hide. I find a large tree and I sit on the other side of its trunk from the voice that grows closer.

And when the voice stops, I hear only the footsteps. The same snaps and pops that my body had made, only louder and stronger. And then everything stops, except the sound of metal on metal.

"What are you doing?" the voice asks.

I look around the tree. The man is there and he holds a shotgun.

I stand but say nothing. I cannot manage to speak.

"You could get hurt out here," he says. "You could get killed."

I stare at him as my body trembles. I pray he can't see the blisters that are forming on my hands.

"Didn't Alice tell you about the bears?"

I shake my head. I study his face. He looks dismayed. He looks concerned, the way a person would, given the situation. The bears. His face becomes a mirror, reflecting back to me my own insanity. How ridiculous I must appear. Have I let the fantasy of a little girl scare me into a frenzy?

He looks around us, swinging the shotgun. Then he sets it against the tree and gives me his hand, helping me to my feet. His grip is gentle and his face holds a smile. It's the smile of a person trying to help a crazy person out of her craziness. He coaxes me and I begin to settle. What caused me to lose control of my senses? Alice said they followed me from the gas station. She knew about my family. But maybe that was all in her mind. Maybe they just saw me there. Maybe I told her first and she only pretended to know how old Annie was.

I consider that my thoughts are not normal. That the death of my child has carved paths inside my head that always lead to the darkest scenarios. Paranoia. *It happened once. It could happen again. Horror.*

But life is almost never horror. It can feel horrible. It can seem horrible. But not like this. Not this kind of crazy horror.

"I'm sorry," I say then, meeting his eyes. "I got lost and then I panicked. I should have stayed in the house."

"No harm done. But come on now," he says. "If we hurry, there might be time to get you back to town."

I want to throw my arms around him and thank him. He's not going to shoot me. He's not going to kill me. He's going to take me to town.

Of course he is. I have had crazy thoughts and now I want to thank him for returning me to reality.

I almost bounce like Alice as I follow him back to the house.

10

Day fourteen

The bartender.

Nic could not remember his name, but she remembered other things about him. Like the calm in his voice, and the surrender in his eyes.

She remembered things about his story as well. A drug-addicted mother. Absent father. Little sister to care for.

He could have gone to college. But he stayed to work—here, and at the Gas n' Go. Anything he could get. His sister was young. Or maybe that was all wrong. Maybe he was older and years had passed since his sister was young and he'd had to support her. Maybe he was still here because the other ships had all sailed.

Nic did remember that he seemed kind. That she liked the way he smelled when she kissed his neck. That he had a heavy pour. Traces of remorse still lingered from that night, the way they always did.

She crossed the street. He didn't see her as he finished opening the doors, turning on the neon sign that hung in the window.

She pulled on the door. A string of bells jingled. He was taking chairs down from tables and he turned at the sound.

"Hey," he said. He looked surprised, his body frozen, eyes wide.

Nic smiled spontaneously. It had been a long time since her face had held this expression. It felt awkward, even as a wave of warmth was released from the pull of her cheeks.

"Hi," she said.

"You're back?" He put down the last chair and walked behind the bar. It was hard not to read into this, how he did not greet her in a more personal manner. And how he chose to put the bar between them.

"I am," she answered. "There was a new tip about my mother." She walked to the bar, took a seat on a stool across from where he stood on the other side.

He asked about the tip and she told him—about the woman and the truck and how they'd just gone to meet her, Nic and Officer Reyes, and did he know Reyes, and of course he did. Everyone knows everyone else in this town. He wiped the already clean counter with a bar towel as they spoke. He was nervous. Something about her return had him unsettled.

"Want a drink?" he asked.

"It's a little early," she answered.

She said it as though the thought hadn't nearly consumed her mind.

"Kurt," the bartender said abruptly.

He poured her a glass of water.

"My name," he continued. "Kurt Kent—and please don't make a joke. I've heard them all."

Nic drank the water as her cheeks flushed.

"I feel like I would have remembered that name."

"You never asked."

"Yeah," Nic replied. And then, "Sorry. I was a bit of a mess."

Kurt leaned back against the other side of the bar, arms crossed, that look of surrender in his eyes as he smiled slightly.

"Understandable."

"Not really," Nic replied. "I was here to search for my mother and I spent every night closing down this bar."

He started to make excuses for her, *people handle fear differently, don't be so hard on yourself, it wasn't that bad. . . .* But it had been that bad.

Vodka had not been able to settle her that night, the night after they found the note and everyone decided her mother had left them. Had walked away. The shock of this had gutted the hollow spaces. It made her cringe to remember now, with him standing before her. How she'd pulled him to the back of the bar, kissed him until he'd kissed her back. Thank God they hadn't been alone.

"I'm sorry," Nic said now. She buried her face in the palms of her hands.

"Don't be sorry. It takes two, you know?" There it was—that calm voice. The kindness.

"So what's next?" he asked her. "How long are you staying?"

Nic unburied her face and opened her eyes to look at him. "I don't know," she said.

"Are the police getting involved again?" he asked.

"They said they would. What do you think? Reyes seems on top of things."

"That's one way to put it."

The sarcasm in Kurt's voice was unmistakable.

"What do you mean?"

"I've never seen him disappoint a damsel in distress."

"Yeah—I kind of got that about him. Lots of eyes linger when he's around."

Kurt moved closer now, elbows on the counter, leaning forward. Nic could smell his cologne, or soap, something, and it pulled from a far corner of her mind the feel of his hands on the small of her back, then tangled in her hair.

"You noticed, huh? Most women don't. Until the next day when he doesn't call."

Kurt the bartender was not that kind of man, and he brought her back, somehow, to the time before. Across that invisible line to the time when life was just life. When her future was nothing but opportunities and the quiet faith that her family would remain as it was. Happy, even when Evan and Annie were fighting over something trivial, when her parents were hovering over them. Her father wasn't perfect—he could be demanding and rigid. But they knew he loved them.

And how he had adored their mother. It was in his eyes, the way he admired her idealism, her passion for her students. They had a special anniversary the first Tuesday in August, the facts of which they kept a secret between them. Her father always bought her something blue. She always made him a chicken salad sandwich. They shooed away the children into another room and sat alone, drinking wine and laughing. They did this every year before Annie died.

On the other side of that line was also her mother—soft on the outside, but strong on the inside. Molly Clarke had never missed a cross-country meet or talent show or football game. She'd crawled into bed with them when they were sick or had nightmares or just because they'd asked her to. She had been the definition of home, the embodiment of family. A sacred symbol of the most primal human connection. Mother and child. How ironic that it had been her dedication that left one of them dead.

Nic had thought of her family as special. Idyllic. Perfect. Maybe Annie had been her punishment.

Kurt the bartender. He had pulled her back across that line to a time when the men she chose, the boys then, were the kind ones.

Kurt busied himself with another task. "So was she helpful?"

"I don't know," Nic answered. "Reyes thinks she might be lying. Something about her E-ZPass records and her story about coming from New York City. Thinks she might be after the reward money."

"Oh yeah?" Kurt asked. "Makes sense. It is strange she waited so long. What did you say her name was?"

"I didn't—it's Edith Moore. Lives in Schenectady."

Kurt's face grew still. "Edith—kind of an older woman's name, right? Is she?"

"Is she what?"

"Older?"

Nic shrugged. "Older than we are. Younger than my mother. Why—did you see someone from out of town that night? Before you closed the bar?"

Kurt looked up at the ceiling as though deep in thought. His hand moved to his chin. His actions seemed exaggerated, like he was overselling his contemplation.

"Don't think so. But I also closed up pretty early."

She asked another question, her eyes fixed on his face now so she could assess his reaction.

"But you've never heard of her? Edith Moore?"

Kurt took her glass and put it in the sink. He wiped the water ring from the counter.

"Nah," he said. His voice was steady. His expression giving nothing away.

Still, something was off.

"I should go." Nic climbed down from the stool, pushed it back in.

But Kurt stopped her. "Hey," he said. "Did you ever follow up on that girl?"

"What girl?"

"The girl who disappeared ten years ago."

She tried to find a trace of a memory but there was nothing. "No. Did you tell me the last time I was here?"

"Yeah."

"Can you tell me again?"

Kurt waved his hand dismissively, now that he had her full attention. Now that Edith Moore and the story of the truck had been pushed aside.

"It's probably not related. She was young, like nineteen. Local girl. Grew up in Hastings. People thought she disappeared but then it turned out she left on her own. Didn't want her boyfriend to follow her. She wrote to him after a while, but I remember people thinking something bad happened."

"Did she ever come back?"

"Would you?"

"Fair enough."

"I guess she was trying to get away—from Hastings. Maybe from her boyfriend. Or both. I didn't know her that well."

Nic was more than curious now. "Which do you think it was?" she asked. "Running from the town or from a man?"

Kurt shrugged. "I've got no idea."

She looked at him until he met her eyes.

"Who would know?"

"Just one person I can think of," he answered. "Her sister."

"Where can I find her?" There was something about this that

had her full attention. Another woman who'd disappeared, assumed to have walked away.

Kurt glanced out the window, across the street at the inn, then back at her.

"I'll take you," he said. "After my shift."

11

Day two

We sit at a small table in the kitchen. It is round and has four chairs. We eat sandwiches. Alice drinks milk. Milk sits before me as well, but I do not drink it. I should have asked for water, but I did not want to upset Alice. She poured me the milk. I hate milk.

The man drinks a beer. His mood has been the same since we walked back from the edge of the property. Helpful. Kind.

Alice makes us hold hands because she wants to say grace. I feel my right hand taken by the man who reaches across the table. I feel my left hand taken by Alice. As she says her prayer, I say my own. I pray that neither of them can feel the blisters on my skin.

"Thank you, Lord, for these blessings. For the food, and the milk," she says. Her eyes are closed as she speaks. But then she opens them and looks at me.

"And forgive us for our sins. Amen."

She was angry when the man brought me back to the house. I had been gone for well over an hour. I had no idea, and I didn't care. I wasn't planning to return. Now I don't know what to think or feel. I cling to hope.

When we returned, the man brought me more clothes from his dead wife. I have not seen my clothes since last night, but he told me he put them on an outside line to dry since the sun was strong today. After dinner, I will offer to retrieve them.

Angry as she was, Alice still offered to give me the mask for my allergies, but I told her I didn't need it. I told her I felt pretty good after such a long walk. This brought a smile to her face. She had been worried about me.

The man brought home lunch. Cold sandwiches and a bag of potato chips. He said that after we ate he would take me back to town.

The power is still out. The phone still dead. The portable generator is running the boiler in the basement so we have heat and hot water. It also runs the stove. It has lasted all night and into this afternoon. Even without the gas. But maybe that's not true. Maybe those cans were full.

Alice swings her legs as she eats. It makes her body bounce and her long hair swoosh from side to side. She wears a pink sweater with purple leggings that are too small. Bunny slippers hang from her swinging feet.

I try to eat. I feel the effects of the exhaustion and hunger and it is not productive. I hold the sandwich in my sore hand and bring it to my mouth. Chew. Swallow. But I am anxious to be done. I want to go to town and see for myself the things I've been told.

First, my car was not on the side of the road. He thinks it probably got towed somewhere. Everything is shut down and the police are too busy to check on it.

Second, he couldn't find my purse. He said I must have left it on the side of the road. Or maybe in my car. But I know this is not right. I can still feel it clutched in my hand as I waved down his truck with both arms, over my head. The way I always do when I'm not thinking about it. It registers in my thoughts because Evan and Nicole find it embarrassing. I reason with myself that some people are not good at finding things, that maybe it is in the truck, under a seat, and that he just didn't look hard enough.

Because, third, he called all the numbers I gave him but no one picked up. He left messages for them. John. Nicole. A few friends. He showed me his phone log—the numbers in black with the little arrow next to them. Then he showed me the voicemail box, which was empty.

I thought that this could not be true. But then I considered that perhaps it is true. Perhaps they didn't recognize his number and did not pick up. We've been getting dozens of robocalls lately, and from all different numbers. Maybe there hasn't been time for them to check their messages.

The man sits back in his chair, legs splayed wide, forearms on the table.

After dinner, we will go to town and call my family again. We will stop by the police station and ask about my car. I will have my clothes from the line. And that will be that.

"I'm sorry I got lost on my walk," I say cheerfully. I direct my gaze at Alice and smile.

"I didn't realize there were bears. That's so scary," I say. "Do they ever come up to the house? I've heard they can be very aggressive when they want food."

Alice looks to the man who nods. Only then does she answer.

"One time they went through the garbage. But it might have been raccoons. They like the garbage too. And they're so big!"

I don't feel like talking, but I want to be polite. I make my eyes grow wide with amazement. "We have big raccoons where we live,"

I say. "My husband put a lock on the garbage cans to keep them from coming. They gave up after a while."

The man's phone sits on the kitchen counter near his wallet. I glance at it now. I have to remind myself that there is nothing to check until we get back in range. Still, it reminds me that he tried to call and no one answered.

It was hard to believe without seeing the phone log. I didn't even have to ask him—I think he knew how unbelievable it was.

I've been missing for twenty-four hours. They should be glued to their phones. They should answer every call—even the robocalls now. Wouldn't they? Wouldn't they answer every single call? Even though my husband doesn't love me. Even though my daughter hates me. They would be desperate to find me. This sickens me, this thought of my family in despair.

And now another thought—maybe they don't know I'm missing. Is that possible? That they haven't even noticed I'm gone?

I struggle to make conversation.

"I saw smoke when I was lost in the woods. Are we close to the neighbors?" I ask.

Alice shrugs like she has no idea. I believe her. My kids never knew how far things were unless they got there themselves, by foot or by bike.

I stop myself quickly from having this thought. Annie was on foot that day. Running to catch the ice cream truck. She'd heard the bells. The jingle. She'd heard it pass by and knew where it would stop—on the corner of our street and the road that heads to town. Our town. There's a small park on that corner. The truck would stop there and kids would come running from the park, lining up to buy ice cream. When I was home, I would walk with them. Down the driveway. Down the street. I would hold their hands and look for cars coming around the bend. We would cross the street to the sidewalk.

But I wasn't home that day.

"It's far," the man says. "Too far to walk without getting eaten by a bear." I wonder how he can say this when Alice is afraid of the bears.

"Alice said your wife got lost in the woods," I tell him. The things Alice told me linger in my thoughts. *That's how my first mommy died.*

The man looks at Alice now. Then back to me.

"It's true," he says. But when he hesitates, I know this is a lie he tells for Alice, and that he knows how ridiculous it sounds. "She went into the woods and never came back." And that was that. His tone has a finality to it and I know to leave well enough alone. Still—he joked about the bears, didn't he?

Finish lunch. Get to town.

Alice seems upset by this talk of her first mommy. I wonder if she was Alice's real mother, and if she loved her. Alice is so hungry for love. It's a hunger that could swallow a person whole.

"It's not as bad as how your daughter died," Alice says.

The man looks between us, curious.

"She was hit by a car. She ran into the street," she says.

I feel violated but I try not to react. I try not to let my emotions run wild. She is just a child.

She is just a child.

Alice now strikes at my heart. "You were driving that car," she says. "That means you weren't a very good mommy."

My eyes stare at her as she stares at me and I can't look away. Suddenly I see Annie's face. Annie's blond hair and blue eyes. Annie's feet swinging beneath the table. And Annie saying those words, the ones she must have been thinking when she felt the impact of the car, hurling metal crushing her bones, sending her into the air, her head smashing against the pavement.

That car.

My car.

I hear her voice. My sweet, sweet girl.

You were not a good mommy.

No, my darling. I wasn't. I let you die. I killed you.

I feel tears streak my face. Alice and the man watch me with curiosity and wonder, and I no longer care what happened here. I don't know what loss they've suffered and how they know these things about me.

I never told her that I was driving the car.

It is inhuman the way they watch me cry for my dead child.

"Should we clean up and go to town," I say with a shaky voice. The hope that this will happen is fading but I don't know what to put in its place.

The man stares at me. Then he says, cheerfully, "Sure."

I stand. I gather plates. My hand are full when a distinct sound stuns us all.

From the kitchen counter comes a ringing. The man's cell phone. A call is coming in. A call reaching this house that he said has no reception.

I look at him now with disbelief as the weight of this information bears down against my chest. I can't breathe.

"Looks like there's service today," I say. I wait for a reaction. He is still. There is no expression. The plates are in my hands. I stand between the man and his phone. I shift my weight toward the counter, toward the phone. My feet are still, but he senses something. My intentions. My desperation. My doubt.

If there is service in this house, then everything he's told me could also be a lie. My car. My purse. The calls to my family. I slide one foot closer to the counter, and it's now that he finally moves.

Slowly, he shakes his head back and forth. The shotgun rests, propped against a wall, within his reach. Alice holds a hand over her mouth, containing her fear. Or is it excitement?

I don't think anymore. I drop the dishes and they crash to the floor. Alice gasps. The man jumps up.

I lunge for the phone and take it in my hand. I should run but I feel desperate to press that little green circle. Before I do, I am on the floor, the broken plates beneath me, scraping against my back. The man is on top of me, the weight of his body pressing me into the floor. Into the broken shards.

"Go to your room," he says to Alice, and she scurries away.

His voice is stern but otherwise calm. He does not yell. He never yells. Even in the heat of this violent moment.

He takes the phone from my clenched hand. He takes it with no effort at all, peeling my fingers away with his fingers, as though all of my strength is not even a bother to him. My body fights now, arms and legs and torso and head, all writhing and flailing like a captured animal in the mouth of its predator.

Helpless.

His legs are outside my legs, pinning them together. His left hand holds both of my wrists as he props himself up and looks at the phone. I try to lift my head, teeth ready to clamp down on his flesh, but he is just out of reach. And he knows this. I can see on his face the satisfaction that he has secured his prey.

He uses his thumb to stop the call before it can be answered.

He slides the phone out of reach, across the kitchen floor. He leans his head in close to mine, his mouth brushes my ear.

"Are you wondering if that was your daughter? The one you didn't kill?"

I freeze now. Terror. They know everything.

Not another word is spoken as he slides me across the floor, pieces of the plates digging into my skin.

He drags me by my arms, even as my legs kick and my body writhes to break free, twisting and turning in futility.

He drags me down the hall, past the guest room. Past Alice's room and his room to the very end.

A door opens to the room that is cold and dark and has a hard tile floor.

The fear descends as he drags me inside and closes the door. I hear a dead bolt click into position on the other side.

It is then I know.

I am never leaving this house.

12

Day fourteen

Daisy Hollander.

Another woman who'd disappeared. Another woman who'd written notes to loved ones, telling them she'd walked away from her life. Nic thought about Daisy Hollander as she cradled a cup of coffee in her hands, looking out at the bar across the street.

Kurt had told her what he knew about the missing girl and her family. Eight children. Poverty. Dismal enough to draw out social services, and that was saying a lot for this part of the state, he'd said. Parents were long gone. He didn't know where. All of the children had left as well. Except for one. A sister named Veronica.

She lived in the family's old house in the deep part of the woods near the river, on land that was owned by the state. No one had tried to chase them off. He'd said he wondered if anyone from the state actually realized it. Nothing that happened in Hastings made much of a difference one way or another.

You'll never find it, he'd told her.

Kurt had promised to take her when his shift ended.

Was that strange, she wondered now? That he didn't just give her directions? That he'd brought it up at all? No one else had mentioned Daisy Hollander. Not even Chief Watkins.

The diner was close to empty, even at noon. Just one man at the counter, and an older woman in the back who came every day and stayed through dinner, reading books and sipping lemon water. Nic remembered her from the last time she was here. The diner was warm and the water was free. It made her think that Roger Booth was a generous man.

Nic waved to the same waitress from the morning who was leaning on the counter, reading something on her phone. Ignoring her. Nic had captured Officer Reyes's attention, so now she would be punished with bad service. Cold coffee.

It was just like the girls in school. She had not been one of them. Not ever. And their petty jealousies had amused her. She'd been an athlete. An academic. She'd had her eye on the endgame, which was getting into college and finding her path in life. Her friends had been like-minded, a small pack of four or five of them, banding together against the invisible social ladder in their school. It was absurd how they were sorted out. Boys who played sports with sticks were at the top. Their girlfriends sat beside them on their thrones. Pretty blondes. Always. Nic was blond and some used to think she was pretty. But she didn't have it in her to sidle up to a jock.

She'd liked the quiet boys. The geeks and runners. The quiet thinkers. The ones Kurt Kent reminded of her of, though he didn't fit into any of those categories. Maybe it was his earnestness. That was how her mother had described her father—earnest.

That life had felt strong and good.

That life had been a gift. A gift that was long gone.

She was about to get up and get the coffee herself when she saw a new text from Evan.

What did that woman say?

Nic started to text a reply, but decided to call.

"Hey," he said. He sounded surprised.

"Hey. How are you?"

"I'm, you know, whatever. What's going on there?"

Nic considered how much to tell him. He needed to keep his shit together. Junior year was important.

"I met with the woman."

Nic told him about Officer Reyes, and how he'd punched holes through Edith Moore's story.

"So she's like the other assholes? After the money?" he asked.

"Everyone wants the money. That doesn't mean she isn't telling the truth about the truck. She would be pretty stupid to make up a story that Mom would know was a lie."

Evan was silent then.

She shouldn't have gone down that path. He was coming to the same conclusion she had earlier with Reyes, after they'd left Edith Moore at the Gas n' Go. If their mother was dead, she wouldn't be able to refute any story. And there was money to be had, dead or alive.

"Ev—I think she did see Mom," Nic said, changing the subject. Giving him hope. "Do you remember how she always waved at us, when she couldn't get our attention?"

"Both arms over the head? Like she was working the tarmac at JFK?"

Nic smiled. "Yeah. It was ridiculous, right?"

"Can I tell you something?"

"Of course, Ev. What is it?"

"She did that at the game. She didn't know I saw her, but after we scored a touchdown, she was standing and cheering and waving like that and it pissed me off because she looked so stupid."

He could barely get out the last few words.

"Maybe she did know, Evan. Maybe she knew you saw her and that even though it pissed you off, it was because you know how much she loves you."

"I guess. What made you think about that? The way she waves at us?" Evan asked.

"Edith Moore said that's how she waved down this truck. And she even had her purse in one hand, so it was flying in the air as well."

Evan's voice was lighter now. "Usually it was with her phone in her hand. It was fucking ridiculous! We told her to stop."

"I know! We did. Even Dad told her. She was so embarrassing."

Nic felt her throat tighten with these thoughts, these memories, of their mother.

"And she saw the letters on the purse. That was never released to the press."

"So she really saw her? She saw Mom that night?" His voice trailed off at the end. Was he crying? Had she made him cry?

"Ev . . ."

"Can you find the truck? Maybe she said something, told someone why she didn't come home." His words sounded fragile, their syllables broken.

"I'm trying, Ev. That's why I'm here. Why I'm staying."

"Okay . . . fuck. I mean, fuck this, Nic! Where is she?"

"I don't know . . ." Nic tried to stay calm, keep her voice steady so she could stop him from unraveling. But it was too late.

"Why? What the fuck! Why did she leave us?"

Nic searched for the right answer. Was it better that he believed their father's lie? That the note had been authenticated? That their mother left them? Or should she tell him the truth—that now she didn't know for sure, even if the police and everyone else in this town still believed it?

Not knowing meant their mother could be dead.

"Ev—listen to me," she said. "It wasn't because of the football game. It wasn't because of anything you did."

"I see her sometimes," he said, his voice beginning to calm. "I see her standing by the door to the field house, smiling at me. Wanting me to smile back. Just one smile, you know? And I just felt so pissed off that she was right there where all my friends could see her. It's not normal that she came all that way for every home game. Other parents don't come until the playoffs. Why did she have to do that? Why did she keep coming?"

"You know why, Ev."

"Why?"

She took a second, let him think about it.

"Because of Annie?" he asked then. "That was so long ago. And it's not like driving eight hours to see me is going to bring her back."

"I know. It's complicated."

"Do you ever ask yourself . . ."

"What?"

"Why we're not enough. Why it's not enough that we're still here."

God, Evan. What could she say to that? The truth was, she had never asked that question. It was shocking to hear this, how their mother's disappearance had resonated so differently inside of him.

"Evan—I'm going to find her, okay? You keep your shit together. I've got this."

"Okay . . ."

"Promise me?"

"I promise," he said.

Nic told him about the broken taillight, and how it was a good lead. She made it sound more promising than it was because she needed him to be all right. He seemed comforted by it, this shred of hope she'd given him.

Then he asked, "Did you ever find out what was behind that fence? If anyone looked there?"

Nic went up to her room. She found sweats and sneakers. Then back downstairs where she found Roger Booth at the front desk.

"Hi," Nic said.

"Hello," he replied. He was in a good mood.

"Are there any trails behind the inn? I wanted to go for a run," she said.

Roger jerked his head back like the surprise had knocked him square in the jaw.

"Not really. The ground's pretty rough. And wet. Why don't you go on the road?"

"I used to run cross-country. I still run in the woods. The trails. How far back does it go—the property?"

"We've got about fifty acres. You could start training for a marathon if you want."

Roger Booth had a sense of humor.

Nic turned and walked to the front door. Roger called after her.

"Wait. I was actually joking. It's not safe out there. The bears are still active. And we've had sightings of wolves."

"Seriously?"

Roger nodded. He was serious, but Nic didn't care.

"You really want to go in the woods?"

"I really do. Besides, I want to check out that fence my father saw."

"Fence?"

"You don't know about it?"

"Not since I've been running the place. Far as I know, it's just woods."

Nic followed him through the door behind the desk. It led to an office, which had another door to the outside. There was a blue-stone patio which was overgrown with weeds. Moss caked most of the stones and a rotten picket fence framed the square. Piled in the corner were an old, rusted-out firepit and some lawn chairs. On the far side was a shed.

"We use this in the summer. Or we used to anyway, back when we had more guests. Some nights, we'd be full up. Kids, parents, everyone sitting around by the fire at night."

Nic could not imagine it. The state of disintegration, of disrepair—it was like a testament to the agony this town had endured since its economic spiral.

She followed Roger Booth to the shed. He opened the padlock, and then the doors.

Inside were some gardening tools and equipment. A John Deere lawn mower sat in the corner, thick with dust. A small generator was beside that. Tiki torches rested against a wall.

And hanging just above them was a row of shotguns.

"You gonna give me one of those?" Nic asked. "To shoot the bears?"

"You know how to shoot?" Roger asked.

"I missed that class at my private school."

Roger smiled. "I was thinking more along this line."

He handed her a small black canister.

"It's just pepper spray. Problem is, you gotta get pretty close before it'll work."

Nic took the spray, examining the nozzle and trigger. Roger adjusted her into the right position. His hands were stronger than she had thought. His fingers long and lean.

"Like this," he said. "Point and squeeze."

"How far will it spray?"

"About six feet."

Roger stepped away and led them out of the shed. He clicked the padlock back on the doors.

"So if I see a bear, I have to let it charge me and then spray and hope it stops?"

Roger nodded and smiled. "He might get in one good swipe."

"Okay," Nic said. "Better maimed than dead, I suppose."

"Exactly."

They walked around the fence where there was nothing but open woods. The trees were tall but bare. Nic could tell she would be able to weave through them.

Roger pointed toward the sun.

"Head toward the sunset. Don't make any turns. When you've had enough, turn around and come straight back. That way you won't get lost."

"I'll bring my phone. Just in case."

"Okay. Good luck."

Roger stood at the edge of the tree line.

Nic turned, took a few steps, then stopped. "Can I ask you something?" she said.

He nodded. "Sure."

"Did you know a woman named Daisy Hollander?"

Booth stared blankly.

"Yeah," he said. "She was a girl from high school."

"Who disappeared?" Nic asked.

"Who told you that?"

"I just heard it around. Any idea what happened to her?"

"She left. Just like the rest of her family, one by one. People do that around here, you know."

Nic watched his face, the nonchalance of his words and the tone of his voice not matching his expression.

"You should get going before the sun is gone."

He disappeared behind the fence. She heard the door to the inn open and close. Then she started to move.

Her legs felt heavy. Her breath shallow. She was tired and she hadn't eaten—her body was protesting now. But the pain felt good. She ran through the trees, watching her feet carefully with every step so she didn't place them down on a branch or rock. It was an obstacle course and it did exactly what she remembered from her days racing cross-country. The physical pain, the mental preoccupation—all of it a welcome distraction.

She checked her phone. Fifteen minutes had passed. Still no fence.

Breathe in. Breathe out.

The pain in her legs had moved into her side. A cramp. She never had to stop. Even after a bad night. Even after miles and miles. This was more than exhaustion.

Suddenly she was standing still, buckled over, gasping for air. Her head was light as she sucked it into her lungs. Words had broken free while her mind had been busy fighting the pain. They were free and singing between her ears. The things she'd said to her mother the morning she disappeared. The things she'd piled on top of *I hate you* and *open your eyes!* The things that surely had pushed her mother over the edge on the anniversary of Annie's death.

You killed my sister!

Oh, God. No.

You killed your own child!

No.

She had said those words. And she'd told no one.

Tears came, running into the sticky sweat on her face. She wiped them with the back of her hand and leaned against a tree.

Breathe in. Breathe out.

The sky was turning orange. She didn't have long until it would be too low to help her navigate.

She looked back at the sunset to make sure she'd squared herself, to make sure of the direction. When she did, she saw something shimmer through the trees. She looked again, then started to walk toward it. Another shimmer. The sun was almost at the horizon and it created a glare. But she kept walking, until she was forced to stop.

Evan was right—there was a fence. She stood before it and looked up. It had to be seven or eight feet. There were barbed coils at the top, and smaller barbs lining every inch of the wire. She touched them gently. They were sharp. They were meant to keep anyone from being able to climb. The barbs would shred bare skin and the holes were too narrow for a shoe.

She looked through it but saw only more woods on the other side.

She started to follow the fence, walking alongside. She remembered Roger Booth's warning—*don't make any turns.*

She told herself she would make this one turn and walk for ten minutes, then turn around.

It only took five for her to reach the small hole someone had started to cut.

13

Day five

The door opens and three days of darkness come to an end.

He has been bringing food after dark. He leaves the light off in the hallway. There are no windows in this dark room where Alice was born. Just the sink, a hand-pump toilet, and the tile floor. He's given me two blankets to stay warm.

I count the days by the pitch of the darkness. Light is like water, always finding a way through the cracks and crevices.

On the third night, he does not bring the food. He waits until morning. When he opens the door, the brightest light pours in behind him. It is so bright it blinds me and I can barely make out his face.

He sets the tray down on the floor while I stand against the far wall. He has made me wait because the last time he brought the tray I was waiting for him. The second night, when I heard the floorboards creak. On that night I stood in front of the door. I heard the dead bolt turn, then the change in the shadows as the door opened into the room. In my hands was a blanket.

Heart exploding with rage, hands shaking with apprehension, I was ready to throw the blanket over his head, pull him toward me, then onto the floor. I had pictured the tray flying from his hands, spilling the food. I pictured Alice screaming as I kicked him in the groin. I would leave them both inside that room, lock the door, and run out of the house. I would take his truck if I could find the keys, or run back to the fence where I would make two more cuts in the wire and then crawl through.

Maybe I would have his shotgun with me. Maybe I would blast a hole right through that fence.

But that was not what happened. On the second night, he was ready for me as I stood on the other side of the door with my pathetic weapon. He stood a few feet back. There was no tray in his hands. Only the shotgun.

I was ready with that blanket and he knew it. He knew the blanket was all I had and he knew I would try.

He knows too much.

Or maybe this was tried before, by the woman who used to live here.

He laughed at me. He ordered me to back away. Then he locked the door. And he made me wait all through the next day, and through the next night, wondering if I would get another tray. Wondering if he was now going to let me starve.

The door opens now, after the third night, and I stand against the far wall. I let the light feed my brain which is starving for it. I watch him place the tray on the floor, close the door, turn the lock.

I stumble as I walk toward the tray. My pupils have narrowed from that quick burst of light and now they can't detect the shadows they have grown used to. I take the tray and sit down. I can feel with my hands the cold sandwich. And something else.

It's small and metal. I feel glass at the top. A button at the bottom. I click it on and light floods the space.

A small flashlight. A gift I don't understand.

I do not deserve a gift after the second night.

I don't stop to think. I leave the flashlight on as I eat the sandwich. I'm thirsty, but there is water in the sink and I decide to eat first because I am sick with hunger.

When I lift the sandwich, I see something beneath a paper towel. An article from a paper he's printed out. The online paper from my hometown.

Warmth floods my veins as I see the logo, the letters forming the name, the familiar print and advertisers. *Grayson's Flower Shop. Buster's Bagels. The Law Offices of Walsh, Sandberger, LLC.* It's always the same. Every day. Every time I open the paper. And for the smallest, most insane second, I feel the safety of home.

But then the warmth turns cold as I read the headline.

SEARCH FOR LOCAL WOMAN
MISSING UPSTATE CALLED OFF

And colder, still . . .

Evidence suggests Molly Clarke left of her own accord after abandoning her car.

Tears burn as they pour down my face.

Emotionally unstable after the accidental death of her daughter . . .

Ran over her own child on her way home from work . . .

"She never seemed right after that," says a source close to the family . . .

I read every word. I read about my abandoned car being out of gas. I read about my phone left behind. I read about my visit to Evan's school and how he ignored me and everyone saw it and how I cried by the side of the field house.

Did I? Did I cry by the side of the field house?

It takes me several minutes to find the answers. It takes until I see a passage underlined in red ink to know what has occurred.

Clarke's daughter, Nicole, and husband, John, participated in the search that was called off yesterday afternoon after four days. Investigators would not give specifics, but a source close to the family said that a credit card charge has been made at a nearby hotel, and some clothing and a note have been found inside the room Clarke rented. Investigators did confirm that it is now believed the subject left of her own accord.

What has he done?

He has my purse. He's found my credit card. He's forged a note—maybe using the names and numbers I wrote down for him so he could call my family.

Rage returns, bringing back the heat. It does not stop the tears.

Those thoughts I had as I walked down that road, the road with the lies and the false promises, that had seeped into my head and my heart. Thoughts about leaving my family. It's as though he read them all and then made them come true. He's done this to me, but I can't stop the rage from turning right back around. Did I do this to myself?

At the very bottom of the page, I see a picture of John and Nicole. They are walking from a car to a police station. I don't recognize the building or the street or any of the people around them. I think it must be Hastings.

I run my finger lightly over the page, touching the image of them.

I hear a creak of the floorboards from down the hall and I shine the light under the door. I get up and walk closer, until I can see through the crack beneath it. The light shifts with the creaks and I know he stands there. Waiting. Listening, perhaps.

The cold, musty air heaves in and out of my chest until it explodes in words.

"You're a monster!" I scream in futility, in anguish, because I know that nothing I can say to him will touch his soul.

But now a voice—

"*Shhhh,*" it's the voice of an angel. My sweet Alice. This is how I think of her right now, in this moment, when I realize it is her little feet making the light change beneath the crack in the door.

I press my hand against the wood.

"Alice?' I say.

She whispers. "Don't worry," she says. "Don't cry."

"I know." I sob. "I just want to go home. I want to see my family."

Alice sighs loud enough for me to hear.

"We all want things," she says. "But we get what we get and we don't get upset."

She giggles and it makes me cry harder. How can I reach her? How can I make her little fingers move to the dead bolt and turn, turn, turn . . .

"She's pretty," Alice says.

And now comes alarm.

"Who is pretty?" I ask. But I already know.

"Nicole," she says.

I choke on my own heartbeat. It pounds my throat closed and I can't speak.

So I listen.

"She has real blond hair and blue eyes and lots of spirit."

I swallow hard to open my throat. "How do you know?" I ask. The picture was black-and-white. And it gave no description of my daughter.

"He told me. He knows her from when she came to look for you."

"Oh," I say. My voice is shaky. I try to infuse it with casual surprise. "When was that?"

"Ummmm . . ." Alice says, and I can picture her face scrunched up as she thinks. "I don't know but she just went home. They're all done looking for you."

And now I am relieved. I do not want my daughter to be here, to be in this town where he can see her. It's as though in some bizarre twist of irony, my prayer has been answered, the prayer that they just let me go.

Even so, the panic is acute. My hand taps furiously against my leg to contain the energy that has nowhere to go. It wants to make my fists pound on the door. It wants to make my voice cry out for help.

None of these things are useful.

"Okay," I say then, hand tapping, hard, stinging my leg. "Do you know what that means?"

"What?" she asks me.

I choke on the words I have to say. But I know I have to say them.

"It means that I can stay now. It means that I can come out of this room and be your mommy because they're all done looking for me."

She is quiet. She doesn't believe me.

"But you just said you wanted to go home."

Clever girl. How I hate you right now.

No, I will not. I will not hate a child. A child who is also a victim. I pull it back and turn it around.

"I know . . . but you are right. We can't always have everything we want. I want to be home, but I also want to be your mommy. I can't have both, and that's okay. I can just be your mommy now for as long as you want. Home will always be there waiting."

Tears, tears, tears as I choke on these words. On the hatred that keeps knocking.

"Oh," she says now. She has perked right up. "Well, you should have wanted to stay this whole time. Because you killed your daughter and she was nine. And I'm nine! And I need someone to teach me, and you're a teacher! You should have seen that this was your second chance."

A piece of the puzzle falls into place.

"Who told you that?"

"It doesn't matter anymore."

A long breath. I swallow tears. "Why is that?" I ask. "Why doesn't it matter?"

"Because he likes her. He likes the way she looks and the way she acts. She's more like my first mommy."

The next word comes out through trembling lips. "Who?"

My lips tremble because, again, they know the answer before she says it.

She says it anyway.

"Your daughter. Nicole. And he wants her to come back."

14

Day fourteen

Roger Booth was not at the inn when Nic returned from the woods. A laminated sign was posted on the reception desk saying that *management is off site for the evening*. He left a phone number in case of emergencies. Where the hell would Roger Booth be for an entire evening?

Nic's mind was still on the thoughts, the words, that had been set free on her run, but also the fence and the small hole someone had tried to cut in it. She had questions that needed answers. She needed Roger Booth.

In the parking lot, she saw a car, then Kurt Kent in the driver's seat. She'd forgotten about their meeting, and ran now, outside to catch him before he drove off.

"Did you find out anything? About the truck?" he asked when she jumped into the passenger seat.

"Not yet," Nic answered.

"Yeah. Things move slow around here. Which is strange since there's not a lot to do. Inertia, I suppose."

He took a left out of the parking lot, heading toward the river.

"Inertia?"

"Yeah. Physics, you know. An object in motion."

"No—I know what it means. I just . . ."

"Figured I wouldn't?" He sounded insulted, like he knew she was making assumptions about him just because he was stuck in this town. And because he felt above all of it—this town and Nic's assumptions.

"I'm the high school dropout," she said, hoping to diffuse him.

He looked at her, then back at the road. It seemed to work.

"Yeah. Okay."

They drove in silence, past the police station, town hall, the auto body shop. They got to the end of Hastings Pass, where the road met the river, and made another right.

"Did you know there's a fence behind the inn?" Nic asked. "It's about a mile and a half into the property, and about eight feet tall. Barbed wire coils. Barbs in all of the wires, actually."

"Did you ask Booth? Maybe it's his fence."

"He said he didn't know. But why would the Booth family need a fence? You can get to the property from either side of the buildings, and through the back doors. Not exactly a steel trap."

Kurt shrugged. "Animals, maybe. Bears, but also wolves and deer. The deer can jump seven feet. The wolves hunt the deer. I don't know."

"There's something else about it," Nic said. "There was a spot where it looked like someone was cutting through the wire. It looked precise, not an animal, but a person. Maybe with wire cutters. Like someone was trying to make a hole to crawl through."

Kurt appeared more surprised now. "That's weird," he said. "Kids, maybe—from a house next door? Looking for a cut-through to town? How old were the breaks in the wire?"

"I couldn't tell. There was some rust, but not a lot. Nothing had grown over it, like weeds, or fallen branches. I don't have anything to compare it to, but I don't think it started before the summer."

"Yeah," Kurt said. "Hard to tell without knowing what kind of wire it is. If it's been treated with something. Rust repellent. I don't know much about fences."

Nic looked out the window as he drove. The road was narrowing, cutting a path between tall trees whose canopy erased part of the sky.

"You know your way around here."

"Hard not to after a lifetime."

"Fair enough."

They made a turn onto Pond Road. Another onto Jeliff. Nic made a point of looking for the signs, some of which were just paint on rough cuts of wood nailed onto a tree. Pavement turned to gravel and then dirt. Another turn onto a road with no name, then a mile or so farther into the woods. The road ended in front of a small house.

The structure was no more than a thousand square feet. One story. Flat metal roof.

"Someone lives here?" Nic asked. There was no car. No electrical wires. An old clothing line ran between two trees. A sheet and some women's clothing hung to dry, though the frost was coming in the mornings now.

Kurt turned off the ignition.

"Veronica Hollander. I told you, we're on state-owned land. Her father cleared the road, built the house. They lived here—all ten of them. Let me go first," he said. "She doesn't get a lot of visitors."

Nic waited in the car. Kurt approached, carrying a brown paper bag. He knocked on the door. It opened a crack. He said a few words, then he turned and waved for Nic to join him.

A woman stood in the doorway as Nic followed Kurt inside.

She was large and unkempt, wearing pajama bottoms and a short-sleeve shirt that curved around her loose breasts. Long, curly blond hair, and skin that did not appear to have seen the sun in quite some time.

She stared at Nic for a long moment, her face confused at first, then moving over her head to toe.

"I'm Nicole Clarke." Nic extended her hand.

The woman blinked, shook her head quickly like a dog shaking off water.

"Veronica," she said. "People call me V."

Nic smiled. "People call me Nic."

They sat at a small round table in the corner by a window. The window looked out at woods, barely five feet from the house. There was no grass, no garden. Just the small clearing for the four-room structure.

Four rooms. That was all. The bathroom and the living area—sofa, kitchen. Two bedrooms on either side of a short hallway.

Nic turned down her offer to make tea. There was hardly space for it. The table was covered with piles of clothing. A sewing machine sat nearby. V made a cup for herself. She had quite a collection of tins which sat on a small shelf above the stove.

"So you do tailoring?" Nic asked.

V nodded. "I do anything people need. Fix clothes. Make clothes. Take 'em in. Let 'em out. I sew draperies and slipcovers. Cushions. Whatever."

She sat down with her teacup and the brown paper bag Kurt had brought. Inside was a bottle of apricot brandy, which she opened, pouring a shot into the cup. The smell of the brandy rose with the steam and filled the room.

"Must be quite a shock," V said. "Seeing a place like this."

Nic didn't know how to respond. Did she mean her place or Hastings?

Kurt intervened. "Nic's mother is that woman who disappeared during the storm."

V's eyes widened. "Oh!" she said, leaning back in her chair. "Chief came by and asked me about that. I was scared to death here. Thought a tree was sure to take this place down. I didn't see a soul that night. Stayed huddled beneath the bed. No one did one thing to protect me. Can you imagine that? The government can't be bothered with folks like us."

V went on then, about the government and Medicaid and how her parents had to live in one of those places that makes old people wish they were dead, and makes them die faster to get them "off the dole." Her mother was trying to outsmart them by suddenly taking an interest in her health after eighty-seven years. V said this part with admiration.

Nic went with it. "Your family sounds strong-willed."

Now V shrugged, less sure. Less admiring. "I don't know about that. My parents had their views. I think they liked having a hard life, liked the fight of it. But the rest of us, we got a little beat down by always fighting for things. My mother used to lock the refrigerator and the pantry. Padlocks. No money, no food, kids piled four in a room, boys and girls. One bathroom. If you really had to go, sometimes you just went outside. Middle of winter, pissing in the snow."

She took a long breath, ready to tell more of her story. Kurt cut her off.

"She wants to know about Daisy," he said.

V was surprised now. "Daisy? Why on earth do you want to know about her?"

"Because she also disappeared from Hastings," Nic said. "Ten years ago."

A loud, boisterous laugh filled the small space wall to wall. "Who told you that?"

V stared now, out the window into the woods. Thinking, maybe, about her sister.

"I did," Kurt said.

V set her elbows on the table and leaned closer to Nic. She looked her in the eye, hard and without blinking, for a long moment.

"Daisy wasn't like the rest of us. Plain folk. Making do. I know where all the others are. Some married. Some got kids. Others like me, just working to pay bills. We like living alone after how we grew up. But Daisy, she was a shining star. Smarter than the rest of us. Resourceful. Always fighting to get out. Get more. She used to use a stick to poke through the crack in the cupboard where the chains couldn't quite pull them together right. She put sticky tape on the end and figured out how to drag boxes of crackers close to that crack. She'd pull out a few. Eat them all herself. Then she'd slide the box back. And she didn't care when it was time for punishment."

V shook her head.

"You think our mother didn't know exactly how many crackers were in each box?"

Nic watched V tell this story of her sister, her mind spinning. There were girls like Daisy Hollander everywhere. Nic knew the type. Scrappy. Resourceful.

"And she finally found a way to leave for good?" Nic asked.

"Sure did. She told most people she was going to Boston to live with our sister. There were four siblings and my parents still here at the time. I knew she was going to disappear, at least for a while. She didn't want to get dragged down."

"So she just never came back? Didn't you worry about what had happened to her?"

"I know what happened," V said. "She texted me. She moved to New York. Begged me not to tell her poor boyfriend. That kid nearly lost his mind when she left."

"But that was ten years ago."

"Look—some of us are close. Talk every week. Others, a few years go by. Daisy texted once in a while. Stopped altogether a few years ago. But there's nothing strange about that."

"And you're sure they were from her—the messages?"

"I know how she says things. How she talks. Why are you asking this?" V was now concerned. "Do you know something?"

"No—it's not that. I guess I'm just in that frame of mind, looking for my mother."

V placed her hand on top of Nic's. "Oh, you poor thing. But Daisy—well, that's not the same situation. She moved to the city. She wrote to her boyfriend, too. And thank God! That poor kid. Went to Boston. Harassed my sister there, demanding to search her house looking for Daisy. Put up flyers all over the city. Did the same in Hartford. Any place he thought she might have gone. You know, he even went up to this summer camp she used to go to."

"Summer camp?" Nic asked.

"I told you she was resourceful. She got herself a scholarship. Up in Woodstock. Some camp for gifted kids. They read plays and poetry all summer—can you imagine? She came back full of herself. Quoting things from people we'd never heard of, making us feel stupid. But it was hard to blame her. Daisy wanted a better life and she was willing to work for it. She said some of the kids at that camp had more money than everyone in this town put together. She got a real taste of it."

Nic looked at the woods now, through the window. It was dirty, like everything in this room. This house. Piles of clothing. Piles of books. Piles of old magazines. Piles of canned food with bright orange value stickers. V was a hoarder, and Nic couldn't blame her after the way she'd grown up. Still, there was nothing here that was going to help Nic find her mother.

She took a moment to be respectful, but then got up to leave. Kurt followed.

"Thanks for talking to me," she said.

"Yeah—thanks," Kurt echoed.

V got up as well. "My sister left ten years ago. Can't see how it had anything to do with your mother."

They walked to the door. Said their goodbyes.

Nic was about to leave, but then she stopped.

"Is her boyfriend still around?" she asked.

"Of course," V said. She looked at Kurt curiously. "Everybody knows him."

Nic also looked at Kurt now.

"Who is he?" she asked.

It was Kurt who answered. "Roger Booth."

15

Day fourteen

My mother used to say that you can only be as happy as your least happy child. She said there was no getting around this if you were a good and loving parent. She said that's why she only had one child. Once she had me and came to understand this about being a parent, she didn't want to further reduce her chances of having a happy life.

My mother was a pessimist.

She never got around to telling me what happens when a child dies. And when you are the one who killed her.

I think about this while I lie in bed staring at the cracks of light that sneak in through the seams of the plywood. It covers the window from the outside. Sometimes I pull the draperies closed so I can pretend it's just a window. Other times I don't want to pretend.

On the frame of the bedroom doorway, he has installed a metal grate—a second door with eight vertical bars and four horizontal ones. There is a small piece that can open at the bottom with a latch on the other side. Another panel is at the same height as the door handle and it, too, has a lock. A lock with a key.

The bedroom is now a prison.

"Sorry about all this," he said on the day he let me out of the back room. "It's my fault, really. I should have remembered to turn off the phone."

It has been fourteen days since the night of the storm. Two days in the house, thinking I would go home. Five days locked in the dark room with the tile floor, knowing I wouldn't. Seven days in this bedroom, wanting to die. But knowing I can't.

Everything now is about keeping this man away from my family. Away from Nicole.

I stare at the streaks of light and assess the state of my mind. On each of these nine days since leaving that back room, it has surprised me and I have come to view it as a separate entity. Separate from my body. Out of my control in every way.

Some mornings, I wake up not remembering where I am and I feel what I used to feel before the night of the storm—what had come to feel normal after five years, but which I now recognize as numb. It only lasts a moment before reality washes through me like a wave of nausea. That is how I feel today, on day fourteen. And I have the answer my mother never told me. What life is like when you have killed your own child. Numb. I see it now for what it is, because now it washes away with the horror of my captivity.

On other mornings, I wake up startled and I jump from the bed and stand with my back to the wall. I let out small gasps of air with cries of despair that I cover with my hand. I am alive with desperation. But I am alive.

Sometimes I don't sleep at all, and so there is no waking up. My mind reels through the night of the storm. Through the mistakes I made. I swim in a pool of self-loathing, for Annie's death, for Nicole's pain, and for what I have now done to my family by walking down that road, trying to escape my life. I bathe in the agony that I feel I deserve, and my suffering soothes the guilt. I cry and shake but then accept my penance as I stare into the darkness.

But that is not the worst of the mornings. On the worst of the mornings, I wake up with Alice entangled in my arms because she is very good at sneaking. She likes to be locked in the room with me. And he allows this because somehow he knows I will not hurt another child. He is good at sneaking, too. At sneaking Alice into my room.

On those mornings, he comes to collect her, opening the gate, closing it again. Locking it shut.

I try to think that this invasion of my bed, my body, is helping me, giving me power. The more Alice needs me, the more power I will yield over her.

And power is just what I need over this little girl, my little prison guard. As long as I am a good mommy to her, there is no talk of finding a new mommy. There is no talk of Nicole.

I have come to call the man Mick. It is the name Alice gave him that night in the truck. Mickey Mouse. And for that split second, I had let myself believe he was harmless like that, like a cartoon character. I let him lead me back into this house when I might have tried to run away, into the woods. I did not know that would be my last chance to escape.

In these seven days, I have learned a lot of things about Alice and her life in this house.

She has lived here since before she can remember. She told me she was born here, in that dark laundry room with no windows, but I have no proof of that one way or another and I will not make any more assumptions.

Her first mommy lived here until last spring. Alice has a calendar and knows how to keep track of time. She has books from a homeschool program, but there is no internet here so she does the work on paper. Mick collects her work at the end of each day and tells her he sends it off to the program and they keep track of her progress.

"Look!" she said to me one day, showing me a handwritten report. It was written by Mick, I was certain.

I studied the report.

"You did very well!" I said to Alice.

The report said little more. *Your work is complete and was very good.*

We pass things through the bottom panel of the prison grate. She brings me food and things to drink other than the water I can get from my bathroom sink.

She is serious about her school work. She is almost at a middle school level, which tells me she is smart and that Mick, or someone else, has been guiding her through the material. The subject matter is easy for me to teach. Simple algebra. Grammar. Earth science. The challenge comes from her impatience when she gets stuck. She is quick to anger and I am learning how to manage her moods.

When she is not doing schoolwork, she watches television shows on an iPad. Mick downloads new shows for her when he leaves the house and she watches them many times. She does not like the days when he takes her iPad with him. It makes her anxious.

The shows are familiar to me, like Mickey Mouse. She also has movies, some of which are too mature for her, but I say nothing. It is not my job to be her mother.

It is only my job to be her second mommy.

"You're a good second mommy," she tells me. And when she tells me this, I feel a heat inside my body. Because on other days, she tells me different things that make my blood cold.

"If you can't be a good second mommy, we will have to get a new one."

It is in these moments that I question what I might be capable of doing.

I have learned that the phone was never dead.

There is no phone line connected. I asked Alice about this and she said she uses it all the time. I asked her how. She said she plays pretend with it. I asked her what kind of sound it makes.

"There's no sound on a phone unless someone calls you, silly. Didn't you ever have a phone?"

"I have a cell phone. And you're right. If you just hold it to your ear it doesn't make any sound. But a phone like the one in the kitchen is not a cell phone. It's an older kind of phone and when you pick it up, it usually makes a sound."

This made her angry too. "There's no sound! I told you that. Phones don't make sounds."

That's when I knew there was no landline.

No internet. No phone line.

Mick and Alice live off the grid. Except for the electricity and the gas. I wonder about this. I wonder who pays those bills and what name holds the accounts. I wonder who owns this property. And why no one came here to search it after I disappeared. The article he showed me said they went door to door.

When Alice calmed down, she considered things.

"You might be right about the phone," she said, shaking her head. Then she lowered her voice to a whisper even though we were alone in the house.

"But it's only because he works in a secret job. No one can know where we are."

I also asked her then, and every chance I've had before, how they knew things about me and my family. How they knew I would be passing through, and that I had lost a child, that I had two other children. That I was so lost in my grief I might actually agree to live with them and be Alice's new mommy.

Or maybe that was just a belief held by this little girl who plays with her dolls.

She never answers. Sometimes she shrugs. Sometimes she says things about how it's important to know secrets about people to be prepared. I wonder now if she doesn't know what he does or how he found out about me.

I hear the knock on the inside wooden door. I know to open it without hesitation, even though there is no working lock on my side. She knocks as a courtesy. Alice stands before me on the other side of the metal grate. She is still in her pajamas, hair not brushed and tangled from the restless sleep of a child who still dreams.

"I want to play a game. Pick one," she demands.

"Hannah and Suzannah," I say. When we play with the dolls, I get to ask questions. The questions bring answers, which are giving me insight into her mind.

"I'll go get them," she says.

Mick is here now. He studies me longer than yesterday. Which was longer than the day before, which was longer than the day before that. In the mornings, I wear the first mommy's pajamas and they cling to my breasts and the curves of my hips. He has been coming earlier so I don't have time to change.

I can't decide if I should sleep in the other clothes he's given me. Her baggy sweatshirts and pants. I can't decide if I want him to look longer. He seems ambivalent about me, as though he is trying to see something in me that he needs, but he can't find it yet. Maybe I'm too old and my body repulses him. Maybe I'm being too good and he wants me to fight so he can exert his strength over me. Maybe he needs me to be more of a victim. I study his face and try to understand. I need him to want me here, with him and with Alice, so he will stop looking beyond these walls.

Pulling Alice close, even having her in my bed, will give me power over her. Of that, I am certain.

But with Mick, I don't know. And that terrifies me.

"Step back," he says. And I do.

He unlocks the bottom panel of the grate and slides me some breakfast. Coffee, eggs, toast. It's the same every morning.

"Thank you," I say. I wait for him to lock the grate again. Then, and only then, do I step forward and take the small tray which holds the food. I sit cross-legged on the floor while I eat because Alice will soon return and this is where I will stay for most of the day. On the floor. Playing with a child through prison bars.

I draw from my work as a teacher years ago. And also as a mother, although those memories are locked away, behind that invisible line. The before and after of Annie's death. They are provoked now by Alice and the things she makes me do. How we would play board games together, me and John and our three children. And how Annie hated to lose, just like Alice when we played Candy Land. Nicole and Evan would yell at her and she would cry. Not every time. It was just a stage. A normal stage that children go through. Learning to play nicely. Learning how to handle disappointment.

I think I was good at this, at teaching them these lessons, because I know what to do with Alice. It comes to me without effort.

With the ease of experience. And it comes to me with the pain these memories provoke.

Alice returns with the dolls. She hands me Suzannah.

I sip my coffee. Take a bite of my food.

"What should we do today," Hannah asks Suzannah.

I swallow as I think through my data and what is still needed.

"I'm very angry today," Suzannah says.

"How come?" asks Hannah.

And then I adjust my voice so it is just right. So Alice will not see the path I am leading us down.

"I had a fight with my mother."

Alice smiles, and tilts Hannah to the side so she can reach through the bars and give my doll a hug.

And I think, *that's right, Alice.*

Keep reaching through these bars. And maybe one day soon they will open.

16

Day fourteen

didn't think it mattered.

That was the first excuse Kurt Kent made. Then, *I felt bad for the guy.*

What did he think Nic was going to do? Laugh at Roger Booth because his girlfriend left him after high school? Torture him with bad memories from his adolescence?

Finally, he gave an answer that rang true.

"I thought you might accuse him of having something to do with your mother's disappearance."

Nic watched the wall of trees pass as she fought to stay calm.

"You're the one who told me about Daisy Hollander," Nic reminded him.

"I know."

"So you must have known it would lead right back to him."

Kurt started to say something but then stopped. A long sigh, a glance out the side window—

"What?" Nic asked now.

"I wasn't thinking about Booth when I told you."

"Well, maybe you should have—he lied to me about it."

"What do you mean?"

"I asked him if he knew about Daisy Hollander and he said everybody knew, but then failed to mention she was his girlfriend—or that he spent all that time searching for her."

"That's not really a lie."

"It's an omission. Same thing."

Yes, Nic thought. Just like her father with the handwriting analysis. And what else? What other things were people not telling her, here and at home?

Kurt fell silent.

"What, then?" she asked. "What did you think it would lead me to?"

The wall of trees opened to the river, then the turn onto Hastings Pass.

"It's probably nothing," he said.

They passed the police station, town hall, the auto body shop. They were at the inn when he finally said the name. A different name. The last name she'd been expecting to hear.

"Chief Watkins."

"Watkins? What does he have to do with Daisy Hollander?"

"The chief has this thing about kids."

"What kind of thing?"

Kurt turned right, into the parking lot at the inn. He pulled to a stop.

"He used to come to the school. Talk about opportunities—scholarships and sports recruiting. Ways to get out of here, get money for college."

"That sounds admirable."

"I guess."

"So did he help Daisy Hollander get the scholarship to that summer camp?"

"Had to be. But it's more than that."

"Okay."

Kurt looked around now, at the inn and then the diner. He lowered his voice even though the windows were closed.

"There was talk that the chief was the one who drove Daisy to Boston. He denied it, but some of her friends told Booth, so Booth got in his face about it. Took a swing at him. The chief said it was a lie, but he couldn't prove where he was that day. That's all I heard. It could all be teenage bullshit. Gossip . . ."

Nic pictured Booth from earlier that day, giving her the bear spray, showing her where to run. And then his abrupt departure after the question about Daisy Hollander.

She pictured Watkins the day before, stretching his arms out like there wasn't enough space in the world to accommodate him. His ego eclipsing the universe. It made sense that he would play God helping kids. Changing their lives. Even helping one of them start a new life with a sister who'd made it out. But then . . .

"Wait a minute," Nic said, remembering something. "Veronica told us that she moved to New York. That she never went to Boston."

"I know."

"So why did people say Chief Watkins drove Daisy to Boston?"

"Maybe that's what she told people so Booth would have no way to track her down."

"And Watkins?"

Kurt shrugged. "I don't know. But people don't change, right? So if he was willing to help Daisy Hollander disappear . . ."

Nic interrupted him. "Then why not my mother."

"Exactly."

A moment passed, Nic thinking. Kurt watching her.

Then, "If she was out of gas, panicking, then the chief came by, felt sorry for her—promised to drop her somewhere and not tell anyone. It happened on the same day your sister died, right? The same day your mother killed her."

The last few words hung in the air. *Your mother killed her . . .*

And Nic felt the reply leave her mouth without a single thought.

"It was an accident," she said.

Kurt tried to go back. "Of course—you're right. I only meant . . ."

"I know what you meant. And why you said it."

She didn't give him time to say more.

"I need to find Chief Watkins," she said. "You must know where he lives. You seem to know every inch of this place."

"Yeah, but he won't be home."

"How do you know?"

"Because it's Thursday. And on Thursday nights he goes to the casino."

Kurt went on explaining, about *free drinks with this* and *double the payoff with that*—all on Thursday nights at Laguna, and every time he said it—*Thursday night*—Nic felt a tightening in her throat.

"Thursday night was the night of the storm. The night my mother disappeared."

Had Watkins been heading there, in spite of the storm? Maybe because of it? Did he lie then, and was he lying now? Had he given her mother a ride? Kurt was writing this new story one line at a time, letting Nic piece them together as though the story was of her own making. He said he'd mentioned Daisy Hollander before, but Nic didn't remember. And she would have, the same way she remembered pulling him to the back of the bar.

Nic reached for the door. Kurt grabbed her. Stopped her.

"Hey," he said. "Wait a second."

Nic pulled her arm from his grasp.

"It was an accident," she said again.

"I know. I'm sorry. It just came out wrong."

That was bullshit.

"She wasn't like that," Nic said. "She wasn't careless, not about anything." Memories flooded in, then spilled out. The sweet memories that had been too painful to remember. "Our mother would wake us up for school by sitting on the edge of our beds and wiggling our toes . . . she used to sing to us—when we were babies . . . I saw her do it with Annie . . . rocking her and gazing into her eyes . . . our mother cried at every stupid concert and school play no matter how horrible we were . . ."

"Okay."

"No—it's not okay. A mother like that doesn't kill her child."

"I know."

"It was a fucking accident!" Nic said it one more time, though the words were more for herself now than for this stranger from the bar across the street.

She caught her breath.

"I'm sorry," she said.

Then she was gone.

17

Day fourteen

annah and Suzannah have very different kinds of mothers. Hannah's mother is perfect. She's sweet, kind, obedient. She has long, real blond hair, wears no makeup. She doesn't need to because she's so beautiful. And her body is thin. Hannah says she feels strong when she hugs her.

Alice never deviates in our game.

Suzannah's mother, who is my invention, is strong-willed and defiant. She hates Suzannah's father and has no problem telling him. It upsets Suzannah because her father has a temper and she is worried about what he might do to her mother.

"Sometimes I think he might hurt her," Suzannah says.

Hannah grows quiet. Alice grows pensive.

The familiar wave of guilt races through me but I do not succumb.

"She should just be happy being my mommy!" Suzannah says. Then she starts to cry.

Hannah wakes up now. She feeds on the emotional turmoil of her friend, and gives back empathy that is exaggerated but also self-serving.

"You are so beautiful, Suzannah! Any mommy would be lucky to have you as her little girl, and she should not do anything that would take her away from you! If she really, really loved you she wouldn't do things like that! Things that might get her killed!"

I hold my breath, waiting for more information to seep out through the cracks of this emotional outburst. But all I get are tears.

Suzannah nods her head. "Thank you, Hannah. You are the best friend I could ever have!"

Alice pulls Hannah to her chest and hugs the doll, lost now in our characters and the game we play. Suzannah and I sit quietly until all is calm again.

We have been playing with the dolls all morning. We have not done any schoolwork and Alice grows antsy.

"I'm supposed to have it done before noon," she says. "Did you know that the morning is the most productive time of the day? It's when our brains are smartest."

We used to talk about these things in faculty meetings and I wonder how she knows them. Someone took the time to become educated about children and how they develop. I can't imagine it was Mick. When he comes now, with the food or to collect Alice, he seems agitated and distracted, like he has too much on his mind. Or maybe his mind is overwhelmed by what he's done and the consequences that are looming. I try to put him at ease with my docile behavior, but then this seems to repulse him. I have been thinking about this dilemma. What does he want from me? What will make his mind settle? He cannot go on forever in the state he's in.

"Okay," I answer. "Why don't we finish this game and then have some lunch. The morning has already passed and the other thing that helps us be smart is food."

I need to finish what I started today. This is further than we have ever come in talking about the mommies of these little plastic dolls and I need to know more about Hannah's. I need to know how old she was, what she looked like, where she slept, and why she wanted to leave. I need to know the things she said and did and how she wore her hair. I need to know how she was like my daughter. Like Nicole. I need to know so I can be more like her myself. Draw him to me and not my daughter.

Their paths can never cross again. Not ever. But what if she comes back here to look for me? What if the search is not really over?

I run through the facts of my disappearance. The car with no gas, my phone still there in the charger. No dead body found, so I must be somewhere. Won't they start to wonder how I am surviving in my new life as a grown-up runaway? If he's used the credit card again, he would have risked being detected. That would be foolish, and he does not seem foolish to me.

I step outside the details and think that maybe they just know. They will know that I would never leave them. Not after I took Annie from them.

Or maybe I'm thinking about this all wrong. Maybe they will see it as a gift—finally freeing them of my presence. The miserable, sad reminder of our family tragedy.

Suddenly, Alice speaks and I force myself to leave these thoughts. These horrible thoughts that have caused beads of sweat to run down my face.

"Let's keep playing," she says.

I continue the game. Suzannah asks Hannah more about her mommy.

Hannah's mommy is a fantasy. She is the mommy Alice wants, the one she might even believe she once had.

Her mommy died because she got lost in the woods. And yet, somehow I know she didn't.

"Does your mommy ever take you shopping?" Suzannah asks Hannah. "Have you ever been to the mall? It's so awesome! They have every kind of store you can imagine. Like the one in that TV show we watched—remember? And they have a whole floor that's just food. All kinds of food! Have you ever had Chinese food? We used to go all the time, but now my father won't let us. I think that's why my mommy is so mad at him."

What does Alice know of the real world? Did her first mommy tell her things about it? How many times has she left the house, wearing her mask?

I want answers to these questions so I can understand my captor. But I also want my little blond prison guard to wonder about the life that Mick keeps from her. I want her to taste it. And to feel angry about it. Angry at him.

I am the one who can give that to her. I am the one who can save her.

Alice grows cold. She slowly drops Hannah to the floor, thinking carefully about what to say to me.

"I know what you're trying to do," she says.

I answer as Suzannah. "What?"

But she reaches through the bars and grabs the doll from my hands. She throws her against the wall behind us, then picks her up to make sure she hasn't been damaged.

I make a note—Mick will not be pleased if she has broken a toy.

"I can't do any of those things because of my allergies and you're using the dolls to make me feel bad!"

I don't let her anger touch me, though it is so hot it radiates from her skin.

"That was not my intention. I was just trying to make Suzannah be a normal girl," I say. *And you are not normal, Alice. Why do you think that is?*

She folds her arms and scowls like a two-year-old. Eyes pinched together. Lips pursed tight. It makes me want to laugh the way I would when my own children would do this. The memory comes and goes, but leaves behind a residue. It's sticky and sweet and I don't know what to make of it. I don't know if I like or dislike it. Still, it lingers.

Nicole was my biggest scowler. There was a drama to it that was so extreme it felt like a parody, like a skit on a television show that was supposed to provoke laughter.

Now comes a memory of John. Being with John. Two young parents with an unruly toddler. Just one precious child in our perfect little family. His love for her bounded past his love for me, but I didn't mind. It made me love him even more, watching him love our child. When she scowled at us over something that displeased her, having to go to bed or not getting more cookies, his laughter was so big he would have to flee the room to stifle it, leaving me to swallow mine while I talked her through it.

These memories come every day now. Memories of my family. My love for them. I don't know if they come because I am finally being punished for what I have done. Or if they come because I spend my days with Alice, in the mind of a nine-year-old girl.

They leave me with the residue which I cannot identify.

In this moment, I decide that I like it. Its sticky sweetness covers the thoughts of the log in the fireplace and Nicole's angry words and Evan's eyes, turning away.

Alice takes the dolls and leaves.

"I'm not bringing you any lunch!" she says.

"Alice," I call after her. "Please don't be angry. I didn't mean to upset you."

My voice is calm. I don't care about lunch. I may be a prisoner, but I am not an animal. I am not one of John's dogs waiting in the kitchen for my bowl to be filled. I will not beg. I would sooner starve.

This defiance is another thing that is unfamiliar, but has become a part of me.

Bring it, I think now. *Bring on the punishment*. The angry little prison guard. The starvation.

I go to my bed and lie down. I begin to think about my next move, the next game I will play and how I will be less obvious. I think that maybe I will watch her shows with her so I can laugh and comment in places that will provoke the same thoughts—recognition that she, too, is a prisoner. And that I am her only way out.

But then she returns. I hear the latch turn on the small panel of the metal grate and the tray scrape the floor as she slides it to my side.

"Here!" she says. "Don't say I didn't do you any favors."

She learned that expression from a TV show and I continue the thoughts of my new plan even as I get up from the bed and walk back to the doorway.

I sit before her.

She has made me a peanut butter sandwich and a glass of milk.

"Thank you, Alice," I say. "You are very kind."

"Eat it," she commands. And I do as I am told. I do not mind this small humiliation.

She watches me eat, the peanut butter sticking to my mouth so I have to drink the milk. She knows I hate milk. I think about going to the bathroom to get a cup of water. To prove a point. I still have some control. Some power. But then I decide to suffer and suffer big. I gag when I drink the milk and I watch her face change. She cannot stop the need to empathize.

"I'm sorry," she says. "I forgot that you don't like milk." This is a lie, but it doesn't matter.

She leaves and returns quickly with a glass of lemonade.

The milk was an intentional act of cruelty. It provoked the intended response—pain and discomfort. That gave her the opportunity to fix it. To make it better. To bring me comfort. And that makes her feel powerful and important. She has few chances to do that, living alone in this house.

She made me suffer so she could get her empathy fix.

Thank you, Alice. Thank you for this piece of information.

She looks at me and smiles. I see tears well in her crystal-blue eyes. Tears of joy that she saved this mongrel with a glass of lemonade.

"Do you want to start your schoolwork now?" I ask her.

She nods. "We'd better or he'll be angry."

"Don't worry—we'll get it done before he gets home."

The man comes home at different times, so this promise is a lie. Sometimes he comes home during the day. Sometimes he stays home late in the mornings. And sometimes he's gone all night. On those nights, he locks Alice inside the room with me with her iPad and food. She seems to like those nights, the nights when we are prisoners together. This is good and this is bad. I need her to like me, but I need her to crave our escape. And I need Mick to want to be with us.

I smile at her. "Just this one time it will be done after lunch. It can be our little secret."

Alice moves closer to the metal bars.

"There are no secrets here," she says quietly. In a whisper.

"What do you mean?" I ask. A chill runs through me even before she answers.

She glances up to the ceiling, then back at me. I follow with my own eyes and try to find what has just drawn her attention.

I see painted molding, simple, running along the crease between the ceiling and the wall. It runs all the way down the hallway that leads to the kitchen and living room and the little room where Alice keeps her toys. It is coated with a thin line of dust, just like the floor, though not as thick.

I let my eyes follow the molding until it reaches the corner where the hallway ends. It is less than ten feet away. It is there that I see a small monitor.

"What do you mean, Alice? Why were you looking at the ceiling?"

"They're everywhere," she answers.

"What are everywhere?" I ask.

She glances again. "The eyes."

A second chill comes and goes.

"What eyes?" I look again at the monitor. It looks like a motion detector for an alarm system. But I know there is no alarm that he sets. I study his movements when he comes and goes. The panel would be by the front door. He never stops there. I never hear the sound they make when they are about to be armed. We've had an alarm in our house for years.

But then I see something in the small box. A red light.

Alice lets my brain process what I've just seen. She can tell by my face that I have seen it.

"Dolly's eyes," she says.

"Dolly?" I ask. Then I remember. "The doll in your toy room? The old doll that sits on the shelf?"

She nods slowly. "Dolly has eyes all over the house. She sees everything and hears everything and she tells him everything."

I hold my breath to keep from crying out.

The red light. I think where else I have seen one. I don't turn away, but I count the places in my head.

The playroom next to Dolly.

The living room in the corner that faces the front door.

The dark room.

This hallway.

The corner of my bedroom.

I ease the air out of my lungs, then take more in to slow my pulse.

"I see." This is all I can manage to say.

So he is watching us, always. I think about the day I went for a walk. It was not a coincidence that he came home in time to stop me. He knew I had left because he saw me leave.

The cameras are everywhere.

And the cameras are feeding to him live. There is internet here, somewhere.

"Go get your schoolwork, then. We don't want to break any more rules."

Alice leaves and I turn my face from the camera in my room. I feel tears wanting to come but they will cause my body to tremble and he will know. He will see.

He watches me sleep. He watches me sleep with Alice. That is why he leaves us alone in this house together.

He sees everything.

Alice returns. She lays out her work and gets started. She can see that I am upset.

"Oh, don't be scared!" she says. "You don't need to worry."

I regain my composure.

"Why is that, Alice?" I ask her.

"Because Dolly can see that you're being a very good mommy."

I smile. And inside, the defiance grows tenfold.

I will use this. I will use the cameras. I don't know how.

But I will find a way.

18

Day fourteen

t was an accident.

Those words had never left Nic's mouth. She'd heard them used by everyone in her life. Her father. The grief counselor. Teachers, before she got expelled.

She'd thought of it the way she'd thought of the words *died unexpectedly* when someone committed suicide. Or overdosed.

No sense adding to the pain of the survivors by saying what really happened.

But now, for the very first time, she felt the words differently. *It was an accident.* Her mother hadn't killed Annie. Nic hadn't killed Annie. Annie had run into the road. Nic had called after her, tried to stop her. Her mother had been coming around a blind corner, she'd slowed down, ready to turn into the driveway. It was a confluence of circumstances, of small decisions and actions that on any other occasion would have left their minds. They were devoid of moral underpinnings, no matter how desperately anyone wanted to believe otherwise.

And when a series of actions come together to create a tragedy, that's what it's called—*an accident.*

She wondered how her mother thought of it. If she still said those words inside her head.

I killed my child.

She wondered if all those conversations with her support group had fueled the fire. No matter how hard people pretended, it would have been difficult to hide their judgment of her. Nic had felt it sprinkled over their kind words in the emails. Even her father— the way he spoke of it, of his wife behind the wheel of that car. It was so much easier to believe that it could never happen to them.

The casino was half an hour from Hastings. Back onto Route 7. Fifteen miles south. Left on Laguna Drive, then another five miles into the alternating woods and fields. Her father had not wanted her to come here when they'd done the canvas. He'd wanted her to go home.

Kurt had been right about Thursday nights. The lot was nearly full. Nic parked in the back.

Through the front doors, across worn, turquoise tile that matched some kind of island-themed decor, she made her way in the crowd past the registration desk to the casino. The bar was at the far wall, after rows of slot machines with people gathered around each one, playing, watching. Loud bursts of cheers came from a craps table through an archway to the right. The noise was oppressive. The air thick with cigarette smoke. Nic could not imagine her mother here. Not for an hour, let alone four days. Or a week. Or longer.

The security cameras were up high, as the police reports had described. Looking straight down, looking for acts of theft more than faces. It would be hard to spot one blond woman among the sea of humanity that now surrounded her. People had seemingly come from all over—skinny blondes in fancy dresses and heels, overweight blondes in jeans, sweatshirts, and sneakers. Plenty of brunettes as well, and men wearing everything from tailored sports coats to muscle shirts.

Nic was looking for Chief Watkins. But her eyes were drawn to the women, each one pulling at her, wanting her to see her mother so she could take her home and have all of this be over.

Her phone rang when she reached the bar. She took a spare stool between two sets of couples and picked up the call.

"Sweetheart? Are you all right? Where are you?"

Nic heard the concern in her father's voice. Yes, she was at a bar. But for once, she waved off the bartender who stopped to offer a drink.

"I'm fine. I'm just out. Meeting someone who might have information."

"What information? Is it about the truck?" He was beginning to panic.

"No. Something else. Probably nothing."

He waited, but Nic didn't offer more. It was hard to hear with the noise in the room, but more than that, she didn't want to say the words out loud.

Chief Watkins may have . . .

And then what? May have helped her mother disappear? Kurt Kent's story felt absurd now.

She changed the subject.

"Dad—Evan told me you saw a fence behind the inn. He said you told him that you had to stop searching the woods because of it."

"Why? Did something happen? Tell me!" His fear was a tinder-box. She chose her words carefully.

"No, Dad. Calm down," she lied. It wouldn't do him any good to picture her like that. Alone in the woods in the town where her mother disappeared.

"Okay, okay . . . yeah, I remember that. I went with one of the search parties. We walked straight back from the road through the property behind the inn and diner. The Booth property. We walked until we hit a fence."

"With coiled barbed wire?"

"Yes. It was pretty tall. One of the locals said it was probably left there by the old chemical company. They thought the two properties might back up to each other. It was hard to tell how old it was. Why? What's going on?"

Nic thought about this, about the property that might be on the other side.

"Did anyone search that property—the one on the other side of the fence?"

"I'm sure they did, sweetheart. They searched over thirty miles of land. What is this about?"

Nic fought for a way to tell him about the hole she'd found, but then she'd have to confess to going back there. Maybe she could say Roger Booth went with her . . .

Something caught her eye before she could decide. A man. Tall. Stout. Full head of hair.

Chief Watkins sitting down at a blackjack table.

"I have to go," Nic said.

He started to protest but Nic hung up the phone. She clicked it to silent, then slid it back into her purse.

What now?

She watched and waited from the adjacent room.

Watkins played blackjack. Then craps. Then roulette. Laughing. Drinking. He wore a button-down shirt and loose-fitting jeans. His hair looked groomed with gel or spray. He had a more youthful look about him, like he was trying not to be the man in charge of a dying town, but a man who could be any man, from any place. Maybe he came here to pretend he was that man.

As he moved from table to table, he was greeted by other patrons, waitstaff, dealers. He was known here. And it filled him up. Nic watched from the far corner of the bar, sipping water. Wanting vodka. Desperately wanting vodka. Thinking about her father and Evan—*God*, Evan and his guilt and tears. Then her mother's email—the one about her marriage and how she couldn't accept love.

I'd rather he punch me in the face.

And the one about her fear—*I can't lose another child.*

Anger stirred, then attached itself to the man who was now indulging himself without a care in the world.

Finally, Watkins got up. He was on the move. A young woman in a tight minidress and thick platform boots had sidled up next to him half an hour before, and now she was convincing him to leave. She wasn't attractive but she'd been wearing him down. Touching his arm. His back. Laughing boisterously when he spoke. He had already bought her two martinis and a pack of cigarettes.

They walked to another table where she'd left her coat. He helped her put it on. She led him to a back door.

Shit!

Nic ran out the front entrance, then turned right to where she thought they might have exited. She saw no one as she walked around the side of the building. Then she heard it—the laughter of a woman. Drunk laughter. Then the deep voice of her companion. The voice of Chief Watkins.

Staying close to the building but out of the lights, she listened until she saw them move from the side of the building into the parking lot. She let them get ahead, then followed them, weaving through the rows of cars so she was out of sight. The laughter stopped. She heard the click of a car unlocking, then she saw headlights. Then a door opening, closing. She hurried now to see the row where the lights were coming from. She walked there slowly, quietly. The lights went off. The car was not leaving.

She got to the row and began to move along the back of each car, looking inside, listening for sound.

She walked until she heard them. The unmistakable sound of a man moaning. It was soft, coming through a small crack in the window. She slid to the far side of the adjacent car and looked through the windows. It was too dark to see, until a car rolled past on the other side, briefly shining a light through the windshields of each car in her row. It was quick, but unmistakable—Chief Watkins sitting in the driver's seat. Eyes closed. Face contorted with anticipation, the melding together of pleasure and frustration as the woman leaned over him from the passenger side, her head moving up and down. The light was gone, but not the sound.

Nic walked around the car that was shielding her view. She could see that Watkins's car was gray, but it was not until she had a clear view that she saw the make. A charcoal-gray pickup truck. Chief Watkins. The woman.

She squatted down behind the truck, heart pounding now.

Think.

The glass was intact on both taillights, but she couldn't tell if the bulbs were out. She would have to wait until he turned the ignition.

Another laugh. The smell of a cigarette from the window. Something about *fifty bucks* and *that's pretty steep* and then, *you should have asked before, asshole.*

A door opening, closing. The woman stumbling away.

Then Watkins in a cruel, mocking voice. *Cheap whore.*

And then the ignition. The lights. Both of them working. Still, it had been two weeks.

She hurried back to the other side of the adjacent car, and managed to snap a photo with her phone as Chief Watkins drove away.

19

Day fourteen

Mick does not come home. This is the first time he has not been home all day and now, apparently, all evening.

He must be comfortable with me, with the way I am with Alice. And, of course, he is always watching.

But then I think that he does not want to be here. That he is still hunting for whatever he lost when the woman who lived here before me died.

"I'm hungry," Alice says. She reaches her arm through the bars and I take her hand and press it to my lips.

"I know, sweetheart. Do you want to tell me what there is in the kitchen and I can teach you how to make something?"

She hangs her head, chin to chest, but then raises her narrowed eyes so I can still see them. Her lips disappear under her teeth and her nose scrunches. I call this expression of hers Angry Face. I don't say this out loud, but I make a note of it, and also what makes it come, and what makes it leave.

"I don't have any better ideas, but if you do I will try to help you with them," I say.

Now she crosses her arms and huffs. I try not to laugh, but it is amusing. I haven't been amused for a very long time. Maybe even for years. There is a new power stirring inside me that has given this impulse of being amused some latitude. Some room to breathe.

"Did he tell you what to do in case of an emergency?" I ask now. "For example, if you got sick, or if there was a fire? Is there a way to reach him? I can help you study and play with you from inside my room, but that's about it," I say.

She uncrosses her arms. Angry Face softens, becomes whimsical, mischievous. She tilts her head and pushes one shoulder, always the right one, a little ahead of her chest. This is Coy Face. She knows a secret and she wants me to get it out of her.

Nicole had this face by the time she was four. Annie didn't have it until she was six or seven, and even then it was more playful than precocious. Evan never had it. My only boy, but I could read him like a book.

I have had time to think these past fourteen days, and not just about the man and Alice and my plan. I think about why I am here, and that perhaps I have finally been sentenced for my crime. I am finally being punished. This has done something to me, shifted my insides.

With this shift has come a reversal of how I had come to see my own daughters. Annie the good girl. Nicole the bad girl. We are not supposed to do that. Parents. Good parents. But I have stopped pretending that I am one. I hate the person Nicole has become these past few years. If I met her on the street, I would thank God she was not my child. I would judge her parents with contempt. Who would allow such behavior? Who would permit their grown child to behave this way?

But now I can see that it was Annie who was also precocious, strong-willed. She could be defiant to her sister when I left her in charge. And she resented her brother. She resented them both, how they pulled her, kicking and screaming, from her pedestal as the baby, wanting her to grow up and be less of a bother. She had managed to become our sole focus. Our squeaky wheel. Babies always need more attention.

The memories keep crossing the line, and the pain they carry lessens each time. Even now, as I speak to Alice about helping her cook, I see Nicole standing on a stool, staring into a bowl of flour and sugar, mixing them together with a big wooden spoon that can barely fit in her hand.

She liked blueberry muffins and we would make them together. I still know the recipe by heart. It never leaves me. Two cups of flour. One cup of sugar . . .

And John, the memories of John . . . they reach back and un-earth feelings that live more in my body than my mind. His hand on the small of my back. The rush that would follow. I thought they were gone forever.

It doesn't change what I did. I do not feel it should commute my sentence. To the contrary. I see now that this sentence, being forced to live here with this man and his child, has scratched an itch. The guilt recedes a little every day. The rock I carry gets lighter.

I suffer now to keep Nicole safe. And possibly Evan. This man could know about him. Maybe he covets him as well. In the suffering, I make amends. And the amends bring a kind of healing.

"Alice," I say with a smile. "I know that face! What are you thinking?"

Alice looks up at the monitor in the corner at the end of the hallway. She positions herself so her back faces it. She lowers her voice as well, for good measure, I imagine.

"I know where the key is," she says.

Her words reach out and choke me with surprise. But I manage a little smile, the smile of only a tepid curiosity.

"You do?" I ask.

She nods slowly, Coy Face firmly lodged.

"In case I really, really need you," she says.

I sit back a little and uncross my legs. They have started to tingle.

It's not easy to sit on the floor all day at my age.

I consider my options now. I could start to cry. Say how hungry I am and how much I need her to help me. But she does not seem to be wanting that. She already saved me once with a glass of lemonade. Her daily fix has been had.

She craves other things, though, as I have come to learn.

Hannah gave it away one day when she was talking to Suzannah.

What do you want to be when you're older? Suzannah is always asking questions.

I want to see a doctor who can help me go outside without my mask. And then I will go everywhere in the world.

Can I come? Suzannah asked.

No, silly. Only my mommy can come.

Only her mommy. She wants to be out of this house, free of these walls. And she knows Mick won't be the one to save her.

Only her mommy can save her.

Her first mommy is dead. The one with the real blond hair and the lean body.

She's stuck with me. And I can only help her if she gives me power over Mick.

"What kind of situation would that be—when you really, really need me?" I ask.

Coy Face recedes, and now comes Sad Face.

"I don't know," she says. I can tell that she means this. Confusion makes her sad. Uncertainty makes her sad. She needs to know the rules so she can keep her house in order. So she can keep another mommy from leaving.

I reach through the bars—something I rarely do—and touch her folded knee.

"It's okay," I say. "Let's figure it out together."

I continue.

"Do you think he just meant if you were hurt or sick?"

She shrugs.

Then comes Happy Face.

"I think if I did something in the kitchen that was dangerous. Like maybe if I burned something."

I go with this idea.

"Like if you burned something and didn't know how to stop the smoke? Like if you tried to boil some soup but maybe there was some butter on the coils of the burner? That kind of smoke?"

She thinks about this. "Yes," she says.

"I've done that so many times back home!" I say. "Butter smokes a lot, but it doesn't catch fire like oil. Still, it's scary."

Alice looks at me carefully. Then she turns her back around so she is facing the monitor.

"I can make us soup!" she says. "Since he's not home and it's so late. We need to have dinner. I've seen him make the soup. I know how!"

She says this loudly. She gets up and walks to the kitchen.

Ten minutes later I hear her feet running down the hall. I return to the edge of the grate and strain to see through the metal bars.

She runs toward me and she can hardly hold back a smile.

"I think I started a fire!" she says. "Cooking the soup!"

I stand now, look alarmed. We both speak loudly.

"Oh no!" I say. "Do you know how to put it out? Did he ever teach you?"

"No! I really, really need you!"

She reaches the grate. Happy Face belies the urgency in her voice.

In her hand is a metal key.

A million things run through me as she puts it into the lock, turns. As I hear the metal click and the bolt release. Thoughts. Emotions. Instincts. There are too many to sort out. I feel dizzy with excitement. The possibilities seem endless, and yet I know there is only one choice that is right. I know there is only one chance.

I step outside my prison cell and run with Alice to the kitchen. The key is still in the grate, the grate that now swings open on its hinges.

In the kitchen, I see the burner coils smoking. I take the pot of soup off the stove. I turn off the heat and go to the sink to get a towel. I wet the towel, then carefully wipe down the burner until the butter comes off, and the heat cools. The smoke stops.

I let my eyes move around the room, looking for one of Dolly's eyes. I don't see one, but that doesn't mean it's not there.

I pull Alice close. "It's fine now. You're safe."

"Thank you so much!" she says. She is not a good actress, and I file this away with everything else I know about her.

"How did the butter get on the stove?" I ask her.

"I was trying to put it on the bread and it just fell off. I didn't think it would cause any problems. I didn't know butter could burn like that." She says this very loud, as though she knows her voice has to carry. I think that maybe there are no cameras in this kitchen after all.

"Okay," I say. "It's okay. How could you know that?"

I finish cleaning up. I heat the soup, butter the bread, and serve us dinner at the table. Alice glances out the door to the living room.

"Alice," I say.

"Yes?"

"Can Dolly see in the kitchen?"

Coy Face comes, and Alice slowly moves her head left to right. *No.*

Then her eyes move back to the living room. I follow them and see a monitor on the wall in the corner near the door. It sits at an angle that can see the table, but not the stove. Not the sink.

And not the cupboard beneath the sink.

The cupboard which I opened to look for a dish towel, and where I found remnants of some household products. Old sponges. Dish soap. WD-40.

And a bottle of antifreeze.

I smile at Alice. I place my hand on her back and gently rub it up and down. Coy Face becomes Happy Face, which has a nice big smile.

And then I smile too.

20

Day fourteen

Nic walked quickly through the parking lot. The air was cold enough to see her breath. And still enough to hear her steps on the pavement. Watkins was long gone. The woman had vanished as well, between a row of cars, maybe to the back of the building.

Inside, Nic stopped, leaned against a wall just beneath one of the mounted cameras. She didn't want to be seen. Not by anyone.

She pulled out her phone but there was no one to call.

Her father had lied to her about the handwriting analysis.

Roger Booth had lied about Daisy Hollander, about being the boyfriend she'd been running away from when she disappeared.

And Watkins had failed to mention he owned a dark gray truck. Now that she thought about it, so had Officer Reyes. And who else? This was a small town. Watkins must drive that truck when he is off duty. Up and down Hastings Pass. Day after day. Year after year. All of them would have seen it—Booth, Mrs. Urbansky. Reyes. Even Kurt Kent, the bartender.

And what about Kurt? He'd driven her all the way into those

woods to meet Daisy's sister, knowing about Roger Booth the whole time.

There was no one she trusted.

Was that true? Or was she just being paranoid? So what if Watkins drove a gray truck? Edith Moore couldn't even be sure of the color. It might have been black or brown. And so what if Watkins picked up a prostitute one day, then helped teenagers with scholarships the next? People were complicated. She'd learned that from all those nights spent in bars. She wasn't a sheltered teenager anymore.

Still, her life these past five years had left her with just one person she could trust—and that person was now missing.

What now? She thought about her car just outside. She could leave—drive straight home. Her father would come and collect her things from the inn. She didn't have to stay here. There was nothing left to do.

The sea of humanity was all around her, coming from or going to the casino that was just on the other side of the lobby. So many faces—happy, pensive, worried, excited. The energy began to seep inside, feeding the panic that had already taken hold.

Maybe everyone was lying to her for this very reason. Because she couldn't handle the facts. The truth. Because she hadn't been able to navigate her life since Annie died.

She drew a breath but couldn't feel it reach her lungs. It felt shallow. Suffocating.

They weren't wrong. After that Sunday afternoon when she'd had that first drink, she hadn't been able to go back. *It's just peer pressure*, the school had told her worried parents after she'd been drunk at a dance. *This will scare her and she'll stop*. After all, she had so much to lose. Williams College had offered her early acceptance. She was captain of the cross country team. In the running for valedictorian.

And then, after they'd found vodka in a water bottle she kept in her locker, the counselors had gotten involved. *It's survivor's guilt*, they'd said. That one she'd read just recently in her mother's emails and it all made perfect sense now. How they made her go to therapy sessions where they talked about how she'd done nothing wrong by continuing to live.

After the third time when she'd passed out in the school bathroom, drunk off her ass, the month before graduation—her grades on free fall—they'd had no choice but to expel her. The new theory—she was looking for attention. She'd tried to get it by being good but it hadn't been enough. Now she had to be bad. The horror that had followed was now a powerful, visceral memory. Therapy sessions with both parents, telling her they loved her and how sorry they were that they hadn't noticed her suffering because they'd been dealing with their own.

No one listened to her about the hollow spaces that nothing could fill. They didn't understand how they'd come to be there if not from some affliction out of their textbooks. She wished she'd had a film of it—of Annie running and Nic screaming and then the car and the blood. The dozens of missed calls on her phone from their mother, begging to know if they were all right. Why hadn't Annie made it to her friend's house for the playdate?

The look on Evan's face. The image of their mother holding her dead child. The harrowing sound that left her body that Nic could still hear.

Guilt. Despair. Self-loathing. There were so many words to describe what lived in those hollow spaces. They laughed in the face of the counselors and their therapy bullshit.

And now she'd caused their mother's disappearance with her wretched words. Gone or dead—there was no way around it, no thinking her way out of those scenarios.

Confusion. Panic—she had to get someplace quiet, alone, before people started to notice.

She walked along the side of the wall, head down, away from the entrance to the casino. There was a hallway on the other side with restrooms, elevators, conference areas. And a business center.

A young man passed and she grabbed his sleeve. Her expression seemed to alarm him as she asked if he was staying at the hotel and if he could use his key card to let her in.

He hesitated, but then swiped the card to open the door. Nic thanked him and he quickly left, looking over his shoulder. Wondering if he'd made a mistake by letting this lunatic into the room. Her breaths were short, her face flushed and wet.

She sat on the floor in the corner and let it out. She wanted a drink. The thought of going back out into the crowd was the only thing stopping her.

So she's dead. So she left us. What now? She could still be found. Nothing had changed since she'd packed a bag and driven to this place. She had to find her mother and bring her home.

The room had a long table with four desktop computers and a printer. Nic pulled herself up from the floor and sat down in front of a large PC. She turned it on, opened to a search engine.

She typed them in, one after the other. The names spinning in her mind. Daisy Hollander. Roger Booth. Charles Watkins. Kurt Kent. Results crowded the screen, faces with the same name, but none of them matching in any way that was helpful. She narrowed Daisy's search to Hastings and got nothing. Then to New York City, and got over thirty faces. She hadn't asked to see a photo. Many of the women in the search could be her—similar age, description. And yet, probably none of them would be. If she didn't want to be found, she wouldn't be blasting her profile on Facebook and Snapchat.

The focus felt good. Her nerves began to settle, the panic sub-siding. She continued.

Kurt Kent was on the social media sites, and all of them were active but private. Booth and Watkins showed up on people finder ads. Most of those were scams and, anyway, she didn't need their addresses. She knew where they lived. She needed social media sites, something that might give her a window into their lives.

Then, a thought about Booth. About his property and the fence with the hole.

She pulled up a satellite image of the Hastings Inn, zoomed out. It was taken in the summer from the look of the trees—full canopies of green leaves. She couldn't see the fence behind the inn, but there was something on an adjacent property. A thin line running across a stretch of cleared land before disappearing again in the dense woods.

She zoomed out and tried to connect the line to other struc-tures—a house or barn or another fence. But it was impossible with all of the breaks into the woods. Still, that line of fence, if it was a fence, bent away from the inn, not toward it.

Fences usually went in a circle or a square, closing off a parcel of land. It would be odd for the fence to veer off away from the parcel where the inn was located, even if that parcel spanned hundreds of acres. No—this fence did not enclose the parcel of land owned by Booth. It belonged to the parcel that sat behind it just like that person from town had told her father.

And then she saw something else—another stretch of clearing within that adjacent parcel. She followed it, zoomed in until it was clear—a house.

A house, and the clearing before it—a driveway.

She zoomed out again, followed the driveway until it disappeared behind more trees. But, assuming it remained straight, it would end at the next road.

Like the driveway and the fence, the road weaved through woods. Still, she was able to guess at the path it carved through Hastings. And the point where it intersected another road, which ran along the river. River Road. And that road eventually intersected Hastings Pass.

Nic held her finger to the screen. She started at the inn, and followed Hastings Pass until it ended at the river. Then she followed it to the left, along River Road, until it met the road with the driveway. Abel Hill Lane. And from there, all the way to the driveway and then to the house—the house that sat on the parcel enclosed by the fence. Farther down Abel Hill Lane was a small cluster of redbrick buildings with flat black rooftops and narrow roads connecting them to one another and to two roads—Abel Hill Lane and River Road. Maybe that had once been the pharmaceutical company that had closed down years before. Or the chemical company before that. Maybe they were the same set of buildings, one company taking over the other.

Nic searched for addresses on Abel Hill Lane. There were seven in total. She pulled them up one at a time, first on the map and then on satellite imagery. There was a small ranch, number 53. Then a cape, number 67. Then five others—none of them matching the satellite image of the house with the fence. None of them with a long driveway. None of them with enough acreage to be that same property.

She leaned back in the chair and closed her eyes.

Everyone was lying about something. And now Edith Moore wanted the reward money. She knew about the purse, the three letters.

But wait—Nic pictured that morning with Edith Moore and Reyes. In her car, looking across the road to where she said she saw her mother. Rain coming down in sheets. That's how she'd described it. Maybe she'd seen the color of the purse, but the letters? Could she really have seen the letters from that far away, through the rain, at night? And yet she knew about them.

She knew, or someone had told her—someone else who knew about her mother's purse.

And what did that have to do with Abel Hill Lane?

Her father said they'd stopped searching when they reached that fence.

Maybe she should just get a drink. Maybe get a few. Calm her nerves. Settle her mind.

But she couldn't stop.

She typed in *Hastings* and then *history*.

And then she started to read.

21

Day fourteen

There is antifreeze in the cupboard. But this is not all that I assess in the kitchen with Alice. Alice and her Happy Face.

I assess many, many things. Thoughts and emotions, but mostly instincts which, as before in the woods, require the closest scrutiny.

Alice has unlocked the grate. She has set me free and it is a gift I cannot squander.

I could run for the front door, to my tools in the woods. But it's dark and cold and I don't know where Mick is. He could be outside in his truck, watching the camera feeds. He could be five minutes away. Ten minutes away. Days of work would be undone.

I could take this child hostage. Put a knife to her neck right in front of the camera. It is not beneath me. It is not out of my capabilities, and I don't allow myself to think about the implications. *It's nothing personal, Alice.*

There are other things, worse things. But nothing gets me the time I need to get through that fence.

I go back to what I have found here—to the antifreeze in the cupboard. I know about this from my other life when I was a science teacher. When I was a good mother. When John and I were still in love. Before we had a child that died. A child I killed.

Before life started to close its hands around my throat.

We finish eating and I clean the dishes and put a kettle of water on the stove.

"We should go to bed," Alice says.

"Yes," I agree. "You go ahead. I am going to make a cup of tea to bring with me."

Alice leaves and I take a teacup from a cupboard. I bring the cup to the cupboard under the sink and pour in the antifreeze. Dolly cannot see the sink.

We go to our bedrooms. She gets ready for bed. I get ready for bed. I change in the bathroom with the door open. I take my time, though I fear it is futile.

Alice comes now to lock the grate. I don't resist. But then she changes her mind.

"Can I sleep with you tonight?" she asks.

Of course you can, sweetheart.

We close the grate but do not lock it. The key remains in the hole.

"What about your tea?" she asks. Nothing gets past her.

Alice snuggles up beside me.

"I would rather sleep now," I whisper.

The heat from her body, her breath, her heart beating—none of it bothers me tonight. None of it pulls from my gut the feeling of my lost child, my precious, precocious Annie. None of it stirs the longing, or the guilt, or the redemption that has begun to appear.

Tonight, Alice and I are one. I absorb her into me while I lay awake, making assessments. Contemplating my instincts.

The grate is still open, and with it, my options.

It is a different kind of prison now that I know Dolly is watching me. Before I knew about Dolly I felt the freedom to release my face. To have my own Angry Face or Coy Face or Sad Face. There was freedom to pound my fists into the pillows, to cry, to hold myself and rock myself to a place of calm, like a mother holding her child.

That freedom is now gone, and the open grate does nothing to mitigate this other type of insidious confinement. I have done things in the line of the camera that should be the cause of humiliation. He has seen me naked, changing into the clothes that he slides through the panel. He has seen me naked and unaware and still, this has not kept him here with us. He still longs for more. I think about my old friends and our battle to hold on to youth. But being a size four can't make you twenty-five. Age is about maturity and knowledge and it seeps out in the way we move and carry ourselves. Here is the proof. I have skinny legs and blond hair and this man has seen all of me. Still, he longs for something more. Something he lost. And knowing this has caused me to reassess. I decide to move on and think about my instincts. Make a new plan.

Alice is also slow to drift off and she rambles now. I want to make all kinds of faces but I hold my expression steady. Pleasant. For Dolly to see.

Alice talks about her first mommy, so I chase away my thoughts to concentrate on hers. I wonder if she is beginning to feel things for me that she felt for her. It's been too long since she's had anyone to have these feelings for.

"She smelled good," Alice says, pressing her nose into the nape of my neck, insinuating that I do not smell good. Maybe I do smell bad to her by comparison, but I am stuck with the cheap body wash that Mick slid through the panel.

"She used to sing to me," Alice says now. Her voice is soft, dreamlike. I decide not to sing to her because that might upset her, although I used to sing to my babies when they still slept in my arms. I could see my voice reach deep inside them, settle their nerves. Mine was the voice they heard as I carried them inside me. It is primal, the way the body reacts to the voice of the mother.

I think that maybe I will sing to myself one day so she can over-hear it, and that maybe she will come to me and ask me to sing. *Yes*, I think. I will lure her into asking me to sing to her like her first mommy. Maybe I can get close enough. Maybe it will reach her, even just a little.

There are other things she says, and I make a note of all of them.

But my thoughts keep drifting back to the antifreeze under the sink in my bathroom, poured into the teacup which I carried back to my room.

Antifreeze contains ethylene glycol, which breaks down in the body by forming sharp crystals. Those crystals shred human tissue, especially the kidneys. I taught some of this to my students when I introduced basic chemistry. Of course, I did not share the rest of it.

How death does not always occur. But severe illness does. In-capacitating illness. The kind that makes it impossible to move, or run. The kind that would allow someone to lock you in a room behind metal bars and then drive away.

It has a sweet taste.

Sweet, like sugar.

Sweet, like Alice. I must believe this. I must hold her close.

And then this sweet girl tells me, in a sleepy voice, "Do you know that it's selfish to have children?"

I am very quiet now as I whisper, "What do you mean?"

"Well," she says, "you had children so you could have someone to love. So you could have football games to watch every other Thursday."

I am still. Perfectly still as I always am in these moments when Alice reveals something new to me. I fear if I move she will stop talking. But she stops anyway.

"I do love watching my son's football games. Do you know where I go to see them?"

But she doesn't bite. She doesn't care about my desperate need to understand what is going on, how they know these things about me—so many things, like he's been watching me. But how?

"That's not the point!" she says. She wants to finish her story. Her theory.

"Okay, Alice. I'm sorry. You think it's selfish to have children?"

"It's not what I think. It's just what is. It's selfish to have children because they're just going to die one day."

I don't know what to say to this. She is right and wrong all at the same time. But then I think she is just right, so I have nothing to say.

But this is not the end of her little story.

"You should know that better than anyone," she says. "You got to watch it happen."

I feel my arms release just a little, wanting to hold this child just a little less. As little as I possibly can without prolonging this night. Without undoing my work.

I wonder who put this thought in her head, and if she knows how deeply she has wounded me. I think, then, that wounding me was her intention. Now she can feel sorry for me.

The muscles in my face quiver as I fight to keep them steady.

I feel her drift off, and then I drift off too, not to sleep, but to thoughts.

Thoughts about how we are born to die. Thoughts about death, period.

And what I have hidden under my bathroom sink.

22

Day fourteen

Officer Reyes met Nic in the business center of the hotel. He was off duty and Nic sensed that she'd pulled him away from something.

"Are you okay?" he asked. He sat down next to her then slid his chair closer to see what had captured her attention on the computer.

"I really don't know," she said. "But you didn't have to come here. I could have explained it on the phone."

Reyes nodded. "I know. But I was just watching a game." He looked up then, around the empty room. "I've been here plenty of times. Never knew it had an office until . . ."

He stopped himself from saying it. *Until your mother disappeared.* Nic moved them forward.

"It's actually a *business center*."

"Ahh," Reyes said, smiling now. "A business center. Very upscale. And clearly a big hit with the clientele."

Nic felt her shoulders drop with an exhale. The bite of sarcasm was soothing.

She pulled up the satellite image of the property behind the inn. Reyes leaned in closer. His arm brushed hers, then pulled away.

"I'm not sure what you want me to see."

Nic pointed to the screen—to the inn, the fence she'd seen on her run, how it turned away from Booth's property and seemed to encircle a large parcel of land behind it. Then she traced the line of the driveway all the way up to a house.

"Okay. So there's a property with a fence and a house on Abel Hill Lane. I don't get why this helps figure out what happened to your mother."

Nic sat back in her chair. "It's a tall fence, with barbed wire. Someone cut a hole into it, making a kind of flap. And the property isn't listed on Zillow. It isn't listed anywhere on the internet."

"Huh." Reyes was curious now. He leaned in closer—again brushing her arm. This time he did not pull it away as quickly.

"It doesn't look familiar—this driveway or fence. I'm trying to think about the houses on Abel Hill . . ."

"Isn't there some way you can search for it—on the police systems or something? I'm wondering if anyone even lives there. Kurt Kent from the bar—he said maybe some neighborhood kids were looking for a cut-through to town . . . which means maybe it's abandoned, and then maybe . . ."

"It wasn't searched," Reyes finished her thought.

"You tell me," Nic said.

"I'd have to check the log of the canvas."

"Can you run the property, see who owns it? I researched the two companies that had plants here—RC Chemical and later, Ross Pharma. One article said Ross bought the plant owned by RC. It looks like the house is on the same land with their buildings—red brick, black roofs."

"Town Hall has all the land records. I searched those buildings myself, me and a trooper—the ones that used to be Ross Pharma. We didn't see a house."

"And utilities? Can we find out if they're servicing that house?"

"Yeah—from the companies who run them. Electric, cable. Or they might have satellite or another provider for internet, if they have it. Then there's heat—natural gas or oil. We get both around here."

Yes, she thought. *That all makes sense. That all seems possible.* She finally drew a breath that filled her lungs.

"Can I show you one last thing?" she asked.

"Sure."

Nic zoomed in on the satellite image of the property on Abel Hill Lane. She'd been staring at it on and off for over an hour, not believing her own eyes.

She pointed at a small object just beyond the house—beneath a tree, but a tree with a missing limb right in the center. From the top, she could see through it to the image hiding beneath the canopy.

"What does that look like to you?"

Reyes squinted, stared. "I have no idea. Maybe a tractor. Piece of farm equipment?"

"Or a pickup truck. Dark color," Nic said. She let the thought sink in.

Reyes looked closer. "I suppose—can you zoom in more? Maybe get a different angle, or a different shot from another day?"

"This is the only one I could find. But think about it, she was seen getting into a truck—heading into town, not away from town. And now there's a property that hasn't been searched . . ."

"That *may* not have been searched. We won't know that until we look at the log."

Nic's thoughts were running wild again.

She wanted to tell him about Chief Watkins, about what she'd seen. She didn't want to drive him away by accusing his boss of something. And what something would that even be?

She couldn't hold back.

"Did you know Chief Watkins drives a dark gray truck?"

Reyes burst out laughing. "Wait . . ." He covered his mouth with his hand, stifled the laughter. "You think the chief's truck is the truck Edith Moore saw?"

"So you do know?"

"Everyone knows. He's had it for years."

"And you didn't say anything?"

Reyes grew defensive. "No, I didn't. Do you know who else has a truck? Mr. Klinger down on Mulberry Street. Henry Drumming on Maple. Let me think . . . oh—I know! Mrs. Urbansky! Sweet Orla Urbansky—now, hers is silver, but we already established that Edith Moore couldn't see a fucking thing because of the storm and is just hoping to cash in when your mother finally decides to come home!"

Nic stared at him now, stunned by the abrupt change. He was just as quick to anger as he was to soften.

"Maybe Mrs. Urbansky helped your mother disappear. Hell, maybe she and the chief are in it together."

"Okay—I get it," Nic said. "I didn't know. That's all. I saw him here earlier and it just surprised me."

"Was he with a woman?" Reyes asked.

"How did you know?"

"Jesus, were you watching? I didn't peg you for that sort of thing."

Nic felt her cheeks burn. "I wasn't watching."

Reyes stared at her, raised an eyebrow.

"Not like that. I saw him walk to the truck and I didn't know what to do."

Reyes was now contrite. "I'm sorry. I don't meant to give you a hard time. Two things—first, the chief has his vices. It's common knowledge. His wife's death did a number on him. But second— the chief is also the man who took me in when I needed a change. Saved my life, really. And the things he does for the community— the kids in this town. You have no idea. Since he lost his wife before they could have children, he's been a man of service. And a man of vice. Every coin has two sides, right?"

Nic ran this information through the other facts she now held back. How he'd helped Daisy Hollander leave town. The contempt Kurt Kent seemed to have for him and Reyes, contempt that Nic had yet to understand but knew was very real. And the tone of his voice when he was done with that prostitute in the parking lot. He'd been cruel and degrading, practically shoving her out the door.

"I didn't know," Nic said.

"It's all right."

She thought then about two sides to every coin. About the two sides of her father.

"I need to tell you something."

Reyes leaned in and listened intently as she told him about her suspicions, the late nights, the car parked downtown and not at the train station.

"I'm sorry about that," Reyes said. "You think it had something to do with your mother's disappearance?"

"I don't know. Except that I all but told her the morning she left. Maybe it pushed her over the edge."

"And now you blame yourself."

He touched her arm. She didn't pull away. And she felt it again, the anticipation of relief that she knew would come if he held his hand there. If she let it linger just long enough to travel through her. A little bolt of electricity. And from there, another touch, and another and another until they were swept away.

"Tell you what," Reyes said, moving his hand. "Tomorrow we'll check the land records and utilities for the property, and the log for the search and canvass. We can even go knock on the door if you want. And I'll do a little looking into your father. Shouldn't be too hard. We have all the bank and credit card statements."

That would all be fine, tomorrow. But tonight—what about tonight and right now? Exhausted, confused, the hollow spaces wanting to be filled. She couldn't fight it.

The words flew from her mouth.

"Let me buy you a drink."

23

Day fifteen

wake up with two bodies beside me. Alice is lodged against my spine, under the covers. One arm over my waist, the other on the back of my neck.

But I feel another hand on my hip. Over the covers, but still heavy enough to feel its weight. The hand of a man. The hand of Mick.

I do not move a single muscle. I do not turn my head to see him, to confirm what I already know. I stare at the beams of light coming through the cracks of the boarded up window. And I wait for them to stir. His touch is repulsive, and yet I am suddenly filled with hope.

Be patient, I tell myself this morning, as the light comes in and the plan continues to form in my mind. Maybe I have more time than I thought. Maybe he is starting to like me the way Alice does.

I feel the hands touching me, the bodies stealing comfort from mine. I lie still.

Be patient.

Alice is the first to wake. She groans a bit and pulls me closer with her little arms, snuggling deeper.

"Hi," she whispers.

"Hi," I whisper back.

"He's here with us," she whispers.

"I know."

I wait for her to giggle or feel her cheeks smile against my back. I think that this should make her happy, that we are all together in this bed. That I am being a good second mommy to her and pleasing Mick.

But her voice grows shaky.

"This is how it begins," she says. "When he gets into the bed with us."

"How what begins?" I ask.

She pulls my hair so my head is forced closer to her ear.

I wince but I do not complain.

Be patient, I say to myself, even as I hear the words she says next. Words that make me gasp in the cold air.

"The end," she says. And then she gives me a kiss.

24

Day fifteen

Nic awoke with a hangover and scattered memories. It was both familiar and unnerving.

She did not linger in bed. Instead, she went straight to the bathroom and ran a shower. She stepped in while it was still cold and let the water sting her skin.

She brushed her teeth, downed four Advil.

Her head still ached from the four drinks with Officer Reyes. From going to bed drunk.

Then she remembered that she'd had to leave her mother's car at Laguna. Reyes had driven her here, back to the inn, walked her to her room.

But that was all. She was certain. Although not for lack of trying.

Shit. What had she done, exactly? Tried to kiss him. Pull him into her room? And he'd wanted to, hadn't he? She'd felt his body respond. Now she was grateful he'd resisted. She needed someone to help her find her mother. Not another stranger she had to kick out of her bed in the morning.

But it had been more than raw need last night. It was the story he'd told her, which she was also now remembering. A story worthy of four drinks and a new perspective on Officer Jared Reyes. It explained why he'd come to Hastings, and why he had such a strong alliance with Chief Watkins.

Reyes had been involved in a shooting when he was a rookie back in his hometown, in Worcester, three hours north of here. A lone gunman had been lurking outside a school. Stalking the grounds, waiting, as it turned out, for the police to arrive. Waiting so he could draw them close, then pull his own weapon, forcing them to shoot. Forcing them to kill him. But his gun had been a toy, a fake. Reyes had killed an unarmed man in a suicide-by-cop. She could have listened to him all night, talking about the emotional pain that was now a deep scar he'd learned to live with.

Nic looked in the bathroom mirror, stared into her own eyes to see if she was remembering all of this right.

Reyes had described his memory of the young man falling to the ground. The blood pooling around his torso. The way it entered his own body as a fantasy, a scene from a movie. And then the rush of something vile as his brain processed reality. And this vile something changed every cell in his body in an instant. *Every single cell.* Those had been his words. But they were also Nic's.

Reyes had managed to describe exactly what had happened to her as she stood on that driveway and watched her mother's car send her little sister flying through air.

Had she started to cry then? She stared into her own eyes now, trying to remember. Yes, she had cried. And Reyes had held her. Kissed her forehead. Then driven her back here, sparing her the degradation of turning their new connection into something sexual. He knew about living with hollow spaces.

I'm not going to help you make them bigger, he'd said to her as he walked away from her room.

No one else had understood why she did the things she did. It wasn't in any textbook. But Reyes knew because he'd lived it as well.

That explained so much about him—how he exuded confidence and swagger, pulling women in. Probably sleeping his way through the county. But also why he was the only one who seemed to give a shit about finding her mother. And why he was so loyal to Chief Watkins, who had saved his life by giving him a second chance at being a cop.

A young woman was at the front desk.

"Can I speak to Roger?" Nic asked her.

She smiled politely. "Is there something I can help you with?"

"No." Nic was insistent. "It's important."

The woman picked up the house phone. "Hold on," she whispered. Then, into the receiver, "Our guest asked to see you . . ."

Then a nod and a smile as she hung it up.

"He's in his apartment," she said. "It's the second door down the hallway."

She pointed to the hallway that began just beneath the stairs.

The door was already open when she got there, Booth greeting her with a burst of surprise, and an "Oh my!"

"What?" Nic asked.

He motioned toward her face, her hair. "It's cold out. Your hair is wet."

"I didn't bring a hair dryer," Nic said.

Booth looked confused. "There's one under the sink."

"I didn't know. Can I come in?"

Booth hesitated, glancing behind him as though checking to see if his home was worthy of visitors.

"Do you have company?" Nic asked. "I can come back."

Booth looked nervously at the floor. His cheeks turned red, and when she studied them they also seemed chapped from a recent shave.

Shaved. Neatly dressed. Smelling of cologne. All just to sit in his apartment or work at the diner. He really seemed to have no idea about what this place was like, Hastings.

"No, no," he said. "Nothing like that."

He stepped aside. "Come in. Please . . ."

His apartment was no bigger than her room upstairs. A bed, a small sitting area. A bathroom. The only addition was a wall of kitchen appliances near the window that faced the odd patio out back.

"Would you like some tea?" he asked.

"Do you have coffee?"

"Instant?"

"Sure," Nic said, taking a seat at the table.

Booth put a kettle on a small gas stove. He prepared two cups on the counter—one with instant coffee grinds, and the other with a loose tea strainer.

"Hangover?" he asked.

Nic felt her heart jump. Had he seen them last night? Nic and Reyes, walking up the creaky stairs to her room? Reyes hadn't stayed—but Booth may not know that. He would have heard them talking as they walked the stairs. He would have heard two sets of feet. And then silence, perhaps, if Reyes descended more discreetly.

Booth studied several canisters of tea before choosing one. They were lined up perfectly on the shelf.

"It's much better, you know? Loose leaf tea," he said.

Nic watched him, lost in her thoughts. And her fears about what he was now thinking.

He filled the strainer. The water boiled and he poured it into the cups.

Milk and sugar were on the table, but he brought saucers and spoons.

Nic sipped the coffee as she looked around the room. Booth was busy fixing his tea just so—one and a half spoons of sugar. A long pour of milk. A meticulous stir.

"Do you live here all the time?" she asked. There weren't many personal effects. And hardly enough closet space for a few days of clothing.

"Yes," he answered. Then he understood why she was asking.

"I have a second room next door. I keep most of my things there. I know it's an odd arrangement, but I don't see much point in renovating. I don't mind it, and who knows? One day we might get busy again and I'll need these rooms for guests."

Nic looked at him carefully. Did he really believe that? After a decade-long spiral into an economic graveyard? How deep into this fantasy was he?

But none of this was why she was here.

"Remember when I went for that run?"

Booth smiled, causing his glasses to slide down his nose. He pushed them up with his middle finger.

"Of course. You escaped the bears and wolves."

Nic smiled. "Yes. But I also found the fence my father saw."

"Oh right. The fence."

She heard Reyes now, in her head, telling her not to do this. Not to speak to Booth about his neighbors or Daisy Hollander or anything else from the past.

What had he said? That Booth was *wound tight as a drum.*

Then—*just wait for me.* The house on Abel Hill Lane had not been on the search log—and it was not a registered address. It had no street number. He'd promised to run the utility searches first thing this morning, then take her back to Laguna to get her car. Then they would go to town hall. He said he would help her get through the *red tape*, whatever that meant. How much red tape could there be in Hastings? It was one parcel. Still, she'd promised to wait and go with him. They would find out who owned the place. Call them, ask about the night of the storm. They couldn't search it without a warrant, but they could stop by. Knock on the door.

Still, Nic couldn't sit around and do nothing all morning. Town hall was two miles down the road. She had no car. Roger Booth was here, right in front of her.

"It's a tall, barbed wire fence," she said, breaking her promise to Reyes. "And I think it belongs to the neighboring property— maybe one of the old plants."

Booth's face lit up then. He seemed happy to be entertaining someone in his apartment, and Nic felt a wave of pity.

"Oh—yes!" he said then. "I'm so silly! I remember now—my father speaking about this years ago. Not about the fence, exactly, but the investors who bought the land and old buildings from Ross Pharma—they were planning to make it some kind of mental facility for criminals, but they never got the permits they needed. The whole town fought it. I remember him saying he'd never let Hastings turn into a prison town. Their property must back right up to mine deep in the woods."

"And you didn't think of this when I asked you before?" It seemed very strange to Nic—how many fences could there be in this town? And how did he not know who owned the neighboring land?

Booth appeared to be embarrassed. "I . . . I'm not sure. You were going for a run in my woods and that made me nervous . . ."

He had looked nervous then. And now as well.

"Do they still own the property?"

Booth shrugged, set down his teacup. "I think they do. It's never been for sale. They probably keep it for a tax write-off."

"There's a house on that property—with a driveway running down to Abel Hill Lane. But it's not a registered address. Do you know anything about it?"

"The foreman who kept the grounds had a house. That must be it. Probably ran the separate driveway for some privacy. I heard it was kind of strange. A ranch but with a porch and false roof so it looks like a farmhouse from the front. I think they started a renovation but then didn't finish after the permits for the facility were blocked."

"Then it might be abandoned?" Nic said. "And then never searched, the owners never questioned about the night of the storm . . ."

Booth contemplated this.

"I know the buildings were searched. Reyes did it himself—with one of the state troopers. I heard them talking about it at the diner, how they were falling apart—those old redbrick buildings you can see from River Road. But the land—all of it? And the foreman's house, I don't know."

Nic smiled politely. Booth picked up a spoon and stirred his cup. He added more sugar. He added sugar like a person who really didn't like tea.

"Can I ask you something else?" she said then.

Booth crossed his legs and leaned away from her. But he still managed a polite, conversational smile.

"How well did you know Daisy Hollander?"

The air became thick between them. Booth froze with that smile on his face. Nic froze as well, acutely aware of the trigger she'd just pulled.

Reyes had been right.

"Daisy?" Booth said softly. "Why do you keep asking about her?"

Nic pushed her chair out and slowly got up.

"You know what," she said. "Let's finish this later—I forgot I needed to call my father."

She started to walk away. When her back turned, she heard Booth's chair scrape the wood floor. Then his feet shuffling.

He grabbed her by the arm and spun her around. And just like that time in the shed, she felt a kind of strength that was belied by his appearance.

"Why are you here?" he asked her.

Nic shook her head back and forth. No words would come.

"Why are you asking about Daisy?"

Her fear seemed to startle him then. He stepped away and released her arm.

"I'm sorry," he said.

Nic went for the door, but he was upon her again, holding it closed with one arm.

"No—wait. Please don't go thinking . . . I'm not like this. I'm not like this."

Nic stood perfectly still as he began to cry. His face was close to her shoulder, warm tears dripping onto her skin.

"You don't understand," he said then. "No one understands. No one knew the truth."

Nic spoke softly but with conviction. "Let me open this door."

Booth stepped back several feet, his head hanging in shame. "I'm sorry," he said. "I'm not like this."

Nic opened the door, her mind screaming at her to run from this room.

But instead, she turned around.

"What is the truth?" she asked.

Booth wept into his hands, his tall frame hunching over like an old woman.

"She was pregnant," he said.

Nic stared at him, mesmerized by his despair.

"That's why you kept looking for her?" she asked.

Booth sat down on the bed. The sobs slowed as he took deeper breaths. It seemed that he had been here before, to this place of anguish over his lost love. His lost child. And he also knew how to make it recede.

"It was mine," he answered after a long moment. "I couldn't tell anyone. I promised her—her family would have been furious. They were strict, you know? Their father used to whip them with a belt over a kitchen chair—and he would wait to do it, sometimes days, to make them suffer from the fear. He'd whip them over nothing, over taking food from the cupboard or being too loud. There's more—so many things. It was brutal, the way they lived."

Nic remembered what Daisy's sister had said about the locked cupboards and how Daisy found a way to get to the crackers—and how she did it in spite of the punishment that followed.

She leaned against the door. She did not move closer to Booth, but she felt safe somehow. And she wanted answers.

"Do you think Chief Watkins helped her leave?"

Booth seemed surprised that she knew to ask this question.

"They were very close. He got her that scholarship to summer camp. When she came back, things were different between us. She had met kids from all over the country. Gifted kids. Kids on their way to college. Kids who didn't get bent over a chair in the kitchen and whipped for stealing food."

"Kids who drank fancy tea?" she asked.

Booth smiled, sadly. "Yes. She thought it made her more like them, if she took on their likes, mimicked their behavior. There was a desperation about it, the way she wanted what they had. It still reminds me of her—the tea."

Yes, Nic thought. *The tea*—it was here, but also at Veronica's house.

"Where would he have taken her?" Nic asked. "A pregnant teenager with no money . . ."

Booth got up then and walked to a small dresser in the corner of the room. He opened a drawer and took something out. When he turned around, Nic stepped farther into the hallway, but then she saw it was a letter in his hand.

He held it out for her.

"I got this about a year after she left. I'd been a maniac— people are right about that. I went to Boston, tortured her poor sister there. I went to Woodstock, posted flyers with her picture. I couldn't let it go. I couldn't believe that she just left with our baby without saying a word."

Nic took the letter. It was folded into a small pink envelope that had yellowed around the edges. She pulled it out carefully. The paper was old, fragile.

It was a woman's handwriting.

Nic read it to herself as Booth continued to tell the story.

Dear Roger,

I am sorry for what I've put you through. It has taken me all this time to find the courage to write. I feel ashamed for not facing you before I left, but I wanted a different life. I couldn't be a mother. Please don't look for me. I hope you can forgive me.

Daisy

"She doesn't say where she went or who helped her get rid of the baby. I'll never understand it. We were in love. And I could have given her things—my family had resources. We could have moved from here. I told her I would work and take care of the baby so she could go to college. I promised to take care of her and our child. And she believed me. I know she did."

Nic finished the letter. It was short, and lacked any trace of the sentiments Booth claimed existed between them.

"There's no postage or return address," Nic said.

"It was left in my mailbox. Whoever helped her leave must have helped her get it to me. She didn't want me to see where it was mailed from."

"Her sister said she went to New York. Did you know that?" Nic asked then.

Booth waved her off. "She told me. But she didn't know about the baby and I never told anyone. Until now."

"But you don't think she went to New York?"

He shook his head then. "She hated the city. She wanted to go north—to a place like Woodstock, a quiet place. People think I didn't know her. But I did. You can't hide love. Not the love we had."

Nic felt it again—pity, sadness for this man. She had never been in love, but people could hide anything if they wanted to. Her father included.

"I should go," Nic said.

"I'm sorry about before." Booth spoke softly now. "I thought you knew something about Daisy. I thought maybe you weren't telling me. It caught me off guard, how desperate I still am to know what happened to her."

"I understand," Nic said. And then, "Why don't you just ask Chief Watkins? You're not the only one who thinks he helped her leave."

"I did. He swore he didn't drive her, but he did say she'd asked him for a ride to Boston. What am I supposed to do? Put a gun to his head? I have to live in this town. Run a business here."

He stopped her one last time as she began to leave.

"Has anyone told you?" he asked.

Nic shrugged. "Told me what?"

Now his eyes, dancing across her face, then over her breasts and hips. All the way down to her feet, then back up to meet her eyes.

"You look like her," he said. His face was flushed with longing that had nowhere to go. "Something about you—your hair and the way you walk. I can't put my finger on it," he said. "But you remind me of Daisy."

25

Day fifteen

Mick wakes soon after Alice tells me about the end that is coming. I fear that my quick, shallow breaths have shaken the bed. Some things must find their way out of the body. Some things cannot be contained. This fear that stirred from Alice's warning was like that. Too big to hold inside.

I feel the hand that weighs heavily on my hip squeeze my flesh. It does not feel intentional, and it pulls away quickly as if consciousness has suddenly taken over. I wonder if he was dreaming about his wife. Alice's first mommy. I wonder if they used to lie in bed like this and if he used to wake with his hands on her body and then fall into the physical pleasures of touch. Maybe more. Maybe they made love while Alice lay beside them, still asleep. Pretending to sleep. Maybe they went to another room to be alone.

Or maybe the first mommy tried as I now do, to lie perfectly still even as the air rushes in and out. Feeling nothing but the fear.

He moves out of the bed. He does not kiss Alice or give her a hug. Instead, he scoops her into his arms and carries her out of the room. He does this quickly as though wanting to remove himself from me.

I am relieved. I am despondent.

Yes, leave.

No, come back.

Want me. Desire me. Let me be enough. Don't leave this house and find my daughter.

I do not move. I do not turn my head. I simply feel the arms slide across me until they are gone, and then the bed gets lighter behind me, and then the floorboards creak as he walks.

There is whispering outside the room.

Then the sound of the metal grate closing. Metal on metal as the key turns the lock.

I hear little feet stomping. A high-pitched voice whining. Alice is not happy about the locked grate.

The front door opens and closes. I hear a car in the driveway. Not the truck engine like before. It has been three days since I heard the truck. Not being able to see outside has made my hearing perceptive.

The car is light on the gravel. Turns with ease. I imagine it's small. From there, I am out of guesses. I do not know this man. Mick. I do not know if he would drive a sports car or a fuel-efficient smart car. I don't know if he's rich or poor or where he goes all day and now most of the night.

I shift my head away from the camera and go to the bathroom. I have searched in here for a camera and have found nothing. Not even in the vent for the shower, or inside the light fixture. I have inspected every inch of this room and have allowed myself to believe I am right. I need to believe.

Still, I close the door and turn off the light before I let myself be free.

I sit on the floor and cover my face with my hands. Alice's words fly through my mind. Ominous words carried on that sweet little voice.

I refuse to hate her, though I feel it creeping in. She is a victim as much as I am. As much as her first mommy, I have come to believe.

I am trying not to hate you, my little prison guard.

This is how it begins.

The end.

I don't know how much time has passed when I hear her voice. I have fallen asleep on the bathroom floor.

"Hello?" It's Alice.

I push myself to sit. I have slept in a puddle of tears. Wet hair sticks to clammy skin. I am exhausted.

"Just a second," I say. I manage to sound perky, though my voice cracks.

I don't know how much longer I can do this. Not with the hatred. It is toxic. Hating a child, a victim. Poison.

"What have you been doing in there?" she asks.

I stand up and find the light switch. The light is bright and it burns my eyes, causing them to squint.

"I had a long bath," I tell her.

"I didn't hear the water," she says.

God help me but it's back. This hatred will kill me before Mick does. I have to make peace with it. With her.

I don't push the hair from my face. I don't wipe away the tears. I open the door and walk to the edge of my cell. And I let her see me.

She is startled.

"What's wrong with you?' she asks.

I sit on the floor and she sits down on the other side of the bars. I reach through them and take both her hands.

I pull from inside me everything I know about children, from being their teacher, from being their mother. It does no good to lie now. She is smart enough to put together the evidence and lying will unnerve her. Children need to trust grown-ups. The moment they realize we are liars is the moment they lose their childhood.

"Alice," I say. "You're right. I did not take a bath. I told you that because I was crying in the bathroom and I didn't want you to know."

Her empathy appetite is strong today so she starts to cry.

"I feel so bad for you. What made you cry for so long?"

I do not let go of her hands.

"Alice," I begin, then pause. I think of how to say the things I want to say to her. The things I want to tell her so maybe she will understand. Maybe she will empathize with the person I really am— the mother taken from her own family, missing her own children and her own husband and her own home. Maybe she will understand, even from what little she knows of the world, that no one can be happy as a prisoner. I've seen the books in her playroom. I know the things she reads for her schoolwork. She has begun to learn about the world, and about human suffering. I think that maybe she can use that knowledge and apply it here, to our situation. The words begin to form. If I can make her see me, then maybe I can rid myself of this hatred.

None of this is her fault.

But something about her makes me stop. Something I know in my gut. The exaggerated sobs. The flow of tears. It is not normal. It is reactive. Responsive, but not like any child I have ever known. Whatever has happened in this house, it has invaded her mind, wired it in a way that I cannot comprehend. And if I cannot comprehend it, I cannot trust it, either.

"Alice," I say. "I'm sad because you told me this might be the end and I don't want to leave you. It makes me scared because I don't know what it means."

Her eyes widen. New tears fall from them.

"Well," she says, trying to find words to explain things, "when my first mommy started to sleep with me, she said it was to get away from him. But then he would sneak in with us anyway, and that was when she got lost in the woods. That was when she died."

I think about what this means—was her first mommy trying to escape him by sleeping with her child? Thinking he would leave her alone? And when he didn't, when he still came into her bed, exposing Alice to whatever it was he did to her—maybe that was what made her try to escape. Maybe she thought it was safer for Alice if she left than if she stayed.

The thought is sickening. And yet, here I am, willing to do anything to keep my own daughter safe. Maybe this other woman thought she could make it out and then come back for Alice.

Alice squeezes my hands tighter and a smile appears. Happy Face.

"But," she says. "I think I was wrong about this being the same thing," she says.

"How come?" I ask. "What's happened?"

She pulls her hands away and wipes her face.

"He said I can't sleep in your room anymore."

I am nervous about the implications. Is he trying to keep me from getting closer to Alice, or does he want me to himself now, at night?

"And," she says, excitedly, "he went to buy us groceries so you can help me cook—things that only go in the microwave so I don't set the house on fire!" She giggles then. "That's what he said."

I smile now. And it comes from my heart. My heart that turns darker every moment I spend here.

"So we can make dinner tonight?"

"Yes," she says. "I even asked him for the Jell-O like you said."

My smile grows bigger. My heart darkens another shade.

"Is he going to come home to eat with us?"

Alice shrugs. "I don't know. I never know anymore. Not since you came."

Information, I think. New information. I have been distracted by thoughts of poison. Poisonous thoughts. I should have thought to ask the questions that are now before me.

"What did he do before?" I ask now. I want to fire them off, all of them, but I speak slowly and wait patiently. I am just making conversation. Passing the time. Getting to know her better.

Alice shrugs again. "Sometimes he would come home and bring dinner. He likes to watch TV until he falls asleep."

Patience. Patience.

"My husband likes to do that. He watches things I don't like so I usually read. What does he watch on the television?"

Alice shrugs. Sad Face now.

"Does he not let you watch with him?" I ask, guessing about the head-spinning change in her mood.

"He doesn't like to be here at night anymore. And I don't like being alone."

I consider this. And I tread carefully forward.

"Is it because of what happened to your first mommy? Maybe that makes him sad to be here without her."

Yes, I think. I need to know these things. Did he love her? Did she live here behind a prison grate? Or did she love him, too? Were they once family that went wrong? Very, very wrong?

I will stay here all day if I have to. Asking questions. Doing schoolwork. Asking questions. Eating peanut butter sandwiches. Asking questions. Playing with our dolls, Hannah and Suzannah.

But she doesn't answer. Sad Face is morphing into Angry Face.

"That's okay," I say, trying to turn her mood again.

"You don't have to talk about it. I bet it makes you sad too. You know what I think?" I ask.

She shrugs.

"I think you loved your first mommy."

Sad Face, and with it are more tears. They are tears I haven't seen before. They run down cheeks that are bright red, with sobs that are uncontrollable. They are real, these tears, and I know I have struck gold.

"Oh, sweetheart! I know. I know . . ."

I do not try to touch her. I do not even want to breathe. I have reached a well of humanity inside this child and it cannot be disrupted.

Even the hatred inside me begins to retreat. Even as I sit in a cage. Even though she has the power to free me.

Patience.

I think about the groceries and the dinner. I think about what I know of the ethylene glycol and how I will put it into food that will be made just for him. I think about how he will collapse and writhe in pain as the chemicals form sharp shards that slice through the tissue inside his gut. And how I will then leave him to suffer. Perhaps even die.

I do not think what I will do with Alice or how I will feel when she watches this happen. I cannot afford to think about that because it might ruin my plan and I can feel the weakness inside me—the weakness for the girl who now cries real tears.

"I know . . ." I say this several times with long pauses. I let her cry.

When she begins to calm, I wait just a little bit longer before I start back in with my questions.

Patience.

"Alice," I say. "What was her name, your first mommy?"

She becomes ethereal now, daydreaming about her first mommy with the real blond hair.

Then she says her first mommy's name. The one who is dead. Who died in the woods.

"Daisy," she says. "Daisy Alice Hollander."

26

Day fifteen

Nic left Booth's apartment and ran across the street to the bar. It was just after eleven. Kurt was opening for lunch.

She burst through the door, sending the string of bells clanging against the wall. Kurt was behind the bar pulling glasses from the dishwasher.

He looked up, surprised to see her.

"Hey," he said. "How did things go yesterday?"

Nic walked quickly to the bar, standing across from him. In the mirror behind the bottles of alcohol she could see herself. It was startling—the wet hair, loose sweatshirt, crazy expression on her face.

She took a breath before speaking. Crazy was not a good place to start.

"I have to ask you something," she said.

Kurt shrugged, wiped a glass. "Sure."

"Do I look like Daisy Hollander?"

Now he put down the glass to study her.

"I mean . . . you have similar hair. Same color, length. And she was thin as well. Long legs which she loved to show off. Even in the winter she would wear short skirts with no stockings. But I wouldn't have thought it if you hadn't said something."

Nic sat on a stool. She felt her nerves calm. Kurt had that effect on her.

"Why are you asking that?"

"Roger said I looked like her. Or reminded him of her."

Kurt scrunched his face. "That's a little creepy."

"And he showed me the letter," Nic said.

"Ah!" Kurt said, his eyes wide with sarcasm. "The infamous Dear Roger letter."

"Do you know about it? What it says?" Nic asked. Booth had told her that no one else knew about the baby.

"Just that he got one. He had to explain why he suddenly stopped looking for her, harassing her family. People were curious. He went from this frantic lunatic—hounding the police, her friends, her poor sister in Boston—to this eerie state of calm. Everyone knew he'd found out what happened to her."

"He's pretty sure Chief Watkins drove her out of town, wherever she was going."

"Yeah, I told you that before. He had this thing about helping kids get out of here."

Kurt's voice hinted of disdain. Nic hadn't picked it up before.

"You don't like him," she said.

He smiled then, a big happy smile. "Everybody loves the chief," he said. Again, with the sarcasm. "Especially his mini me."

"Reyes?"

Now he looked surprised again. "Haven't you noticed it?"

"Not really. Not like that," Nic thought about the casino, those four drinks. The story that had kept her glued to her seat, drinking those drinks late into the night.

"I know Watkins helped him get a job here."

She didn't know what more to say. How much was public knowledge. How much Reyes had spilled out over drinks right here, at this bar. Reyes had been here for eleven years—that was a long time to hide a story from the past that changed your life.

Kurt answered her question before she could ask it.

"Don't worry," he said. "We all know the story. How Reyes was a rookie up in Worcester. Shot and killed an unarmed kid."

"Wait a second," Nic said, feeling an urgent need to defend Reyes. "The kid had a toy gun. And he wasn't a kid. He was almost twenty. Untreated schizophrenia. Living in the bus station—he drew the gun outside a school and wandered around until the police showed up."

Now Kurt studied her face, the way she'd expected him to do before, when she asked about Daisy Hollander.

"He's gotten to you, hasn't he?"

"What?"

"He is a charmer. I'll give him that." Kurt's tone turned bitter and Nic had a sudden realization that the things she knew about this town and the people who lived here were next to nothing. Like background music distracting her from what was really going on.

"That has nothing to do with the story. And, no, I have not been charmed or 'gotten to.'"

"But he got you drinking, didn't he? With his sad tale? I can still smell it on you."

Stunned by the truth that had just left his mouth, Nic continued with her defense. "What does that matter? If I had some drinks? It doesn't change the facts—four cops came to the scene. He was just one of them. They were waiting for the SWAT team but the kid kept pointing the gun at them, and then at the glass windows of the school. Three of the four opened fire. It just happened to be Reyes's bullet that caught him in the chest."

"I know the story."

"It was suicide-by-cop. It wasn't his fault, but it messed him up."

"And there was the chief, coming in for the save."

"No—that's not what happened. At least, not how Reyes told it."

"Look," Kurt said, leaning on the counter so he could get closer to her. "I know all of it. He needed a new start. Applied for the job. The chief took a chance on him, got him all straightened out in his head. But that's the point. That's why Reyes has his back, whatever the hell he does."

Nic had a flash of Chief Watkins with that prostitute, pushing her out of the truck. Calling her a cheap whore.

The dark gray pickup truck.

"And what is it he does?" Nic asked.

Kurt stepped back, threw his hands in the air. "Doesn't matter. He helps kids, right? He helped Reyes. They run the town. The cops with their authority. And Roger Booth with his money. People like me working two, three jobs. I just left the Gas n' Go after an all-nighter—and now I'm here. It's all a fucking joke. Because this town's a fucking joke."

Nic didn't respond. These were relationships that went back many years. Kurt had wanted to get out but got stuck here. Booth lost the love of his life. Reyes lost his future to a horrible misfortune and now had to be grateful for the scraps Watkins threw his way. And Watkins—Nic couldn't even begin to unravel him.

Her phone rang.

"Excuse me a second."

It was her father's number. She closed her eyes, shook her head. She didn't want to deal with this now.

"Hey, Dad," she said.

He did not return the greeting.

"Where are you right now?" he asked.

"Back at the inn. I was about to go upstairs," she lied. She didn't want to explain why she was at the bar at eleven a.m. "Why? What's wrong?"

"I'm sending you a photo. It's from Mark."

Mark—the PI her father had hired.

"Did he find her?" The world stopped for one short moment.

"No, no—I'm sorry, I should have explained this better. I had him look into that woman, Edith Moore. It's just too strange that she waited this long to come forward."

Nic had been so preoccupied with Chief Watkins and Daisy Hollander, Reyes and Booth and Kurt Kent, she had nearly forgotten about Edith Moore and the lie she'd told about having been in New York.

"Listen—she met with a man in the parking lot of the hospital where she works as a nurse. I couldn't place him, but I swear he looks familiar. Like someone we met in Hastings. Schenectady is a long way to go for a visit in a parking lot."

Nic felt a shiver.

"Can you send it?"

"I just did. Put me on speaker. I don't want to lose you."

Nic hit the speaker button, then opened the text from her father. She could easily make out Edith Moore. The other figure was slightly hidden behind her, but she had no trouble making him out either. He was unmistakable.

No . . .

"Nic? Did you get it?"

Nic took the phone off speaker and held it to her ear. She smiled and slid down from the bar stool. Her cheeks were trembling.

"Do you know who it is?" her father asked.

She held her hand over the receiver as she started to walk toward the door. Kurt was watching her carefully, curious now.

"I have to go—something back home," she said to him.

But he didn't believe her. She could tell by the expression that didn't change.

"Nicole!" her father said again in the phone, pleading with her to answer.

With the phone still pressed to her ear, she bounded the last few steps until she was at the door. She swung it open and walked outside, then raced across the street.

"Nic? Are you there?"

Finally, she stopped moving.

"I'm here," she said, standing at the edge of the parking lot for the inn.

Her father repeated the question.

"Nic—do you know that man?"

She exhaled to calm her voice. Then she answered.

"Yeah, I do."

27

Day fifteen

hear the car outside. So does Alice, and she leaves me to run to the front door.

We have been doing her schoolwork through the bars, making sure Dolly sees us.

I hear a high-pitched squeal of excitement. Then a man's deep laughter.

They go to the kitchen. Cupboards open and close. Voices muted. Plates. Glasses clanking.

I sit with my back to the camera and make no motions. I am perfectly still on the outside.

On the inside, I am racing—to the end of this day, to my escape.

Time passes. I hear footsteps and turn. It's Alice with a tray of food. Not the usual peanut butter sandwich. Today I have grilled cheese and tomato soup.

"It's so good if you dip the sandwich into the soup!" she explains.

She opens the bottom panel. She slides the tray through, then relocks it.

I wonder now why she has brought me the food and not Mick. Usually he does it when he's home with us.

"Why did you bring the tray?" I decide to ask her.

Alice shrugs. "I don't know. He asked me to do it."

This, and he hasn't looked at me since he slept in the bed with us.

She stands now, watching me.

"Do it!" she says.

I look up at her from my spot on the floor.

"Do what?" I ask. And I ask so nicely.

"Dip the sandwich in the soup!"

"I will," I say. "You don't have to watch me. I know he's waiting for you in the kitchen. He came home just to see you, right?"

It was not easy to remember to ask a question. I feel anger boiling up as I sit behind my bars. An animal trapped. There is no way around it, the feeling this provokes.

"He came home with groceries so you can make dinner later. Just like he promised! And besides, he's busy cleaning up."

Alice crosses her arms defiantly.

"Do it!" she commands again. "Take a bite!"

I force out a smile. I take the sandwich and dip a corner in the soup. I put it to my mouth and insert it and close my lips around it and pull off a portion with my teeth.

I gag as I chew and swallow, making facial expressions and sounds of culinary delight.

Mmm.

I used to make this for my kids. We first had it at a ski resort in Vermont where we went in the winter months. John and I both love to ski. *Loved* to ski, I should say. I can't remember the last time we went skiing.

It was different after we had children. Our days were spent

tethered to little bodies that grew heavy with the pull of gravity, and we would become exhausted after a few runs on easy trails. John liked to hold Nicole's poles and ski beside her, forcing her to make turns and learn how to control her speed. I would hold the back of a harness tied to Annie's waist and snowplow behind her. Evan—he always went with the other kids in the group lessons. It was too embarrassing to learn from his parents.

Oh, how Nicole had the taste for speed! She would scream into the cold air, *faster, Daddy!*

When they were settled in the hotel room, John and I would sneak down to the pub and drink cold beer and listen to country music cover bands. It would remind us of our time together before the kids when we would ski hard all day, get drunk on beer, make love, and fall asleep. Spent and happy.

There was one day that could make us laugh even years later. A man had ridden up with us on the lift, bragging about his proficiency, his house on the mountain, his brilliant children. Then he'd fallen just sliding off the chair, poles, skis scattered around him; the lift stopped, people rushing to help him. Only his ego was hurt, and we laughed so hard it made us cry.

The thought of this takes my breath away. Makes me gag on the food in my mouth which provokes these precious, painful memories.

The mountain had a hut near the lodge that served grilled cheese and tomato soup. People would stand in line for half an hour, sometimes longer, even in the cold and the snow, and they would eat standing up, helmets on, gloves on sometimes. It was the kind of thing that when we met someone who skied there, it would come out simultaneously—*grilled cheese and tomato soup!*

We stopped skiing after Annie died. I don't know why I think of that for the first time only now. We stopped skiing, and I stopped making grilled cheese and tomato soup.

"I told you," Alice says precociously.

I swallow it down.

"It's delicious," I say as though I have never had it. As though I am just a silly little animal behind the bars. As though she is my master.

Hours pass. I play with Alice. We finish her schoolwork.

And finally it's time. Alice brings me a bag of food and some plastic bowls and dishes.

Mick has bought a small roasted chicken. He has also bought a bag of frozen peas and carrots. I place the chicken in the largest dish. I sprinkle the carrots and peas around it and add some water.

"You can put this right in the microwave," I say. "For three minutes. Do you know how it works?"

"Yes!" Alice says. "We got the microwave from the Gas n' Go. They got a new one so they gave their old one to us. It has instructions on the front. You can microwave hot dogs at the Gas n' Go."

Now I pause. *Information*, I think.

"You've been inside the gas station? I thought it was dangerous for you to go outside?"

"I haven't been inside it. But he told me about the hot dogs when he brought the microwave home. Cause I asked him why you needed a microwave to get gas."

Slowly, I tell myself. *Ease into it.*

"Well, that's very nice that they gave him their microwave."

I take more things from the bag. The instant Jell-O is there and I let out a sigh of relief.

My words linger inside her. I haven't asked a question so she is not afraid to give an answer. She likes to tell me things when she feels like it. And tonight she does.

"Do you want to know a secret?" she says, in a whisper now.

Always.

"Yes," I say.

"Dolly has eyes there." Her face is full of mischief.

"At the Gas n' Go?" I ask, thinking now about all the times I've stopped to get gas.

Every other Thursday in the months of September through November. Again at Thanksgiving and Christmas, several times during the winter and spring, though not on an exact schedule. For three years in a row, I have been making this trip to see my son. Stopping for gas many times. I've always been alone. When Nicole came with me, she reminded me to get gas before we left the school. She liked to fall asleep and not have to stop.

"Yes," she says. "All kinds of people come there. They're all heading north to get to the their kids' schools. They all have a lot of money, so it doesn't matter if they have to pay when they crash into his truck."

I think about all the times I stood at the counter, buying coffee, candy for Evan, or a bottle of water. How many times I swiped my credit card. How many times my car sat parked at the pump, with my Connecticut plates. You can find plates on the Internet now. People have hacked DMV records and they sell the information. It happened to one of the parents at Nic's old school in our town. Someone found her name and address from her plates and tried to break into her house. My car is registered to John's company. Still, there would be a trail.

Maybe Mick works at the Gas n' Go. Maybe he owns it. Maybe he knows the owners. He managed to put cameras there. And he has their old microwave oven.

I am stunned, but grateful for this new information.

Alice starts to laugh harder than I've ever seen her laugh. "One time," she says. She laughs so hard she can barely get the words out, just like me and John that day we were skiing. "One time, this man was looking at some sodas in the back . . . and he. . . . and he . . . he picked his nose! Right in front of Dolly!" She laughs so hard her eyes begin to water.

"That is very funny," I say. I think about how many times I stood right in that spot, looking for a bottle of water.

Her laughter slows quickly, as though she's caught herself. I can see now that she's done with this secret because her eyes glance at the camera down the hall and her face grows apprehensive.

I change the subject.

"Do you like lime?" I ask, forcing myself to remain neutral. Normal, whatever that is under these circumstances. I hold the Jell-O pack in front of her.

"No!" she says. "I hate lime."

Yes, I think. I already know this because she's told me before.

"I like orange," I say. "Do you want strawberry?"

She nods.

"Okay—you bring this to the kitchen and heat it up, and I will mix the Jell-O."

She picks up the chicken and walks carefully down the hall. When she is out of sight, I take the Jell-O and the bowls and I go to the bathroom.

I close the door and I grab the antifreeze from beneath the sink. I pour the small amount that is in the coffee cup into one of the bowls, thinking about Mick as he watched me pick out water.

I mix the antifreeze with the powder of lime Jell-O, thinking about Mick as he watched me at the register.

Then I make the orange and the strawberry and pour them into separate bowls, thinking about Mick as he wrote down my license plate number and researched my family.

Alice returns with the chicken and some plates and silverware. Then I send her back to the kitchen three times, carrying with two hands each of the bowls so they don't spill. My life may be in one of them.

Then we eat. And we wait for Mick to come home.

So we can have our dessert.

28

Day fifteen

W here are we going?" Reyes asked.

He'd done what she'd requested the second she'd jumped in his car—*drive!*

Nic was breathing hard. She managed to get out one word.

"Laguna."

"Okay," Reyes said. "But I thought you wanted to go to town hall—to look up that property."

Nic shook her head *no*. Then she said more words. "I need to get out of Hastings. I need time to think."

Reyes jerked his head back quickly. "Okay. Here . . ." He placed his hand on her back. "Lean forward—head between your knees. You're hyperventilating."

Nic leaned down and rested her head in the palms of her hands. When her mind cleared, she pulled out her phone and studied the photo—making sure she was right.

Then she told Reyes.

"Kurt Kent and Edith Moore," she began. "They know each other. They met in a car outside the hospital where she works."

Reyes looked at her quickly, then back at the road. "Whoa!" he said. "Slow down. Start from the beginning."

Nic told him about her father's PI. How he'd gone to Schenectady to look into Edith. How he'd followed her from the moment after they'd met with her in Hastings.

Reyes pulled over then, parking on the dirt shoulder just before the entrance to the Gas n' Go.

He motioned to see the photo.

Reyes looked at it closely. "Damn. That's Kurt, all right."

The phone rang. Nic took it back, picked up the call.

"Dad—I'm fine. I'm with the police."

She listened patiently then as he told her to come home, to get the hell out of there, to let the PI handle things from here. She agreed to everything, though she had no intention of going home without her mother. She would get out of Hastings, as far as the casino. But that was all.

Kurt was a liar, and he had tried to cast doubt on Reyes's story and his intentions. He'd tried to implicate Watkins in her mother's disappearance. The truth was, Reyes could have fallen into her bed last night. But instead, he'd turned around and left.

She hung up the call, then looked at Reyes.

"This is what my father thinks. And the PI," she began. "After my mother went missing, Kurt knew to wait until all the other calls led to nothing. Until everyone stopped calling in tips and the case got cold. Then he had his girlfriend, or whatever she is to him, come out of the woodwork with this bullshit story about passing through town the night of the storm."

Reyes continued the story.

"And now—whenever you happen to find your mother—Edith

Moore is first in line to collect the cash. That's what I feared when we found out she was lying about being in New York."

"And how could she have seen the letters on my mother's purse? From across the street and through the rain?"

"Shit," Reyes said. "I can't believe I missed that. I was so focused on trapping her in the lie about her E-ZPass records."

Nic nodded but then felt her face tighten.

"What?" Reyes asked, leaning forward, reaching for her hand.

"What if he knows where she is? What if he's known all along and he waited for the other leads to die down so that now he could lead me to her?"

Reyes squeezed her hand tighter and smiled. "Well, who cares, right? If he helps you find your mother, that's all that matters! We can go after the little prick later. I think we have to play this out—pretend you don't know a thing about it and let him lead you to her however he plans to do it."

Nic pulled away.

"What if it's not that? What if he knows where her body is? And that's why he knew it was safe to wait. That no one else would find her and that she . . ."

"Stop," Reyes said. "Don't let yourself go there."

But Nic had to say it out loud.

"No one else would find her because she's dead."

Reyes reached in his pocket and took out a piece of paper. It was a copy, white on one side and folded in quarters. He held it out for Nic.

"What's this?" She took the paper and unfolded it. It was some kind of invoice, something billed to the police department.

"I wanted to close the door on the truck with the missing taillight. I wanted to close the door on the chief. Move on to another truck. Another theory. Maybe the property with the fence."

Nic looked closer at the receipt. It was for thirty-seven dollars and change. Billed from an auto parts store in Waterbury.

The item on the invoice was listed only as a number.

"That number," Reyes explained, "it's for a taillight bulb and cover—fitting a Chevy Silverado."

Nic grabbed her phone and pulled up the photo of Chief Watkins's truck.

"Watkins drives a Silverado," she said, staring at the photo of the truck that may have picked up her mother. "You think he fixed it himself?"

"Yeah. Which means he knew someone saw him, saw the truck that night. Otherwise he'd have gone to the auto body shop right in town. And he didn't drive that truck the whole time you and your father were here searching for your mother. I didn't think much of it, but . . ."

"Now it fits."

"Which means," Reyes continued the thought, "that Edith Moore probably did see your mother that night. She told her boyfriend she was going to New York to meet friends. Then came to see Kurt—maybe they're lovers. The storm rolled in and she knew she had to get out of it so she didn't get trapped here. She waited until the last minute, then drove toward Route 7."

Nic picked it up from there. "She saw Chief Watkins pick up my mother, but she thought nothing of it. Then the next time she saw Kurt, he mentioned the missing woman and she told him what she saw."

"That could have been the next day or a few days ago. Look, Kurt Kent may be a loser bartender, but I don't see him plotting such a complicated crime. It could be that everything Edith Moore said is true, except for the small detail that she was here visiting Kurt before the storm."

"What about the purse? And the letters?"

"She could have seen them. We can't know without recreating the scene."

"And Watkins?" Nic asked now.

"I know . . ."

"What did he do with my mother?"

Reyes started the ignition and pulled away from the curb.

"Let's find out," he said. "First, we get your car. Then we find the chief and ask him straight up what's going on."

Nic felt a wave of relief.

Reyes was right about everything. Kurt Kent was not a bad man. Edith Moore was just lying to her boyfriend, that was all. Maybe she had come forward as soon as she found out about Nic's mother—or maybe she waited to make sure she was the one to get the reward money. But either way, it didn't mean they knew where her mother was. Only what Edith Moore had seen.

It was Watkins with his truck. The broken taillight. No way that was a coincidence.

Edith Moore saw her mother get in that truck. Watkins's Silverado.

Watkins was the one who knew where her mother was.

Reyes was smiling now. "You feel better? Your breathing has slowed."

Nic smiled back. "I think she's alive. I think Watkins drove her somewhere. Helped her leave. I don't even care that she walked away, or why she did it."

Reyes patted her knee. "I know. And we will get her . . ." He stopped speaking but Nic could tell he was holding something back.

"What?" she asked.

"I found something else. On your father's credit card statements."

"Just tell me." Nic braced herself for what she knew was coming.

"There are some hotel charges. Local ones, in your town."

Nic stared out the window, feeling the traces of hope leave her. "I knew, but I still didn't believe it. Not completely."

"There's one other charge that I can't explain. At a gas station near West Cornwall."

"That's just south of here. When was that?"

Reyes didn't answer. And then he didn't need to.

"The same day. The day she disappeared," Nic said.

"Look, maybe it was her—the charges are on the same statement."

"But then she wouldn't have run out of gas," Nic said. "If she'd filled up in West Cornwall, she would have made it well past Hastings coming home."

Reyes was silent again. He'd come to the same conclusion.

"This can't be right," Nic said.

"I can call them, find out the exact time of the charge."

Nic closed her eyes, hard. This couldn't be happening. Her father couldn't be involved.

"Do you want me to call?" Reyes asked.

Slowly, but with conviction, Nic nodded.

Yes.

29

Day fifteen

We lie on the floor. I am on my side of the bars. Alice is on the other. She wanted to sleep near me even though we are not allowed to sleep together anymore, so I told her to get some blankets and cushions from the sofa. I showed her how to make a pillow bed and she liked it very much. Of course she did. My kids used to love pillow beds. When we would go to a hotel, all of us, as a family—oh, that was another life—we would share a room. Me and John in one bed. Two kids in the other. And the third on a cozy bed between them, made from cushions or extra pillows—whatever we could find in the room.

The trick is to tuck a sheet tightly beneath them so they don't come apart.

Evan usually chose the pillow bed. Even as he grew too big for anything we could make, he would sleep on the bound pillows, arms and legs hanging off the sides. He didn't want to sleep with one of his sisters. Girls were *yuck*. Thankfully, I wasn't recognized as being a girl. These memories flow now, freely and with the semblances of joy. Leaning over to kiss him goodnight, he would pull me to him with both arms and hug me tight. Still a little boy inside, but with the strong arms of a big boy. He needed me. And it was blissful. Even as the memory retreats to the other side of the line, the joy lingers. But it does not last. This night has ended in disaster.

Alice sleeps soundly in her pillow bed, even though I have untangled her arms from my waist and moved beyond her reach.

It is not far enough.

I let the feeling flow through me, still and silent, because Alice has left the hallway light on for Mick and now Dolly can see my face.

It is probably for the best. I don't know what I might do if these feelings are set free.

We waited for Mick for a long time. We waited until we had watched all of her shows on the iPad and grown bored and tired.

"I want my Jell-O," she'd said then.

I told her it was okay. She could bring us our Jell-O but she should leave the one for Mick, the lime Jell-O, in a place where he would see it. Maybe he would want dessert when he finally came home.

I can still see her face as she told me, "No!"

It was Coy Face, speaking with defiance.

Then she said, "I threw it away."

"What? Why?" I asked, because it was all I could think to do. The hatred surged. Pulsated. Took over every inch of me and crawled over my skin, making me shudder.

"Because he didn't come home so he doesn't deserve Jell-O," she said.

"Alice—that's not nice!" I was so close to reaching through those bars and shaking her, violently. "Go and get it right now—out of the garbage and bring it to me!"

It was a ridiculous request. The Jell-O would be scattered among the remnants of the chicken and coffee grinds from the morning and who knew what else. Still, I needed it. I needed her to bring it to me.

But then she said, "It's not in there. I can't even stand the smell of it."

"What did you do with it?" I asked, my mouth bone dry.

Coy Face answered, and my only plan for escape disappeared before my eyes.

"I put it down the drain."

Alice has killed my chance to escape. She has done it over her frivolous hatred of lime-flavored things and she has done it in a way that demonstrates the extent of her hatred.

It does not matter that in any other set of circumstances I would not care about her actions. It does not matter that she did it without knowing what her actions would cost me.

I find this all ironic. How her hatred of lime-flavored things has caused me to feel hatred for her. Truly feel it for the first time, in depths that are beyond the reach of my ability to pull them back. The hatred is deep inside my bones. Inside my mind. Inside my heart.

I am too tired to reach for it. Too tired to fight it. I hate a child.

It is hard to think straight. I had a plan which is now gone. New plans swim and swirl, but there are too many unknowns.

I do not know where we are, and what is beyond that fence. I do not know how far away he is, and whether he could get to me while I run there, back to the hole and the tools I left beneath the dead leaves.

I don't even know if the tools are still there. And yet, I could get another knife from the kitchen. Maybe there are more scissors as well.

I think through the steps. I would have to convince Alice to open the grate. I would have to find the boots, maybe a coat. The air is still cold at night. I could run through the woods this time, in the direction of the fence to the right side of the driveway, not down the driveway. But then—what if I overshoot the place where I cut the fence and hid the tools? I could just make a new hole.

No, no, no.

This plan will not work unless I can be sure he's far enough away. He will see me leave. He will know.

I can't go back to that dark room. I can't go wherever Daisy Alice Hollander has gone.

I have to stay and be a good second mommy to one child to protect another—my daughter. To protect Nicole.

I fight to keep my face calm, though the tears fall down my cheeks and into the pillow around my ear.

Stillness brings chaos inside my mind.

Nicole.

You used to be a glorious warrior. That was how I saw you, though I never said it. I didn't want you to become something simply because I put the image in your head. My mother did that to me.

You're a smart girl, Molly. Not the prettiest girl, but smart. You need to use that to get ahead of the other girls who have their looks.

Maybe it served me well to hear those words. I studied hard and made a career for myself. And John always told me that's what he loved most.

I remember now how my husband once loved me. I don't know how, but it just happened and it was glorious. And now that glory is agony.

It would be easy to tell myself that he stopped loving me because the scale tipped too far to his side. That I got older and less attractive. That I stopped working, stopped being interesting. Up, up, up, my side of the scale drifted, losing the weight of these things.

But that would be a lie. There is no scale that can bear what I have done.

I feel my lips part, taking in air as the tears fall. I taste the salt on my tongue.

I hear the argument for the first time in years. The argument I lost then and will always lose.

No—I was not speeding around that corner. I had slowed down, of course I had, because the driveway was just around the curve.

No—there was nothing more I could have done. My eyes were on the road. My hands on the wheel. I wasn't adjusting the radio, or using my phone, or reaching for my coffee.

No—I could not have slammed on those brakes any harder than I did! The forensic report confirmed all of this. The skid marks. The air bag. The turn of the wheel away from the object in the road. From the child. My child. My Annie.

Six more inches and I would have been clear. I would have slammed into the mailbox and the boxwoods and the flower bed. But the wheel turned only so far.

Six more inches.

People say things. Things beyond *put one foot in front of the other*. They pose questions and force you to answer. *Would it be your fault if you gave up your seat on a plane and the plane went down? If you ducked from a gunshot and it hit someone else?*

There is no logic to the guilt.

But you gave her life.

Yes, but then I killed her.

I killed her.

I killed her.

It never goes away. God, help me. It never leaves.

I'm sorry, John, for falling off the scale. For being unworthy of you.

I'm sorry Evan, for infusing you with anger. It seeps from my pores. I should have known it would reach you.

And Nicole—my fierce warrior. You had everything! You were beautiful and strong and brilliant. You were that glorious firstborn child who saw the world as a thing to behold, and a thing to be conquered. And now you live behind a sword and shield but the enemy still comes for you. To vanquish you. To kill you as well.

My chest rises and falls quickly now as I gasp for air. I cannot hide it any longer. The tears are now sobs as I lie here in my prison, unable to see a way out. I am forced to surrender. And it comes. It all comes, storming the unarmed gates.

Nicole.

I see your face as you stand in the driveway. I see your face staring at your sister as she lies in the road. I see your face when you realize what has happened.

I prayed that the warrior in you would conquer. I did not have the strength to carry you through the storm of our grief. And our guilt.

I will not sleep tonight. And without sleep, I will not have the strength to fight him. I will not have the mental agility to make a new plan.

The tears have stopped though I cannot stop the panic.

There is no evidence of an imminent fight. No need for an immediate plan.

And yet it is here. This panic.

I sit up then. Not caring about the camera, about Dolly. Not caring if I wake Alice. I sit up because I have to shift the blood that has pooled in my head and caused this chaos.

I let it all settle, recalibrate. I can't make any sense of it. But it does not leave.

I allow my gut to weigh in, the feelings I have had these past fifteen days.

Mick was cheerful when he picked me up that night. He was almost giddy. His plan had worked. His stalking and scheduling. Using Alice to lure me into this house.

And then he was hopeful as I was kind to Alice and then returned to the house after going into the woods.

And then I tried to take that phone and he wrestled me to the floor, dragged me to that room. There was excitement in his eyes, from the physical violence. From the dominion he then had over my body, but also my emotions. He provoked terror and relief each time he walked down the hall to that dark room.

But Nicole had arrived and he had seen her in the town. She reminded him of his dead wife and the thought got in his head. Under his skin.

Still, he gave us some time. Me and Alice. But also me and him. He watched me changing. He watched me standing before him, and sitting with Alice. He slept in the bed with us. I know he tried to want me. But hope turned to frustration. I was not enough. I have not been enough.

And now, he is planning something. With his avoidance of me, but his leniency with the food. He makes accommodations to appease me and Alice.

I must accept the truth now. The kind of truth that is known from inside, without the need for objective evidence.

I see Alice squirm on the other side of the bars. Her little arms reach through them for my body. A little octopus. I lie back down and let her wrap them around me.

I feel it.

The truth.

The fight is coming.

30

Day fifteen

The day turned to night in a heartbeat, it seemed.

She and Reyes arrived at Laguna just after noon.

She texted with her father to avoid having to hear his voice. She didn't want him to know what she'd found out, about the affair and the credit card charge in West Cornwall that day. She texted him what she knew about Kurt Kent and Edith Moore. He texted back that his PI was looking into the connection. Reyes called Mrs. Urbansky at the station, asking her to find out about the utility bills at the property on Abel Hill Lane. He asked where Chief Watkins was, said he needed to speak with him.

Then came talk of Nic going home, but she refused.

Then stay here.

Reyes insisted. He didn't want her near Booth after the incident in his apartment, or across the street from the bar and Kurt Kent who could very well have read her expression when she saw that picture on her phone of him with Edith Moore.

It's safer here.

He checked her into a room, then went back to Hastings to gather her things from the inn. She gave him her key—the one with the giant wooden ring. He returned a few hours later and they went to the bar.

Watkins is nowhere, Reyes reported. *Not at the station or at home.*

Mrs. Urbansky said he was taking a personal day. He hadn't answered his cell, and Reyes didn't want to alarm him by having Mrs. Urbansky track him down on the police radio. Confronting the chief would have to wait until tomorrow.

But he did have news—and a document. A title copied from the land records at town hall for a property on Abel Hill Lane.

It is a corporation—a group of investors like Booth said, he explained. *A holding company.* They would have to search the records with the secretary of state to get the names of the investors. Reyes said he hadn't lived here back then, but remembered there was talk of turning the buildings into a mental facility for criminals. Again—just like Booth had said. It never happened—but that explained the fence with the barbed wire. He said the same corporation also owned the Gas n' Go.

There was nothing online. The corporation was no longer active. But that made sense—Booth had told her the investors probably only held on to the property for tax reasons.

Reyes and the state trooper had searched the redbrick buildings, but not the house where the foreman once lived. They didn't know it was part of the same parcel. It had a separate driveway but no registered street address. It was as though it didn't exist at all.

Except it did.

And then . . .

Vodka.

Reyes talked about his childhood and what had happened to

him after he killed that boy. Nic had confided in him about Annie. The afternoon became evening.

I guess we're the same that way.

And then . . .

I can't believe my father . . .

Don't go there. Let's see what more we find.

And then . . .

I can't believe Kurt did this . . .

Don't take it personally. It's just money.

And then . . .

Easy for you to say. There was a night—when I was here the first time.

The night at the bar?

Yeah.

You were pretty lit.

Something happened.

I remember.

What do you mean?

In the back. You and Kurt.

How did you know that? Did he tell you?

Then silence.

Then recognition.

You were there? You saw us?

Reyes motioned to the waitress.

"Another round," he said. Then to Nic, "I think we're going to need it now."

Nic protested. "No, no—I can't. Not after what you just told me. I can't believe you saw me with Kurt, with anyone, like that."

Reyes drained what was left in his glass. Then his face got serious, mirroring hers. He reached out and took her hand. "It's no big deal. So you made out with a complete stranger in a completely strange town. It happens."

This got a slight smile out of her. Thank God for vodka. Her father was receding from her mind as the conversation turned to flirtatious banter.

"It shouldn't, though. It shouldn't happen. That's not who I am." Then she reconsidered. "It's not who I used to be, anyway."

He leaned back and nodded. "I was just trying to make you feel better."

"Not possible," Nic said. "These past five years have been such a mess. *I've* been such a mess."

The drinks came. Reyes took his, but then waved off the vodka tonic for Nic.

"No—wait." She reached for the drink, grabbing it from the tray before the waitress could leave.

"It wasn't right away," Nic explained. "After my sister died, I felt like I had to make up for her being gone, you know? I actually tried harder. Got better grades. Stopped going out with my friends, doing things teenagers do. Shopping, movies, texting all day about stupid shit on the Internet. But it didn't last."

"Is that when you started drinking?"

"Yeah. It's so strange how all of it, the drinking, the men, it gives you this relief, you know? In the moment. But then it just makes it worse."

Reyes leaned forward and took both of her hands in his.

"Listen, I was a disaster before the chief brought me here. After killing that boy, leaving the job—it was like I wanted to die, only I didn't have the courage to do it, and more than that . . . there was this annoying part of me that wanted to live, that kept whispering that it wasn't my fault and that I deserved to live, and I hated that part."

Every word he said resonated inside her.

"I know—you're not really trying to kill yourself, you want to kill that annoying voice that keeps telling you to let go of the guilt and start living again. That's the thing I've been trying to kill— with the drinking and the . . . the men."

"If you keep degrading yourself, maybe that annoying voice will finally shut the hell up and let you drown in the guilt."

"Yes," Nic said. "The first time I ever had a drink, I was so desperate to stop feeling. I actually had thoughts of wanting to die. Of jumping off this bridge that runs through our downtown."

"Jesus, Nic. That's horrible. Did you ever tell anyone? How you wanted to kill yourself? Jump off a bridge?"

"I told the counselor they made me see. I don't think she really got it. I don't think anyone gets it unless they've lived it. They were just words to her, when I tried to describe it, the hollow spaces wanting to be filled, but never could, because that day can't be unlived. I can't get my sister back. And now my mother . . ."

Reyes pulled her close. Stroked her hair.

Then he repeated what he'd said earlier.

"We are the same, Nicole. And I understand everything you're saying."

Nic closed her eyes and let herself go. She let the alcohol settle in, warm her blood and blur her thoughts. There were too many of them, and none she liked.

Except this one. This one thought he had put in her head.

We are the same.

She liked that thought very much, even though she knew, before they even left the table, where it was going to lead.

31

Day sixteen

The morning begins with chaos. The sound of a drill. Then silence. Then the front door banging as it swings so wide it hits the wall.

Alice sits up, startled, arms pulling away from my body on the other side of the bars.

She lets out a holler of surprise, but says nothing.

I sit up now and see Mick reaching for her, scooping her in his arms and carrying her away from me.

She is quiet as she looks at me from over his shoulder, as they move down the hall.

It is a new face I see. I do not give it a name because I don't ever want to see it again.

It is a face of terror, as though she knows she is about to lose me.

I take a breath now because the chaos seems to be over. At least for the moment. I get up and walk to the far side of the bed. Something has drawn me there. I hear no more sounds. It is quiet.

The light is different somehow, brighter and sharper.

I can see now, I can see why the light has changed.

Mick has drilled a hole in the wood.

I slide the glass panel down and touch the little hole with my finger. It's been drilled from the outside. It is no wider than my pinky.

But it is wide enough to let in the light.

And it is wide enough for me to see outside.

I look through the hole, I can see one side of the driveway circle and realize the room must face the front of the house.

I feel relief at first that he has given me this gift of light.

But then another thought enters. A thought that fits better with the chaos that has just occurred.

Mick has drilled this hole so that I can see outside.

I don't know what it is he wants me to see.

But I suddenly long for darkness.

32

Day sixteen

Nic awoke, startled by her surroundings. She sat upright, her eyes slowly taking in the things that were visible in the dim morning light.

Stiff white sheets. A fluffy duvet. Blackout shades behind thick beige curtains.

She heard a quiet hum from the heating unit above the door to the bathroom.

It crept into her brain, this fog carrying information about where she was and how she'd come to be here. Hungover. Naked. Alone.

"No," she said out loud. "This isn't happening. I didn't do this. Not again."

She pulled the sheet tightly around her. There was no one to kick out of her bed. No one to hold on to.

Hand shaking now, she reached for her phone. It was nearly ten. She needed something, someone.

Her mother was gone. Her father was lying. And this new man who had made her feel so good last night—the man and the vodka, both gone now.

"Evan?" she said, her voice trembling into the phone. He was all she had left.

"Nic? What is it? What's happened?"

His name was the only word she could get out.

"Where are you?" he asked.

"At a hotel. At that casino. The one where Mom used her credit card."

She cried the words. Evan was confused.

"What are you doing there?"

"Ev—I think I know who gave Mom a ride here. I think she may have left."

Evan was quiet for a moment. But then—

"I don't care! We still have to find her. You're still going to look for her, right?"

"Yes. Of course. I promised you I would."

More silence. She couldn't tell him why she'd called, that she had dug herself into a hole and didn't think she would survive it. Not this time.

"Evan?" she said.

"Yeah?"

"Just keep your shit together, okay? I'm sorry I called. I'm so sorry . . ."

Then a knock at the door. And Reyes's voice.

"Are you decent?"

Then Evan again. He'd heard it—the man's voice.

"Who was that?"

Then Reyes.

"Are you ready?"

Nic jumped out of the bed, raced to the bathroom for a towel which she wrapped around her body. She called out to Reyes, covering the phone with her hand so Evan wouldn't hear her.

"Just a second . . ."

Then to Evan on the phone, "I'm fine. I have to go . . . I just needed to hear your voice." She made quick excuses, then hung up the call.

She opened the door, her hand still clutching the phone.

Reyes stood there with two cups of coffee and a disarming smile.

He walked inside, his eyes moving over her, head to toe, wrapped in the towel.

"Good morning," he said. He set down the coffee and pulled her close.

She buried her face into the crease of his neck. She wanted to cry, with despair, or relief. All of this was disorienting.

He held her until she let go first. Then he handed her a coffee and sat on the bed.

"Are you all right? You seem upset. Is it about what happened last night?"

She told him the truth. "I don't know."

Had it been like all the others? She had told herself it was different somehow.

Sweet and tender. Wasn't it? She could still hear his soft voice on warm breath. *We are the same. We are just the same.* Whispering in her ear as they fell onto the bed. And then the silence of his voice, but the words his body spoke as he touched her and kissed her and held her. They were kind words. Loving words. The silent conversation of lovers, not just people fucking, but making love, connected by the role they'd played in the death of another human being. It was something few people could understand.

"It's okay," he said to her. "Why don't I wait outside. You take your time. Get dressed. Come down when you're ready and we'll head back to town."

When the door closed behind him, Nic took a shower. Got dressed. Drank the coffee he'd left for her.

It was different, wasn't it? How could she not know?

They drove half an hour back to Hastings, then another fifteen minutes through winding roads before arriving at the parcel on Abel Hill Lane that Reyes had found in the land records. It felt like they'd been driving in circles.

"It's such a maze of woods and cornfields," Nic said.

Reyes nodded. "It's a small town, but you'd be surprised how easy it is to get lost."

They pulled into the dirt driveway. Then they stopped in front of a metal gate. On either side was a tall, wire fence with coiled barbed wire lining the top.

Nic stared at it for a long moment, then got out of the car.

Reyes joined her.

He went to the gate and swung it open. It was not locked, though a loose chain hung from one side.

"Strange," he said. "Why go to all this trouble to hang a lock on the gate but not close it?"

Nic looked up at the fence, then touched one of the wires. She could feel the small barbs.

"This is the same fence!" she said.

Reyes started walking back to car. "I guess you were right about it."

They got back in the car and drove up the long driveway to the top of a hill. They stopped just past the front porch of a house. It was exactly as Booth had described it. An old ranch with a partial renovation.

"Stay here," Reyes said.

Nic didn't argue. He walked around the car, but then stopped by her window. She rolled it down.

"What?" she asked.

He leaned in and gave her a kiss. It was the first kiss all morning and it made her want more.

"Is that okay?" he asked.

"Yes," Nic answered.

She leaned out the window, watching as he walked to the porch steps, then up the steps to the front door. He rang the doorbell and waited. He knocked, and waited. He looked back, shrugged. Rang again. Knocked again. Waited.

He placed his hand on his holstered gun.

Then he turned the doorknob. It opened. He looked back to motion that he was going inside. Nic nodded at him, and watched as he disappeared into the house, closing the door behind him.

33

Day sixteen

hear a car in the driveway. Mick has been gone for two hours. Alice has not come to me, not even to bring me food. I have listened to her play alone in her toy room, making the voices for both Hannah and Suzannah. I cannot hear what they say to each other but it worries me that she stays away.

I get up and walk to the window. I look out the hole to see what it is Mick wants me to see. There is no point in avoiding it.

I have been looking out all morning and I have already turned his plan to my advantage. Beyond the driveway, I see my new weapon.

A row of apple trees flank the side of the driveway. They are mature trees and I imagine they were planted before Mick took over this house. He does not seem to have an interest in property maintenance.

The apples have ripened and fallen days, maybe weeks ago.

Apple seeds contain amygdalin.

Amygdalin can convert to cyanide.

Cyanide can make you sick. It can even kill you.

I have been back and forth to the hole in the window, studying the trees, counting the apples that have fallen to the ground.

Plotting how I can get to them.

I watch now as the car pulls around the driveway just enough for me to see.

It takes a moment for the image to settle in my brain. And then it explodes. A police car.

A police car!

I hear footsteps. Alice is coming. She is at the bars of my cell. She pushes the wood door open so she can see me. I look back at her, and I know I cannot change the look on my face.

Desperation.

She shakes her head sternly and raises her finger to her lips.

Shhhhhh! She makes this sound. I look back out through the hole.

I have to be careful. I will have one chance to call out before Dolly's eyes see that I am being a bad mommy.

I don't know how far away Mick is. He could still be in the house, though I thought I heard him leave. He may have returned.

Think, Molly! Think!

I wait for the officer to open the door and step outside. He walks around the back of the car and I lose sight of him. But then I see his back as he walks to the passenger side. A window rolls down. A head leans out. It's a woman, I can see her blond hair. He kisses her and I think how strange this is.

Is he not here to save me? To look for me?

He stands up straight and steps away. I think that I will press my lips to the hole now and scream out for help.

Alice taps nervously on the metals bars.

"Stop!" she screams in a whisper.

I look back at her, then once more through the hole, ready to call out for help.

Alice leaves. I hear her feet running now toward the front of the house.

The officer turns. I am ready to do it, ready to look away and press my lips to the wood. But then I see the face of the woman. I think my eyes have gone crazy. But I stare long enough to know that what I am seeing is real.

I do not look away. I do not scream for help.

Because the woman in the car is my daughter.

And the man in the uniform is Mick.

Day sixteen

Nic stared at the house. There was no movement now. No sound. Apple trees lined the driveway, then woods. More woods, as far as the eye could see. Probably all the way to the edge of the fence.

She thought then that if no one was inside the house, they would track down the owners, those investors from New York. Maybe they had someone check on the place the night of the storm. They owned a black truck. Or a gray one. But a truck, like the one Edith Moore had seen her mother get into.

How this fit with Chief Watkins and his truck, his broken taillight, was still a question. But she would follow every lead until it brought her to her mother.

She looked back to the house and noticed a window to a room in the back. It was boarded up—from the storm, she imagined— only it was fortified with steel bars.

She stared at the one boarded window. It was odd. Out of place.

And for a second, she wondered what was behind it.

Day sixteen

hear the doorbell and the knocking and the waiting. Then more ringing and knocking until finally the door opens and closes. I look out the hole and pray Nicole is still in that car. That she is still unaware.

Footsteps bound the hallway. Smaller ones scurry behind them. Then the lock turns. The grate opens.

Mick walks in, wearing a police uniform. He is calm and steady.

He wears a face that is smug and laden with the power he has just acquired over me. Just like the moment when I heard his cell phone ring on the kitchen counter. The moment I knew I was his prisoner.

I have a flash of memory, provoked now, by the uniform. A traffic stop somewhere along Route 7. I don't remember the name of the town. I only remember now how John hired a lawyer to make it go away because he was worried about our insurance. And how it was never submitted by the officer. It was as though it had never happened. I thought I'd gotten lucky.

I had been traveling twenty miles over the speed limit. I had been trying to get away from these dying towns, trying to get home. I hadn't noticed how fast I'd been going.

I study his face and know it is the same man.

How long has he known me? How long has he been planning this? That stop was last spring.

Mick is a cop. Everything I have come to think about him now unravels. I try to put the pieces back in a way that fits with this new one.

Mick is a cop—a real cop. He has access to records. He can get people to pull over, the way I did. To give him their information.

What else? The cameras—at the Gas n' Go. Mick watches people coming and going. He can see their license plates and credit cards. I think about how these pieces fit together—how perfect it is. How he can gather information, and then use it however he wants.

He knew I came every other Thursday in the afternoons from the cameras at the gas station. He got my driver's license and car registration from the traffic stop. And how easy it was from there—one Google search and my whole life unfolded for him, like a nicely wrapped present.

I want to fight against it. I think that maybe my rage is finally big enough to overtake him, but that delusion is dispelled the moment his hands take hold of my wrists. His physical strength is undeniable.

He pulls me back to the window. Presses my face to the wood until it scrapes my skin. I can feel the small splinters as they enter and dig their way through the flesh.

"Look," he says calmly, though his strength feels like an explosion against me.

I do as I'm told. I look at my precious daughter through the hole.

"I have her now. Nod if you understand."

I nod. I do exactly as I'm told.

"I think she would make a good mother, don't you? And a good wife."

A cry leaves my mouth. I can't hold it in.

"She is so lovely. Every inch of her, so, so lovely. And she is in love with me."

He lets go of me and I fall to the floor.

"Nod if you understand," he says again.

Again, I do as I am told.

Of course I understand.

If I am not the best mommy to Alice, he will take my daughter.

But then I also know the truth.

He is delusional, thinking she loves him. Thinking whatever it is they've shared will last beyond this morning. She will grow tired of him before the sun goes down.

And yet, it doesn't matter.

He will take her anyway. But first, he will kill me.

Unless I can stop him.

36

Day sixteen

t was only a few minutes before the door opened again and Reyes appeared. He shrugged once more, then walked back to the car.

"The place looks abandoned. No heat. No water. I checked every room in case . . . but no sign that anyone's been living there."

Nic stared back up at the house.

"We have to find out what the story is with this place."

"We will," he said. Then he leaned over to kiss her again.

He started the car and pulled forward.

Nic looked back one last time, at the window with the wood and the metal.

"Did you see the room with the boarded window? There are metal slats on the outside."

"Yeah," Reyes said. "Strange, right? But the window inside was broken. Maybe they didn't want to pay to replace the glass. I told you, no one's lived there for a while."

They drove through the gate. Reyes stopped. Got out.

"I'm just going to close it. Leave things the way we found them. Probably shouldn't have come without a warrant."

Nic didn't turn around to watch him, though his image in the side mirror caught her eye.

He closed the gate.

But then he replaced the chain—which was not how they'd found it—wrapping it three times as though he knew that would be the right number. And then he did something else.

Something that made her gasp one breath of air.

He took a padlock from behind a post—as though he knew it would be there, just like he knew about the chains—and he put it through the loops of the chain, locking it shut.

37

Day sixteen

watch the car drive away. I watch the man, the monster, drive away with my daughter.

Now, more clanking on my prison bars. Alice is there with her Sad Face.

"Come over here," she says.

She wants to comfort me. The chaos of the morning, the violence, has made her hungry.

I don't move. I can't.

"Come here!" she demands, and I see Angry Face coming. She points to the camera in the corner of the room, reminding me that he is watching.

She does not need to say the rest. That he has my daughter. That he will take her and kill me if I do not behave.

I manage to walk across the floor to the grate. My skin stings in the places where the splinters of wood have entered.

"Sit down," Alice says. Sad Face has returned. She is volatile now, and I have to calm her. I have to feed her need to empathize with me, to comfort me.

So I sit.

"Give me your hands," she demands.

I give her my hands.

She holds them tight and presses her cheek into them.

"What will happen to you if I have to have that new mommy? What if she's not as good a mommy as you are? What if she only loves him the way you only love me?"

She begins to cry now, tears of empathy as I knew she would, and I can feel her calming. She presses my hands to her wet little face and cries into my skin.

"Don't worry," I tell her. "I will be better. I will make him happy so you don't have to get a new mommy."

She looks at me as though I've just tried to tell her the sky is purple. We both know what Mick wants.

He wants Nicole.

But I remind myself that Mick is not the only one in this house with power.

He has physical strength. Metal bars. Locks and keys and Dolly's eyes. But I have those apples and inside of them, in their tiny seeds, is everything I need to take him down.

I watch Alice melt in my presence. And I think something else. Something about power.

"Have you ever tried an apple muffin?" I ask her. She looks up at me with wonder. As though it sounds delicious, and like something we will do together. And I think, Mick may have my daughter. But I have his.

38

Day sixteen

'm sorry that was a dead end," Reyes said to Nic as they turned back toward town.

Nic was confused. He'd just said something entirely different not five minutes before.

"What about finding those investors? And the utility companies? I thought we were going to see if anyone checks in on the place—they left the gate open, right?"

Nic had just watched Reyes lock the chains as they were leaving. And now this sudden shift in his demeanor. He was distracted, like his mind was now preoccupied, unable to even remember what he'd just said to her.

"I think it's futile—I know you don't want to hear that," he said. "It was cold and dark in there. No utilities running. And that broken window . . . we can still check if you want, but it's a dead end. The fence is there because of that loony bin they wanted to build. Trust me," he said. "I am the cop, you know." He let out a slight laugh.

Nic was dazed. Things were moving too fast now. Why had

they even come to this house? Because no one checked it. Because no one knew it was here. And now it was checked, with no sign of her mother. Reyes was right to be dismissive.

"What about Chief Watkins?" Nic asked.

"Don't worry. I'll speak with him as soon as I can. And I still need to find out about that credit card charge your father made in West Cornwall."

Nic let all of this sink in.

She wasn't losing her mind. Reyes was the same man who'd held her all night, who'd brought her coffee and taken her to this house. He'd told her about Chief Watkins even though it was likely to hurt him in the end. And he would find out the truth about her father.

"Thank you," Nic said.

"And what will you do? Where do you want to go?"

"To the hotel, I guess. I don't know. Where should I go? What should I do now?"

How pathetic she sounded, even to herself. But that was how she felt.

"I think you need to figure things out with your father."

"Yes."

"Who do you think it is? This other woman?"

Nic had her suspicions. "He has an office manager who's divorced. Same age. He wouldn't look for someone younger. He would want someone like . . ."

"Your mother," Reyes finished the thought. "I get it. He lost her the same day he lost your sister. It makes sense he'd want to get that feeling back. When you lose someone you love that much, you want someone who was just the same. Because you know that's the kind of person your heart desires and nothing else will satisfy it."

Nic studied him now, curiously.

"Did you lose someone you were in love with?"

Reyes sat up straighter. His face flinched. She'd hit a nerve.

"I'm sorry," she said. "That's none of my business."

"It's okay."

But then, he didn't answer.

When they reached Laguna, Reyes pulled the car up to the curb. He handed her a piece of paper and a pen from the center console.

"Here—do me a favor. Write down your father's full name. Make and model of his car. Where he works. The name of the office manager. Anything else that might help me look into this for you."

"I don't know . . ."

"Just write it down and then call me later if you want me to do something about it. I'll wait to hear from you—promise."

Nic wrote down the information, though each stroke of the pen felt like a stab in her father's back.

"Do you want me to go up with you?" Reyes asked, folding the paper into his pocket.

"No, I'm fine. Will you come back later?" It was strange how she wanted to be alone but how it also terrified her.

"Of course," he said. "You can't get rid of me that easily."

And then the anxiety shifted. As she got out of the car. Watched him drive away. And remembered the gate that was now locked at that house.

And who was this woman he'd loved and lost and was trying to replace? Maybe with her?

She walked into the lobby and smelled the sickening sweet pull of the bar, and the instant relief that was waiting for her there.

39

Day sixteen

Cyanide.

I taught this in one of my eighth grade chemistry units.

Hours pass as I sit on the floor and help Alice with her homework. She is very sorry about my daughter but life must go on. I must be a good mommy.

Thank you, Alice, for reminding me of what's important.

She does a math problem on the other side of the bars. I sit cross-legged and pull from my memory what I learned years ago about cyanide. I steady my expression because Dolly's eyes are surely watching very carefully now.

In small doses, the body will change cyanide into thiocyanate which can be excreted in urine. In larger doses, it prevents cells from using oxygen, causing those cells to die.

The heart, lungs, and central nervous system are the most susceptible. Symptoms can include shortness of breath, vomiting, dizziness, weakness, and confusion. Seizures. Cardiac arrest. Death.

Apple seeds contain amygdalin, which will turn into cyanide when exposed to the enzymes in the human gut. They must be crushed or chewed for the amygdalin to be released. It can take thousands of apple seeds to kill a grown man. But how many, I wonder, to make him sick?

The time does not go to waste. I do not allow myself to indulge in the panic that is at my door. I have removed the splinters from my skin and applied some ointment Alice found in her bathroom. I have changed my clothes which were drenched in the sweat of the morning's terror. I have showered. And I have cried the last of the tears I will cry.

I think about cyanide. I also think about Nicole as the clock ticks away.

There are only two things that would bring her back to this town. The first is a man. The second is me. I know my daughter. I understand her suffering. A man would not hold her attention for long. The newspaper article said she was here for four days. That's long enough for her to get drunk and meet a man. A man like Mick. A cop, probably involved in the search. I remember those first few days—how he came and went. And now—she has returned, maybe for him. But it won't last.

She will peel him off of her like the rotten skin on the apples outside. Even if he was wonderful. Perfect. Even if he offered love. Especially if he offered love. She cannot accept love. Not from anyone.

Oh, how I understand her suffering.

That leaves one reason for her to stay now. Me. Finding me.

I remember her words the morning I left for Evan's school. I remember her face when she said them, and how they jabbed at my heart in quick bursts as they left her mouth.

I hate you—but that was just a small one. A little jab. But then, *You killed my sister!* The first big one, and then, *You killed your own child!*

I know my daughter. She has carried her own guilt from that fateful day. Not answering her phone. Not driving Annie to her friend's house. Not being there in time as her sister ran down the driveway.

And now this—the belief that she caused me to walk away from them. Not just her, but Evan and John. This thought nearly breaks my steeled expression. This thought causes the blood to surge into my face, pulsing around the scrapes.

Evan. John. Nicole. My life.

In these long hours I have thought about the possibilities. I know how Mick learned about me. The cameras at the Gas n' Go. The traffic stop. There is a lot of information online because of Annie's death.

But then my family came to look for me, and everything changed. Now he wants Nicole.

Why did he bring her here? Why did he drill that hole so I could see her?

I know about human nature, about need that overcomes reason. Teaching children who were on the cusp of maturity has given me this tool, which I now use. Mick needed me to know what he's done. What power he wields.

He wanted this more than he feared what I might do.

Or maybe he doesn't know how fiercely a mother will fight to protect her child. Maybe he never learned that.

Either way, he has misjudged me like an adolescent child. I will not yield to his power. I will not behave when he has set his hands upon my daughter.

Alice looks up.

"I can't get this one!" she says. Angry Face is here.

She shoves the paper through the bars and I see what she's done wrong.

"Two negatives make a positive," I remind her.

I hand the paper back. She takes it and resumes the problem.

"I have an idea when we finish your homework," I say.

"Shhh!" she commands.

Fine, Alice. But we will talk about my idea. About the apples in the yard. The ones that have fallen and begun to rot. We will talk about how you and I are going to make a special treat for Mick and how you are going to sneak around Dolly's eyes to get outside, and put on your mask, and collect as many apples as you can find.

Maybe I was selfish to have children, knowing they would have to die one day. Maybe I deserve to suffer for it. More than I already have.

But further punishment will have to wait. Because today, we are going to talk about those things.

We are going to do those things.

And we are going to save my daughter.

40

Day sixteen

t took sheer will to walk back outside, away from the bar. She needed the fresh air. She needed to drive, and to push aside the thoughts that were twisted up in her mind.

Reyes, the tortured soul who truly understood her—who might be strong enough to save her from herself.

Reyes, the damaged man who used women the way she used men—and who might just pull her into his despair as well as her own.

She couldn't possibly know the difference. Not in two days' time. And not with all that had happened.

She found her mother's car where she'd parked it the day before. She wasn't sure where she was going. Not back to Hastings. Not home.

She checked her phone and the texts that had been piling up. Three from her father—all with the same message. When are you coming home? Come home, sweetheart. Where are you—you need to come home.

One from Evan. Did you find her? What's happening?

It was the final one from her father that provided the most distraction. Edith Moore is Edith Bickman. Moore is her boyfriend's name. Probably used it to hide the fact that she worked at the bar in Hastings four years ago. And Kurt Kent did time for a gun offense. Two bad apples. Scam. Also—Mrs. Urbansky said she did not give out your number to anyone. Another lie! Call me or answer your phone!

She had two missed calls and voicemails from him as well. She responded with a text. I'm fine. Will call soon.

But was she fine? Drinking and sleeping with strangers again. Infusing her reckless actions with meaning that might be pure fiction?

We are the same . . .

How could he say that when they'd just met? How could she have believed it. And yet it had felt so real. She wanted it to be real, even now, as the doubt crept in.

She sat in her mother's car. Smelled her smell, which was fading more every day. She turned on the ignition and closed her eyes. The list of loose ends—what was on it now? Edith Moore—or Bickman—and her plot with Kurt Kent, her father's PI was looking into that. But what about the lie she'd told about getting Nic's cell phone number from Mrs. Urbansky? It had been Reyes who'd put those words in her mouth. She remembered that now. Maybe he'd assumed it, and then she jumped on board, not having a better answer.

Her mother had not been at that house. No one had, and it was a long shot anyone had been there the night of the storm. Next, Watkins and the truck—but Reyes said he was going back to find him. Her father and his affair, and the stop he'd made at the gas station in West Cornwall. She should call him, ask him for the truth, for once. But he had already lied to her about the handwriting analysis.

And then, Daisy Hollander—the woman Chief Watkins helped get a scholarship to a fancy summer camp in Woodstock, whom he'd supposedly driven out of town when she'd needed to escape the fate of becoming Mrs. Roger Booth. Watkins and his truck. Watkins and Daisy Hollander.

Daisy Hollander. She remembered the way. The names of the roads, and even the road with no name.

Down Laguna Drive to the end. Then right on Route 7. She was a mile from the Gas n' Go when she saw the dark gray truck— the Silverado—with Chief Watkins in the driver's seat. She turned her head and sat low as he drove by. Then she picked up speed, turning onto Hastings Pass. She drove through town, past the police station, until she got to the end—to River Road. Then right onto Pond, left onto Jeliff. Then the road with no name. She remembered the way.

As she made the final turn into the dense woods, those words were still ringing in her head. Making her stomach turn now.

We are the same.

41

Day sixteen

Alice has been such a good girl.

"Can we play Hannah and Suzannah?" she asks me.

Of course we can, you good, good girl.

"Of course we can," I say, hiding my excitement.

She runs off to get the dolls and I return to the bathtub to check on the rotting apples Alice has collected from the yard.

There are forty-five of them. And they all have seeds.

Alice went to the kitchen like I told her. She went to make us lunch. Peanut butter sandwiches and milk. Yes, milk today, because she wants to make me suffer a little. She wants me to suffer because somewhere inside her little brain is the knowledge that I am lying to her about the surprise for Mick.

Still, she climbed out the back window of the kitchen. The back window near the sink, where Dolly's eyes can't see.

She wore her mask and carried two brown grocery bags. She scurried like a little bunny rabbit, picking up the apples and filling the bags. She had to make two trips to bring them back to the window. They were heavy.

She did all of these things. And she did them fast. She brought the apples to me in the bags, along with some groceries she placed on top. I emptied the groceries, bread and milk and peanut butter, then pulled the bags with the apples through the bars and brought them to the bathroom. I put the apples in the bathtub, then threw the bags in the garbage.

I try not to think about where he is. And when I do, like I am now, I look at the apples and think about his cells suffocating. I think about his lungs closing. I think about his heart stopping.

"Hey!" Alice calls out now. "Come out and play!"

I have been too long in the bathroom with my apples.

"Sorry," I tell her, resuming my spot on the floor.

We make lunch and eat. Then she hands me Suzannah and I straighten the doll's hair.

Half an hour passes slowly. It is late afternoon and there is no sign of Mick. Flashes of him kissing my daughter in the police car come and go. But mostly come and stay.

Hannah and Suzannah have been discussing their mothers again. Alice likes this and I need this. Yes, I have my apples, but I will not waste one opportunity to gather information. To make inroads into my little prison guard. Into her head. Into her heart.

What she did today was extraordinary. Not because of the logistics of getting the apples. But because she knows I am planning something devious. Wrong. Hurtful. She knows, and she helped me anyway.

Then she served me my milk and I drank it down.

Oh, the games we play, Alice and I.

"It makes me so sad," Suzannah says. She has been telling Hannah a terrible story about a fight her parents had and how her mommy still won't be happy. Now she's run away and Suzannah is afraid she will never come back.

"I know," Hannah says, and she reaches through the bars to give Suzannah a plastic doll hug.

"Thank you, Hannah. You always make me feel better." Suzannah pauses long enough for the sweet moment to pass. Then—

"Do yours ever fight?" Suzannah asks.

I swear I can see Coy Face run all the way down from Alice's face, through her arm and fingers and onto the stupid plastic doll.

"What do you mean?" Hannah asks.

"Do they ever get mad at each other? Do they yell sometimes?"

I am desperate to get back to my apples. I need to take out the seeds and grind them. I need to do this before we can bake the muffins.

Time passes. Mick is with my daughter. A bead of sweat rolls down the side of my face.

Hannah finally answers.

"He loves my mommy," Hannah says finally. "He loves her so much it makes him cry."

The image of Mick with my daughter leaves for a brief moment as I try to think about what this means. I can't picture Mick crying.

But then suddenly I can. Suddenly, my perspective shifts. Love can make people crazy. It can make them do crazy, evil things.

"Because she's so beautiful?" Suzannah asks.

Hannah nods.

"With her real blond hair and her thin body?"

Hannah nods again.

Alice reaches through the bars and takes Suzannah from me. She lays her on the ground, and then lays Hannah down beside her. Alice leans in close and so I lean in close. She doesn't want Dolly to hear.

"I have to show you something. It has to be a secret."

Yes. Please. Tell me your secrets.

"I promise," I say to her. Then she gets up and leaves. I hear her walk softly to her room. A moment passes and she returns.

She sits down casually. Too casually, like she's acting. And I can feel that her heart is exploding.

She carries a small book of nursery rhymes. She hands it to me through the bars.

"The story on page twenty-three is my favorite," she says.

I open the book and carefully turn the pages until I find what she wants me to see. On page twenty-three, tucked into the crease, is a picture of a young woman.

A young woman with real blond hair and long, skinny legs.

I stare at the picture, trying to hide the surge of adrenaline as it pulses through my veins, turning my face crimson.

I am looking at a woman who resembles my daughter.

Alice picks up Hannah.

"That's my mommy," she says. "Daisy Alice Hollander."

I look at Alice, then to the picture. Then to Alice again. Her face is transformed from that of a child to a grown, wise woman.

A woman who understands and wants me to understand what's happening here.

Alice's mother is dead. The mother that Mick loved so much it made him cry.

And now he's found a way to bring her back to life. He's found a woman who has long blond hair and a sleek body and is young.

He's found my daughter.

I nod slowly to Alice. She reaches through the bars and takes the book from my hands.

Yes, Alice. I try to say with my eyes. I understand.

42

Day sixteen

Nic stopped just beyond the clearing where she could see Veronica Hollander's house. The trees were thicker here, evergreens mixing in with the pines and oaks, filling up the sky. The house seemed dark inside but smoke billowed from a chimney. She could smell the wood-burning even with the windows closed.

A text broke through the silence. It was Reyes.

> At the station with Watkins. Will sort everything out.
>
> Heading back to see you.

Nic stared at it, remembering she had just seen Watkins leaving town—back to the casino. And she had just driven past the police station. Reyes's car had not been there.

Something about this was all wrong.

She got out of the car and walked to the same door she'd been at the day before, with Kurt Kent.

She knocked, waited. She could hear the creaking of floorboards inside, someone walking. Maybe deciding whether to let her in. She was alone this time. And she'd been asking questions about the past that had made Veronica uncomfortable.

"Hello?" Nic called out. She knocked again.

"It's Nicole Clarke. From the other day—with Kurt? I just have a few more questions."

Finally, the turn of a lock, and the door opened.

Veronica was just as she'd been the last time. Long, tangled hair. Loose clothing hanging from her body. She was barefoot this time, and her skin glistened from the heat that was coming from the fireplace.

"It's hot in here," she said. But she stepped aside and let Nic enter.

"Damn fire either won't stay burning and I freeze my ass off, or gets hot as hell."

Nic smiled. "Thanks for letting me in."

"At your peril." V laughed then. "Want some tea?"

Nic wasn't sure if she was serious. The place had to be eighty degrees. The windows were closed, and Nic wondered why she didn't just open one, even a sliver, to let in the cool air.

"No thanks," Nic said after V went to a kettle and poured hot water into a cup with a tea strainer. When she returned, she moved a leather jacket from the back of a chair, then pulled out the chair for Nic to sit. The table was just as cluttered as last time.

"Did you make that?" Nic asked. She motioned to the jacket which now lay on top of a pile of fabric.

V shook her head. "Just doing a repair. Ripped pocket. I'd be rolling in dough if I could make clothes like that."

"So," V said quickly after. "Is this about Daisy again?"

"I hope that's all right."

V titled her head, studying Nic closer now. "I guess we'll find out. What more do you want to know?"

"I was hoping you had some pictures of her. I couldn't find anything on the Internet. She doesn't use social media, at least not under her real name. Images come up, but I have no idea which one is her."

V nodded. "You want to know how much you look like her."

Nic hadn't expected that. Booth had told her she reminded him of his lost love, but Kurt had not seen it.

"Do I?" Nic asked. If anyone would know, it would be her sister.

V shrugged. "Some," she said. "But you can judge for yourself."

She got up and walked to the small hallway which was lined with three doors. She opened one and disappeared, then returned with a cardboard box. She needed both arms to carry it.

She placed it on the small piece of table that was clear just in front of Nic.

"We didn't exactly do family portraits. We didn't even have phones until we could pay for them ourselves, and believe me, they were the shittiest little phones you could buy. We weren't snapping selfies and posting them on those sites they have. Facebook, right? I listen to the news."

"So what's in the box?" Nic asked.

"Daisy's things. Junk, mostly. But it's not my place to throw it out."

Nic stood up so she could see over the top of the box. "Can I look?" she asked.

"I didn't haul it out here for my health."

V watched, sipping her tea, as Nic opened the folded cardboard flaps. A musty smell escaped in a quick burst, then dissipated. This box hadn't been opened in many years.

V was right—there was some clothing, which Nic carefully removed and placed on the chair where she'd been sitting. A concert T-shirt, a pair of sequined jean shorts. Beat-up wedge sandals, one with a broken strap.

"See what I mean?" V asked. "Look at that stuff—crap, right?"

Nic pulled out more things from the box, costume jewelry, a makeup bag, a stuffed bear. And then something more promising.

"What's this?" Nic asked.

V looked at the small book Nic was holding. On the cover was a photo of about fifty girls, posing in rows by a lake.

"That's from the fancy camp she went to one summer. The chief helped her get a scholarship for it. She was happy as a pig in shit, that girl. And don't think for one second she didn't rub all our faces in it." V shook her head from side to side. "She thought she was something else, getting out of Hastings, hobnobbing with rich girls from fancy schools."

Nic read the small print at the bottom of the photo. *Woodstock Summer for the Gifted.* The date was from twelve years ago.

The girls were crowded together, all of them smiling ear to ear. Long hair. Straight teeth. Shorts, tank tops, flip-flops. Nic could have been one of those girls at that age. It was only a few years back for her. The memory of it grabbed hold of her for a fleeting, but brutal, moment.

"You all right?" V asked.

"Yeah." Nic looked up, smiled sadly.

"They're young, aren't they? But don't let them fool you. Those girls would eat you for breakfast."

No kidding, Nic thought. Her school had been full of girls like that. Not one of these "friends" had stuck around after she'd fallen off the social ladder. And it had not been gradual. The day she was expelled was the day her phone stopped ringing or buzzing or pinging. It was as though she'd caught a deadly virus. A social virus that no one wanted to catch. And the strange thing was, she had welcomed it. Still, it made her wonder how Daisy had survived them. Maybe she was good at pretending to be like them—maybe she'd just taken it, knowing she was going to get out of Hastings and be just like them one day. Maybe it ignited a fire.

Nic scanned the faces in the picture but she couldn't pick out anyone who looked particularly like her. She moved closer to V and placed the book in front of her, next to the tea.

"Which one is Daisy?"

V opened the book past the first page. "They each have a page, I think. Like a yearbook. I remember when she came back late that summer and made us all look at it."

She turned a page to a dark-haired girl from Boston. "Look at this one—Cindy Coughlin. *She attends The Milton Academy and rides horses.*" V said the last part in a mocking tone. She turned more pages, stopping at others, reading their profiles with that same tone, only with increasing anger.

Finally, she stopped—at the page for Daisy Alice Hollander.

"There she is!" V said. "Look what she wrote—*attends Hastings High School and studies ballet.* What a joke! She never took a ballet class her whole life."

Nic leaned in closer, taking in the face of the girl who'd disappeared ten years ago. Long blond hair. Big white smile. Skinny arms sticking out of her shirt.

"Well? What do you think? Are you looking in a mirror or not?" V asked.

"I don't know," Nic said. "Am I?"

"It's all in the eye of the beholder," V answered. Then she handed the book to Nic and got up from her chair. "Here—sit down, look through the rest of it. There's other pictures in there—small groups of them out on the lake, by the fire. Camp shit. I think Daisy is in some of them."

V took her teacup to the sink and started washing dishes. Nic turned the pages, one after the other, scanning faces of girls. Daisy was in several of them, front and center, posing, smiling. She was beautiful and that was the last word Nic would use to describe herself. Though there was a time when she might have felt that way. When she might have felt the way Daisy seemed to in these pictures—talented and beautiful, with the world at her feet.

At the very front of the book were headshots of the teachers and counselors. At the very back, pictures of staff. Nic started to skim them quickly, but then found herself slowing down. The photos were small and faded. The features of the people were hard to distinguish. In the kitchen. By the boathouse. In the rec room. They caught her attention at first because they had faces of men and women. The campers were all girls. But the staff—especially in the kitchen—included men, and of all ages.

She was about to turn a page when she stopped. Cold.

She leaned in closer, not believing her eyes. But then she could not deny them. The cheekbones. The chin. The hairline. Even the smile on his face.

She looked up at V, still at the sink, keeping busy with her dishes.

"Veronica?" she said. The woman turned. Nic started to ask the question that was dying to come out. But then she pulled it back, acutely aware now of where she was. Alone with this stranger in the middle of a forest. One way in and one way out. And no one knew she was here.

V turned around. "What? You find something?" she asked.

Nic got up and managed a warm smile.

"No. I just realized I'm late to meet someone."

V stepped away from the sink, a look of doubt on her face.

"What did you find in there?" She took a step closer. Nic put the book back in the box.

"Nothing. I should go."

Nic walked quickly to the door. V didn't follow.

"Thanks," Nic said, pulling it open, stepping outside.

She didn't look back as she closed the door behind her. Then she walked to the car, quickly, sucking in the cool air, turning around, then driving through the woods, back to the main roads.

And thinking about the face she'd just seen in that book.

The face of Jared Reyes.

43

Day seventeen

t took most of the night to grind the seeds. The amygdalin is beneath the hard shell. Alice made soup for dinner. I slid the spoon
under my leg when she went to the kitchen to get more crackers.
When she returned, I drank the soup from the bowl, slurping it
loudly. *That's bad manners!* she scolded me, but it made her forget
about the spoon when she cleared our dishes.

I still had the knife from when we made the sandwiches. Now
I had one spoon, which I bent at the top. One spoon and over two
hundred seeds. I lay them in the sink, ten or so at a time. I pressed
both thumbs into the head of the spoon, twisting and pressing at
once, into the seeds. Grinding them between the metal and the
porcelain. I collected the mash in a cup, sifting out as many of the
hard shells which broke into larger pieces but would not grind.

Thumbs aching, cramping. Arms begging for rest. I did not
stop grinding those seeds, making the mash, until I had a small
cupful.

I pray now, in the morning light, that it will be enough to make
him sick. The amount of amygdalin, and then cyanide, depends

on the type of apple and how much evaporates before it can be ingested. It depends on his weight and how quickly he consumes it. There are so many factors. It is not likely he will die. Not at all. But I don't need him to die.

I hear the car on the gravel outside. I look at Alice and she looks at me. Maybe I am misreading her. We are soldiers about to enter a field of combat.

Alice and I have been very busy this morning. First, we cleaned up the pillow beds where we slept on the floor together, the bars between us.

Then, Alice brought the flour and sugar, the baking soda, butter, milk, and eggs. She brought, too, a metal bowl, measuring cup, and mixing spoon. She brought all of it, and with Dolly watching us, I was the best mommy—showing her how to make muffins.

The apples were tricky. There was not much of them that wasn't rotten. I salvaged what I could and left it in the bath tub. I flushed the rest down the toilet—a little at a time.

I knew the recipe by heart. Muffins are muffins when it comes down to it. Alice measured and mixed. We laughed and pretended to be having fun. She spilled the flour. I went to the bathroom to get a towel. And in the towel were the bits of apple I was able to save. I slid them into the bowl with my back to the camera, to Dolly and her watching eyes. Then I wiped the flour from the floor.

I sent her to the kitchen to get a wet sponge. And when she was gone, I filled the muffin tins.

When they were baked, we put frosting we made from powdered sugar just on one special muffin—the one in the middle on the edge of the tin with a brown stain. I told her it would make Mick feel special. Like we cared about him.

And then we sat and did Alice's homework. We sat and played with the dolls. We sat and waited.

When the front door finally opened, it closed again with a loud bang. His footsteps were heavy, pounding the floor. He walked past us without saying a word. Not to Alice. Not to me. He went to his room in the back of the house and slammed that door as well.

We said nothing, Alice and I. We pretended not to notice him, though my heart was heavy and light all at once.

Heavy because he needed to be happy and calm and eat his muffin like a good boy.

Light because he was angry. And that meant something had gone wrong with Nicole.

Good Lord, is it terrible? Is it twisted that I feel a laugh rise inside my chest as I picture my strong-willed, tortured daughter sending him away after an unfortunate night? I am filled with joy where there had once been despair that my daughter uses men to fill the hollow spaces she spoke of in therapy.

I thought it would kill her, this behavior. But now I think it might just have saved her.

The door opens again and Mick emerges. How different he seems to me, now that I see his pathetic, broken heart.

Alice rises slowly and walks beside him to the kitchen. I told her not to mention the apples. He could grow angry that she went outside to get them. I told her to say that we made *special* muffins, with *special* ingredients.

I hear him getting a mug—the cupboard opening, the ceramic clanking as he pulls one out. I close my eyes and picture him pouring his coffee. The coffee in the coffeemaker. The one with the white filter, which we filled with coffee and turned on for him so he would not have to wait.

I told Alice how to do this as well. I have been a very, very good mommy today.

Moments later, Alice walks quickly back to my room. Sad Face is here and she holds back tears.

"What?" I ask. "What's wrong?"

"He won't eat the muffin. He said he's not hungry. He said he had a very bad night and he just wants to drink his coffee and be left alone to make his phone calls."

I sit on the floor and Alice sits as well. She is curious now that my face does not grow sad. Or disappointed.

We worked hard on those muffins.

"It's okay," I tell her.

Now she is confused. "It is?" she asks.

Then I ask her a question. "Is he drinking the coffee? The coffee that we made?"

She nods. "Yes. In the big cup."

And I can't hold back my smile.

44

Day seventeen

Reyes had been at the casino, parked in the back.

Jared Reyes. The boy from the kitchen. The boy who knew Daisy Hollander before he'd even stepped foot in Hastings.

Jared Reyes. The man who'd lied to her—about everything, it seemed.

The house on Abel Hill Lane—he'd known where the lock was, and then chained the gate closed. Edith Moore—he'd given her the answer to the question about Nic's phone number, then failed to ask her about the small black letters on her mother's purse and how she'd been able to see them. And he'd claimed not to know Daisy Hollander well, said he didn't see a resemblance between her and Nic.

It all made sense now, why he'd lured Nic into bed. It was just as he'd said—how people try to replace the ones they loved with replicas.

His messages had not stopped all day and all night and she'd had a bad feeling—one she was now glad she'd heeded. It had made her stop before she'd pulled into the casino. It had made her look for his car.

She'd backed up, turned the car around, and started to drive. It had been late, but she'd needed to call her father.

"Daddy," she'd said, her voice trembling. She hadn't called him that for years. Not since she was a little girl.

"Nicole? My God! What's wrong?"

"Are you having an affair? Just tell me. I have to know the truth. Why did you lie to me about Mom's note?"

There'd been a long pause, and then, "Pull over, Nic—I can hear the car. Pull over before you get in an accident."

Nic had pulled to the curb. Put the car in park. Then she'd let go, sobbing into the phone. Screaming. "Tell me the truth!"

"I will, I promise. Just calm down. Take a breath. Where are you?"

Nic had looked up. She'd been on Route 7, heading north, back toward Hastings.

"I'm still here," she'd said.

"You said you were coming home! Jesus, Nic—you promised. I'm coming to get you. I can get the next flight out . . ."

"I don't need you to come get me. I need you to tell me the truth!"

"No, okay. The answer is no. I'm not having an affair."

"But the late nights, the way you stopped looking at her . . . I was so sure. I told her! I told her the morning she left!"

"Oh, Nicole—no, no—this is not about you. It doesn't matter what you told your mother that morning. She already knew the truth."

"What truth, Daddy? What did she know?"

Another pause. A breath.

"That I couldn't find my love for her."

"But there were charges—at hotels . . ."

"Please, Nicole. This is so hard for me to say. Sometimes I just couldn't come home. But there were no hotels. I never made any charges."

It had sounded crazy, but yet Nic understood completely. She had stayed out all night when she could.

But then—

"Why were you in West Cornwall the day she disappeared. I know about that charge as well."

His voice had changed suddenly. "What are you talking about? I was at work that night and then I went home. Went right to bed. You can ask anyone at the office . . . what is this about? What charge did you find?"

Reyes. Another lie? But why? How could she not have seen it? Or felt it? The thought had disgusted her.

"Promise me, Daddy. Promise me you don't know where she is. On my life. On Evan's life. Promise me right now."

Thirty miles north of Hastings, Nic had found a shopping strip. It had employee parking in the back, hidden from the road.

Nic had climbed in the back seat and laid down on her side, curled in a tight ball like a child. She'd closed her eyes, and heard her father's voice in her head. Over and over.

I promise.

It was morning now, and she called Chief Watkins. He came within the hour. He parked his truck two spaces over, the gray Silverado, then got out and walked to the blue Audi.

Nic turned on the ignition and opened the window.

"Are you okay?" Watkins asked.

Nic unlocked the door. "Can you get in?"

Chief Watkins went back to his truck, then returned with two Styrofoam cups. He opened the door to the Audi and climbed into the passenger seat. He wore the same uniform as the day Nic had returned to Hastings—just three days ago. Three days. So much had happened.

"Here," he said, handing Nic a cup of coffee.

"What's going on?"

Nic wiped her eyes which were sticky with exhaustion. She breathed in the smell of the coffee. Then took a long sip.

"Thanks for coming. I'm sorry if I was cryptic."

Watkins shrugged. Drank his coffee. "That's one way to describe it."

Nic had told him where she was and that she needed to see him. She'd asked him to tell no one.

She looked straight at him now. "I'm going to ask you some questions and they're going to sound really strange but can you try to just answer them without asking me why or what for . . ."

Watkins held out his hand gently as though he could magically slow down her racing mind and the words that were pouring from her mouth.

"Okay," he said. "I'll answer. Just take it easy. You seem a little wired."

Nic started with the little ones.

"Did you know Daisy Hollander?"

Watkins's face changed abruptly. She could see the questions begging to come out, but he held them back just as he'd promised.

"Yes," he answered.

"Did you get her a scholarship to a camp in Woodstock?"

"Yes."

"Did you drive her out of town the day she left and never came back?"

Now a long pause. But then an answer. "No."

Nic was surprised. "You didn't drive her to Boston?"

Watkins exhaled loudly. Hung his head.

"You've been talking to crazy Roger Booth."

"Yes," Nic answered.

"Okay—truth is, I was going to drive her to a train station, Hartford, most likely. But then she said she had a ride."

"Did she say who it was?"

Another pause.

"Do you know? Tell me if you know."

Watkins answered. Reluctantly.

"Officer Reyes. Look, I know he lies about that. But I would have lied too. Daisy was desperate to get away from Booth. The only reason Reyes took her and not me was because he had the time to take her all the way to Boston that day."

"I don't get it. Booth doesn't seem like a bad guy."

"He's not—it's just that she wanted a different life. And after the childhood she endured, and the gifts she had—she was brilliant, you know. And pretty. She was the only one of that lot, those crazy Hollanders, who had a chance. Booth would have pestered her for the rest of her life. You think he'd ever get a girl like that again?"

Nic let this sink in. Reyes knew Daisy from that camp. But had Daisy known Reyes then? Was it a coincidence that he moved here the following year?

Watkins was the one who'd hired Reyes. Saved him from his guilt after he shot that unarmed man. The suicide-by-cop.

Or did he?

"Tell me what you know about Reyes," Nic asked.

Watkins rattled off the same set of facts Reyes had given Nic the night she drank with him and let him into her room. Into her bed. The thought made her shudder.

It was the exact same story—the shooting in Worcester, how Reyes had quit his job, fallen apart. How he'd applied for an opening in Hastings and Watkins had hired him, pieced him back together.

Only now, a new fact—he'd arrived three months after Daisy Hollander went to that camp.

Nic didn't tell him what she'd seen in that yearbook. But she pressed on with her questions about Daisy and Reyes.

"Was there anything between them? Maybe something Roger Booth didn't know about?"

"Reyes? No way. Never saw them together. Daisy didn't give any man the time of day unless he could do something for her. She had gifts but she was also wily as hell. A survivor, you know?"

"And what about you?"

"Me? Me and Daisy?" Watkins laughed then. "Look, I have my vices, especially since my wife died. But she could have been my daughter. I'm not one of those creeps."

Nic thought about what she'd seen in the parking lot of the casino. The way he'd treated that prostitute. He may not be one of those creeps, but he was something.

She moved on.

"The taillight on your truck."

"What about it?"

"You fixed it six days ago."

"I did."

"How long was it out?"

"Not a day before I fixed it. I'm the chief of police—can't exactly go around with a broken taillight."

"Broken cover and light bulb?"

"How would you know that?"

"Just tell me."

"Okay. I walked out of the casino on a Thursday night, the way I always do, and someone had smashed the glass cover and the bulb. I figured it was some drunkard who backed into me. The thing is, there was no other damage to the car. You'd think maybe there'd be some scratches to the paint around the casing. Anyway, I went to the auto body and they fixed it."

"The one in town?"

"No. I use one up the road. Got a friend there. Why?"

"So you didn't order parts through the town? Charged to the department?"

"Hell, no. That's a sure way to get my ass fired. What is all this about—wait a second, is this about that woman? The one who saw a pickup truck the night your mother disappeared?"

Nic didn't answer. She didn't need to.

"Just ask it, then. Ask the question you really want to ask."

"Okay," Nic said. The words choked her at first, then exploded. "Did you see my mother the night of the storm? Did you take her somewhere? Did you help her leave us? Did you do something else? Did you hurt her?"

"Jesus Christ," Watkins said. "I mean—Christ! No. No, no, no. A thousand, million times. No. How could you even think that?"

Nic told him then about Edith Moore and the truck and the taillight and the invoice Reyes had shown her. She told him about the house on Abel Hill Lane and how Reyes had known about the lock and the chains. And she told him about the fence that backed up to the inn and how there was a hole someone had tried to cut open. Finally, she told him about Edith Moore, or Bickman, and how she knew Kurt Kent and how he met with her the day after she came back to Hastings and told the story about the pickup truck.

When she was finished, Watkins stared at her for a long moment. Thinking. But then—

"You should go home," he said. "This is not for you to sort out anymore. No wonder you asked me those questions. Everyone you turned to for help has been lying to you, or hiding things . . ."

A wave of relief pushed out the adrenaline. She saw their faces; Reyes, Kurt Kent. Even her father who had lied to her about the handwriting analysis. Then she saw Roger Booth.

"He's the only one—Roger. The only one who hasn't lied to me."

Watkins drained what was left of his coffee in one giant swallow.

"Go home, Nicole. The hotel can send your things. I'll check up on that house. Find out who takes care of the property. See if utilities are running. I'll go there myself if I have to. And our friendly bartender—don't you worry. I'm gonna find out what he has cooking with that waitress."

"And Reyes?" Nic asked.

Watkins shook his head from side to side. "That's a tougher one. Can't see that he's done anything wrong here. Don't know about that invoice. Or Daisy. Let me think on it. He's been a good cop. Kind of took him under my wing, you know? I don't want to accuse him if he's done nothing wrong."

Nic thought about the messages on her phone and his car parked outside the casino. She hadn't told Watkins about any of that, and she didn't want to. What did it matter? She'd brought that on herself. It was humiliating.

Watkins said goodbye. He got in his truck and drove away.

Nic checked her phone. Her father had called three more times.

She couldn't sit here, do nothing. They all wanted her to leave, to go home. Then what? All she had were Watkins's promises.

No, she thought. No way.

She sent one last text before heading back to Hastings. Another lie to her father. I'll be home tonight.

45

Day seventeen

Coffee is bitter. On this morning it was bittersweet.

I hear him call out from the kitchen.

"Alice!"

She looks at me with a new face. I don't give it a name. It is a face of terror.

She knew what I was doing. She helped me do it. Now it is real.

"Alice!"

I nod at her. I motion for her to go to him and she obeys me.

Yes, that's right, I think. She obeys me.

He cries out now, in pain. In agony. And even as I try to feel joy that his cells are suffocating, the sound of human suffering is difficult to take. My heart pounds against the walls of my chest. My vision blurs for just a second as my body adjusts to the fear that his cries provoke.

She comes back to me now, feet pounding the floor, voice calling out.

"He's sick! He's lying on the floor! He's throwing up!"

I picture the vomit, his body trying to rid itself of the poison.

I try to calm her down. I lie. "He's going to be all right. It will be a few hours, but he will be fine. You can bring him some towels and some water. Turn him on his back."

The water will make more vomit. If he's on his back, maybe he'll choke on the vomit. Maybe that will be what kills him.

"But he didn't have the muffin! He didn't eat it!" she cries out, and I can see that part of her was relieved when he didn't eat it. She is ambivalent about my plan. She is ambivalent about him.

Which is why I didn't waste the seeds on the muffin. I couldn't trust Alice to give it to him.

"I know, sweetheart," I say. "But he drank his coffee, didn't he? All of it."

Her eyes get big now as she remembers how I had her bring me the coffee tin, and then the white filters, and then made her go back to the kitchen for a measuring spoon, the little yellow one that scoops out the coffee.

When she was gone, I put the apple seed mash beneath the filter, coating the plastic basin, then sprinkled some coffee into the filter and placed it on top. When she returned, we measured more coffee from the little yellow scoop.

She cries harder. Terror Face. I give it a name now because I am no longer reacting to it. To him, and his suffering.

"Alice," I tell her. "Do as I say now. It's very important. But then go and get that key."

She moves her head back and forth, no.

I reach through the bars and grab both of her arms.

"You will get the key and bring it to me. Do you know why?"

She shakes her head with Terror Face. No, no, no.

"Because," I tell her. "He knows you helped me make the coffee."

46

Day seventeen

Nic did not go home. She drove right into the heart of the storm, this new storm that was brewing in Hastings.

She got to the intersection of Route 7 and Hastings Pass, to the Gas n' Go. Kurt's car was in the parking lot. She drove across from it and parked. He'd been working the night shift here, then was probably heading to the bar to open for lunch. That was what he'd told her before, about his schedule.

Now was better. Here was better. Customers would be coming in and out. They wouldn't be alone for long.

Kurt was behind the counter, sitting on a stool, reading a magazine. He was surprised to see her, but he smiled warmly. Covering up his guilt.

Nic did not waste time with small talk. She took out her phone and pulled up the photo of him with Edith Moore.

"So what was your endgame with Edith *Bickman*?"

"Shit . . ." Kurt mumbled, hanging his head. "Not here—they have cameras."

Nic followed him to the back of the store, behind a row of shelves.

"This is the only spot they don't cover," he told her.

"Who is they?" Nic asked.

"The people who own this place. Some corporation. I don't know. I just know where the cameras are because they have monitors up front."

"So tell me now, away from the cameras."

Nic waited as he thought about what to say. She could see him struggling for words.

"Okay. Look—it's not what you think."

"What do I think?" Nic asked.

"I didn't know what she was doing, okay? When you came in here and told me about this witness and then told me her name—I mean, how many Ediths are there who could be connected to Hastings?"

"But she worked with you. At the bar."

Kurt nodded. "She did. I knew her. I knew where she'd gone. So I went to find her, to ask her what the hell was going on. I didn't want to get her in trouble. It's not like she's a criminal. And you were convinced she'd seen your mother. I wanted to find out why she was lying about her name and why she was here that night."

Nic was frustrated now, all of the threads tangled together, and her mind too exhausted to sort them out.

"Just tell me everything. Please. You can start with your arrest for gun possession if you want."

He looked back to the front of the store, then out the window to the gas pumps.

"I'm scared, okay? I didn't want to go up against Reyes. I can't go back to prison, and I can't leave this town. I have two jobs and about fifty bucks in the bank. I'm an ex-con. Are you starting to get it?"

"Why would you have to leave town?"

"You don't see it? You still don't see what he is?"

"Who?"

"Reyes. Officer Jared Reyes."

Now a rush to her head. A wave of nausea.

"He's the criminal, Nic. A con man." Kurt let this sink in for a moment, but not a long one. Not long enough.

"Three years ago, he pulled me over for supposedly running a light. It was bullshit. Next thing I know, I'm out of the car and he's holding a handgun, saying he saw it in plain sight in the back seat of my car. He didn't even pretend to look back there. He didn't even bother to go through the motions of the setup."

Nic stared at him now, her perception of Reyes taking a new turn.

Kurt continued. "Then he said it could all go away for ten grand—like I would have ten thousand dollars. He said I could borrow it from my family. He gave me until the end of the day. I thought, *fuck him*, you know? I was young. I believed in justice and the people in this town who'd known me my whole life. I believed in the chief and his bullshit about helping kids . . ."

"But you were convicted," Nic said, finishing the story for him.

Kurt nodded. "The chief backed Reyes. His pet project. His prodigy. The son he never had. Who the hell knows. Doesn't matter. Reyes is a con man, Nic."

"I'm sorry. I really am. But what does this have to do with Edith Bickman? Reyes was the one who made me suspect that she was lying. He found a hole in her story about being in New York."

Kurt looked up and crossed his arms, like he was preparing to tell her something she wasn't going to like.

"I went to see her to find out what the hell she was doing. She was a decent girl, but she had an infatuation with Reyes, and he knew she needed money. Always. Had a mountain of debt from college and now nursing school. She said he called her a few days after the search ended. Said he knew where your mother was hiding but that he couldn't collect the reward money because he was a cop, and it was his job to find her. He said it would be easy—she would call you with the story about the truck. He said you were the only one who would come back and try to find her—it had to be you. Then he would help you find your mother, your father would pay her the million bucks, and they would split it."

"So Reyes did give her my number," Nic said, remembering what Mrs. Urbansky had told her father, and how Reyes had put that lie in Edith's mouth the morning they'd met.

Nic couldn't help it, but this almost made her giddy. "Then she is hiding somewhere? Reyes knows? I don't care about him or the money—this means my mother is safe!"

But Kurt's face did not lighten. "Wait—there's more. Whatever Reyes said to her in front of you, the holes he pointed out in her story, they were all meant to keep you here, to keep you frantically looking for your mother."

Nic suddenly knew exactly what he was saying. "No, you're right—if he knew where she was, why take the chance that she would leave? Why not let me find her the first day?"

"I don't know. But he wanted you here. He wanted you to stay."

"And he wanted to set up Watkins," Nic said now, fitting two of the pieces together. "I think he broke Watkins's taillight. Forged an invoice for the replacement parts because Watkins didn't get it repaired in town like Reyes thought he would. Maybe he wants his job."

"I don't know, Nic. That's strange that he would betray the chief. And why you? Why did it have to be you?"

Nic drew a quick breath, her hands crossing at her chest. "I know why."

She thought about those photos from the summer camp year-book. Her resemblance to Daisy Hollander. Reyes being the one to drive her out of town. And his growing obsession with her after she let him into her life.

"Nic? What is it?" Kurt asked.

She turned suddenly. "I have to go," she said. Kurt followed her to the door.

"Wait," he said. "Where are you going?"

"I have to check something out."

He grabbed her arm. "I am sorry," he said. "I should have come right to you after I spoke to Edith."

Nic stopped, turned. "It's okay. But I have to go," she said again.

"Wait—there's one last thing," Kurt said. "Edith never saw your mother. But the thing she knew about your mother's purse—Reyes told her to say that. How did he know?"

Nic realized then what must have happened. The only explanation. "Reyes knew because he saw my mother that night."

She pulled away from Kurt Kent, and raced back to her mother's car, down Hastings Pass to the inn. And the fence. And the hole that someone had started to make.

47

Day seventeen

Alice does not get the key. Instead, she sits in the kitchen with Mick for hours, it seems. I hear him moan and choke. I hear her sob. I think I have miscalculated. I think that now I am surely going to die.

But then another sound. A car.

I race from where I stand by the grate and look out the small hole in the wood. I see another police car. Another police officer. This one wears short sleeves and patches. He walks to the front porch and I think, *call out! Call for help!* But then I wonder Mick is a cop. What if they're in this together?

I return to the grate when I hear the shuffling. Mick is on his feet, and he drags Alice toward me. He is pale, his shirt covered in sweat and vomit. But he has survived the poison. This will not end well.

He says nothing because the doorbell has rung and now the new cop is knocking. He calls out a name.

"Reyes? You in there?"

Mick has a name. *Reyes.*

He is worried. I can see it on his face. Worried and weakened by the cyanide.

The cop again—

"Reyes—come on. I see your car out here. . . ." A pause as he listens outside the door. And then—

"I spoke to the owners. I know you take care of this place. Listen—it doesn't matter, okay? You've been working on the side for them. Right? Moonlighting? Doing security here and at the gas station? I've seen the utility bills—buddy? Are you in there? You been living in there when you're not supposed to be? It's okay, we can work it out. We can work everything out."

When the cop falls silent again, Mick, Reyes, the man—he opens the grate with the key that he wears on his belt. He shoves Alice inside the room with me, and locks it shut.

I pull Alice close. We are one now, in our fate. And we move as one back to the grate where we can see what's about to happen.

48

Day seventeen

Nic ran through the lobby of the inn to the back door. Then across the patio to the shed where she took a rock to the padlock, beating it until it opened.

Inside the shed, she found a pair of wire cutters. Then she ran to the fence, straight back like before, though it was harder to navigate with the sun so high in the sky.

Nic was out of breath when she reached the place where the hole had been cut. Nerves, exhaustion—all of it was crashing down.

She'd forgotten about the barbed wire and she didn't have gloves. She took off one sneaker and put her hand inside it. She pushed the fence to see where it needed to be cut. The wire cutters were strong and they cut through it in seconds.

When she was on the other side, she put her sneaker back on, caught her breath.

She had just one thought now—Reyes knew where her mother was. He'd known the entire time. And he knew she was in a place that she couldn't leave. That was why he risked waiting to get the reward money. He knew he had the time.

And the reason he wanted the time? It was absurd, this thought, but his behavior, his obsession with her had to go back to Daisy Hollander. Nic and Daisy—that had to be why he waited. He wanted Nic to come back to Hastings. And come back alone.

Be smart now, she told herself. She took out her phone and pulled up the photo she'd taken of the satellite image. The one showing the house and the fence, and the inn. She took her best guess at the direction and she started to walk, through the woods, along a path that was most likely to get her to the house.

Be smart.

Reyes was a con man. He used his position as a cop to extort people. No chance it was just Kurt Kent who'd been on the receiving end.

Through the trees, over the wet brush of dead leaves and soil, the extent of his lies, his planning ran through her mind. Edith Bickman. The truck story. How he pretended not to know her, not to trust her, giving her a string of facts that he could then punch holes through—giving Nic a reason to stay. He knew she would find out about Watkins with his gray truck. And when he couldn't figure out where Watkins had gone to get the broken light repaired, he created a fake invoice. Framing Watkins—but why? When he finally led Nic to her mother, she would tell them the truth—that Watkins wasn't involved. And that would prove Edith Bickman was a liar, keep her from getting the money—and Reyes his share. Did he do all of this in the hope that Nic would fall for him? That he could have her as a replacement for Daisy Hollander?

The house wasn't as far as she thought. Maybe an eighth of a mile from the fence to a clearing where she could see it, and the scene at the front door.

Watkins knocking. His car was parked in the driveway.

She stopped dead in her tracks as she heard him call out—to Reyes.

Reyes was the caretaker of this place. Reyes managed the security cameras at the Gas n' Go. Reyes was using the gas and electric, living here.

The boarded window with the metal bars holding it in place.

Her mother would know the truth and would tell them Watkins wasn't involved. Edith never saw her. Maybe there wasn't even a black truck.

Unless—*no*—the reward money.

It was one million if they found her alive. But five hundred thousand if they just *found her.*

That was it. She was already dead. Or about to be.

And now Watkins—not knowing what might be behind that door.

She started to run, calling out to him—"Chief!"

The door opened just as his name left her mouth. There were no more words. Just one shot. And Watkins, hand to his chest, stumbling backward until he reached the steps. Falling, crumbling down to the gravel, where he lay still.

Day seventeen

A lice and I watch as Mick stands on the other side of the door. We watch as he draws his gun and steadies himself. He is still weak.

I turn Alice to face me, pull her from the grate. Fear blankets my face. I know what is about to happen.

And I think—I have done it. I have killed another child. The hatred I thought I felt for her was not real. It was anger and frustration. But she is a child. She is a victim of this house and whatever has happened here these past nine years.

"Alice," I say. "This was my fault and I will tell him that. I will save you," I promise. I lie. He will surely kill us both.

Her face doesn't change as I say these words. It is another new face. It is determined.

Alice holds my eyes as she reaches in her pocket. And slowly, very slowly—she pulls out the key. I fold my hand around hers and I gently take the key and turn the lock.

As we push the grate open and walk out into the hallway, to our freedom, we hear the shot.

Day seventeen

Reyes saw Nic, heard her call out to Watkins.

Now he called after her as she ran away, back into the woods, back toward the inn.

She ran the way she'd come, watching the ground, her feet taking small, quick steps on patches that were steady. She weaved through the trees, dodging the branches.

Then another shot and a pop against a trunk not five feet from her.

He called out again.

"Stop!"

And then—

"I have your mother!"

I have your mother.

Her feet kept moving. But not her will.

I have your mother.

Nic could smell the wood burning from the fireplace at the inn. She was almost there. But then what?

Reyes wanted her.

She wanted her mother.

She wanted her mother to be alive. She wanted her to be freed, finally, of the pain she'd suffered. She wanted Annie back. She wanted to feel her hands grabbing hold of those little arms before she reached the end of the driveway. She wanted the past five years to be over.

Her feet stopped moving then. She was too tired. It was time to stop running.

51

Day seventeen

pull Alice back into the room where she can't see. I go to the window and look out the hole. I see the other cop on the ground. Lying still. Blood pooling around his torso. And Mick running into the woods. Running with his gun drawn, calling out to someone. Was there another cop? A partner?

"Come with me!" I say to Alice. I grab her arm and pull her out of the room and down the hall and through the open front door. She stops at the threshold.

"My mask!" she says. "I need my mask!"

I take hold of her arms and look her in the eye.

"Do you trust me?" I ask her.

She doesn't know. I can see the doubt and the debilitating apprehension it brings.

"You don't need the mask."

I do not give her time to think. I pick her up in my arms and bury her face in my chest as I run down the stairs and over the body of the man. I set her down, facing away from the house. Away from the violence.

"You need to run now, Alice. You need to run down that driveway until you reach the road. The gate must be open because that policeman came through it. You need to turn to the right and follow the fence on the other side—do you understand? Stay in the woods. Do not go onto the street. The fence will lead to another house. You need to look for it carefully. If you smell a fire, or food or gasoline—go toward it. Okay?"

Alice cries. "What about the bears? What about the wolves?"

I shake my head. "No—the bears are sleeping during the day. You will be fine."

She won't leave and my heart is going to burst. I must get to the dying man. I must use his radio to call for help. But Alice must leave. Mick could come back at any moment.

"My first mommy died in the woods," she says now. "I don't want to die!"

I pull her close to me again and squeeze her so hard as if I can squeeze the doubt right out of her.

"Alice—that was a lie. Your first mommy didn't die in the woods. I don't know what happened to her. But it wasn't the woods that took her from you."

I look at her now and I can see that she believes me. She believes me because it is the truth.

"Now go! Run!"

She nods, turns, and her feet begin to move, to fly, kicking up dust from the driveway.

I can't remember feeling as happy as I do right now, watching this child go free.

I turn back to the man on the ground. I feel for a pulse. He is still alive. I go to his car and find the radio. I push a button.

"Help! I need help! There's an officer shot!"

A woman's voice answers. "Who is this?"

"It's Molly Clarke."

Silence now as the woman recognizes my name.

"This is the chief's radio. Has the chief been shot?"

"Yes!" I say, frantic now for help. "I don't know where we are. I've been held here for two weeks!"

"I have your location," the woman says. I hear her voice tremble.

"I see keys in the car. I might be able to get him inside . . ."

"No—stay where you are. He could bleed out. Seconds matter now—are you able to provide assistance to the officer?"

No! I think. I see keys in this car. I need to leave this place! I look back at the man, bleeding on the ground. All I want to do is run like Alice, away from this house. But I can't let him die.

She tells me what to do and I do what she says. I leave the radio and the keys and look for a first-aid box in the trunk. I leave the car, my means of escape, and I go to the dying man. I do what I can to stop the bleeding.

It's now that I hear the shot in the woods.

And the scream. The unmistakable scream of my daughter.

52

Day seventeen

Reyes walked closer. Close enough not to miss again if he pulled the trigger. Still his face was soft with a warm smile.

"Mom!" Nic screamed, her voice filled with rage, rising up through the trees. Then to Reyes, "Where is my mother!"

Reyes spoke calmly as he took a few more steps.

"Right inside that house. She's been waiting for you all this time. Waiting for you to find her. She's perfectly safe."

Nic knew that was a lie. Her mother would never have willingly stayed with this man.

"I know about Edith Moore."

"I just wanted to see you again," he said.

"What happened that night? The night of the storm?" Nic didn't want to hear about anything else. She wanted to know what happened to her mother.

Reyes kept walking, the rustling beneath his feet breaking the silence.

"I love you. That's all that matters. From the first time I saw you. That very first day. All of this has been about you, can't you see that? It could have been so easy!"

He stopped then, but the sound of footsteps remained. Only it wasn't coming from his feet. It was coming from behind them, from the fence.

Nic saw Reyes's eyes move from her to the source of this new sound. And then a new voice.

"Yes, Officer. Why don't you tell us what happened that night."

It was Roger Booth. And he held a shotgun that was pointed squarely at Reyes.

"Roger—that's not the right question," Reyes said. His words were confident, but his voice shaky. He was panting. Sweating in the cold air.

"What is the right question, then?" Booth asked, moving closer.

"You know, don't you, Nicole?" Reyes's eyes remained fixed on Booth.

Nic took one step to the side. Then another, slowly moving out of the line of fire.

"I do," she said.

"Well, tell him, then," Reyes demanded. "Tell him!"

One more foot. Then another.

"The right question," Nic said, "is what happened the day Daisy Hollander disappeared."

Booth flinched, but then caught himself. "What does any of this have to do with Daisy?"

Nic was three steps away from a tree. From cover. She took one of them and stopped.

"He drove Daisy out of town that day," Nic said. "He knew her from summer camp. He worked there, in the kitchen. That's why he came to Hastings. He was obsessed with her. And then with me because I remind him of her."

Reyes blinked hard as though his vision was starting to blur.

Nic kept talking, buying time.

"He went there after that shooting in his hometown. The suicide-by-cop that messed with his head. He worked odd jobs like the one at the camp until he met Daisy. And then he played on Chief Watkins's sympathy to get a job here, so he could be close to her."

Another step. She could touch the tree.

Now Booth was panting as well. "What are you saying? Daisy barely knew him. She used to make fun of him, how he thought he was such a ladies' man."

Now Reyes—

"That's what you thought. But I was the one she loved. Not you. She was using you for money. All those free dinners and trips to the city. You made her skin crawl, Booth. She couldn't stand the sight of you, or your hands on her body. She was strong and she did what she had to do. But she was not about to give you a baby. So she left you. She left you for me."

Booth's face was twisted with anger. "You're a liar!" he screamed.

"And you're pathetic," Reyes yelled back.

Nic took one more step. She was almost behind the tree.

But then more footsteps. And a new voice still.

The voice of a woman.

"You're both pathetic," the woman said.

Nic froze, her eyes now glued to the image that was so like her own.

Only now that image was flesh and bone. And she was wearing the same leather jacket Nic had seen at Veronica's house.

Daisy Hollander walked toward them through the woods.

Holding the hand of a little girl.

53

Day seventeen

run like I'm on fire.

I run through the woods to find my daughter.

Now I hide behind a cluster of small trees. I do not know what I am seeing, but it has led me into a deep pool of confusion.

A well-groomed man, neatly dressed, holding a shotgun on Mick.

Mick, staggering from the poison, trying to steady a gun on the man.

And Nicole! How the sight of her makes me want to cry, makes me want to run to her and throw my body between hers and those men.

I force myself to stop. To think. I can't afford another mistake.

I watch her move until she is almost safe, just beside a tree.

Go! I want to scream. Why doesn't she take that last step?

And now I hear the voice I have come to know so well. To hate at times. To love at times. To fear at times.

"Mommy!" she says. Alice tries to pull her hand away from the woman who holds her. The woman who was her first mommy until she left last spring. Whose clothes I wear even now.

Daisy Alice Hollander.

"What?" she scolds Alice. "They are pathetic. Both of them."

"Daisy? Is that you?" The man with the shotgun looks as though he's seen a ghost.

But Daisy doesn't answer him. She walks to Mick, dragging Alice with her. He, too, is mesmerized by the sight of her, and suddenly another piece falls into place.

"What the hell have you done?" Daisy asks. "We need to clean this up. I never should have left. I can see that now. I've been watching for two weeks, hoping you'd stop this nonsense. Seriously—how did you think this was going to end?"

She was never a captive in this house. And she's been watching us. All of us, through those cameras. Through Dolly's eyes.

Daisy strokes his face, runs her hand down his arm to his fingers which release the gun without the slightest resistance. He is in a trance. And he is weak and sick from the poison.

She steps away, five or six yards. Alice is dragged along with her like a pet on a leash.

She points the gun at the man with the shotgun, who trembles. Her face is stone cold. It shocks me more than anything else in these woods.

She sees Nicole, she sees her, but now really sees her. And she laughs, loud and hard. She laughs at Mick.

"I get it now. You thought this girl was going to replace me? That she would want to live with you? My God, it is beyond pathetic."

Mick stumbles, drops to his knees. I can't tell if it's the poison or his grief. But he lets his head fall into his hands and he begins to weep.

"You didn't come back this time," he cries.

Alice tries to pull away. She wants to go to him. She loves him. I can see that now. Even though she helped try to kill him to set me free.

Daisy sighs like she's annoyed. "I told you if you kept getting into my bed I would leave for good. And that's what I did."

"I kept waiting. We kept waiting . . ."

Alice cries. I see that she is confused, and confusion is her worst enemy. Mick told her Daisy died in the woods. Now she knows that Daisy is alive, that she left on her own, and that Mick knew the whole time.

I think about what Alice told me—how the beginning of the end was when Mick got into bed with them. Now I understand. Daisy had simply had enough.

She continues her rant as though she and Mick are the only ones in these woods. "But then you gave up, didn't you? You found that old woman, and then her daughter. Why didn't you just go fuck a waitress at the diner? Why did it have to be like this?"

Mick has a second wind, rises to his feet. "You know why— because of her!" He points to Alice. "How was I going to explain that? I had no way out. You left me with no choice."

Daisy takes a step closer. "Did you even consider moving away? Making up a story about the girl? You could have gone anywhere. Started over. It just pisses me off! I used to think you were so smart. That we were going to build a little fortune and get the hell out of here together. But you had no imagination. Just your little cons and scams. I told you I wanted more. You promised to give it to me if I stayed with you and had the kid. But no—that was all just a con you pulled on me, making me need you. Making me have to stay!"

She pauses, looks to the sky, and back at Mick. She is cold

with rage. I think about the photo in that book, and the way Alice loves her. She wanted something that Mick had promised her— something she believed in once. Something that made her stay and give things to this little girl.

"It's all so clear now. How weak you are." She speaks with an eerie calm. "I should have gone to the train station with the chief. Gone to Boston and gotten rid of it. I could have been anything. I could have gone to college. But I believed you—and you promised me. You said we would make it out. That's all I ever wanted. To get the hell out of Hastings! But you're a coward and a liar."

The woods are dead quiet. The man with the shotgun, and my daughter—they are statues listening to this story. And Alice, how she weeps and buries her face into the side of her mother.

Daisy gets ahold of herself. Her face changes the way Alice's does. In an instant.

Now come seconds that blur. Seconds that leave me stunned.

First, the words.

"Well, it's done—so now we have to clean this up."

And the shot. One shot, fired at Mick. Hitting him dead-on.

Day seventeen

aisy!" Booth yelled out to her. Nic felt her head spin. She reached for the tree.

Reyes was on the ground. His eyes were open. His body still. He was dead.

The little girl was screaming now. "No!"

Daisy slapped her clear across the face.

"Stop it! Do you hear me? Mommy has to take care of things now."

She turned the gun on Booth. He held the shotgun on her, though his arms were trembling.

"Put it down," she said to him.

But even as his whole body began to shake, he did not let go of the shotgun.

"Roger—think about it. Do you know what's been going on? We've been here this whole time. For ten years. Right under your nose. Living in that house through the woods. Running the cons—on the roads, at the casino, it's been so easy—and raising this girl. *Your* girl. Don't tell me you're not happy he's dead."

Booth was breathing hard, but said nothing.

"You wanted him dead when he said those things to you, right? Just now, when he told you how I never loved you? How I would never have your baby? He wasn't lying. I was going to get rid of it. I kept it for him. I kept it because I thought he was a big man. I gave him your baby."

Daisy laughed.

"You wanted to pull that trigger just now, but you couldn't. That's why I could never love you."

Nic moved farther behind the tree. The little girl pulled hard against her mother's hold, even as her face began to swell.

Then, suddenly, Booth cocked the gun and held it higher. Aimed right at Daisy's head.

"Why did he do all of this—kidnap Molly Clarke, then lure her daughter here?" Booth asked.

"Well, I'd tell you to ask him yourself but that ship just sailed." Then, "It's like I said—because I left him for good. I've left him before, plenty of times, when I needed a break from him, from this." She looked quickly at her daughter. "But this time I didn't come back. I couldn't stand the sight of him anymore. He made my skin crawl. Every night, breaking into my room, getting into my bed. I even tried sleeping with Alice, right? Alice—you remember that, don't you? How he came into bed with us?"

The little girl nodded, her entire face now red, trembling.

"That was the last straw. It was like living with a puppy dog who follows you everywhere you go. It had been ten years. I did my part, and still—no fortune. No better life, still in this place where my father beat me and my mother starved me! I wasn't going to stay for one more second."

Booth took a step closer.

"So why did you come back now?"

Daisy took a step closer as well, Reyes's gun pointed at Booth.

"Because he got himself into all this." She waved the gun quickly at Nic, then back again, aimed at Booth. "We have cameras in the house to keep an eye on the girl. I still see everything going on—do you know what's been happening? That woman got into your daughter's head. I've been watching it for days. They tried to kill him today. And then what? I've started a nice life, now that I'm free of him and everyone thinks I'm somewhere else. I don't need this—I don't need people looking for me again."

Nic listened carefully to every word, thinking through what they meant. Her mother tried to kill Reyes—today! She was alive.

"So what now, Daisy?" Booth asked. He seemed to be calming, the clarity settling his nerves. He wanted to keep her talking. She had his daughter. And she held a gun.

Daisy studied the situation. Reyes, dead on the ground. Nic behind the tree. Booth with his gun aimed at her head.

"Well, let's see. How does this sound to you? Reyes held me captive for ten years until I could escape. Then he kidnapped Molly Clarke. Then he lured her daughter here so he could kidnap her as well. Chief Watkins came to investigate and he shot him dead. They poisoned him with apple seeds just as I came back to save my daughter, and I chased him through the woods, got his gun away and shot him. Unfortunately, not before he killed the other captives."

Booth looked scared but determined. Nic realized it was now all about the little girl. Booth's little girl. He had something to fight for.

He called to Nic. "Run!"

Nic hesitated, but then bolted into the woods. Daisy took a shot, but there were too many trees to get off a clean one.

Nic heard Daisy scream as she ran through the trees.

"I will kill you!"

55

Day seventeen

will kill you!" Daisy screams. The man with the shotgun is not more than five yards away now.

I watch my child escape. I watch her until she disappears and I want to laugh out loud with relief and joy.

I hear the sirens. They've found us.

Daisy's face changes. "Okay, see—now I have to leave. Do this shit all over again. Do you know how hard it is to disappear?"

The man shakes his head. "Like hell you are. Don't move," he says.

Daisy looks surprised.

But there's little time now.

She pulls Alice in front of her. A human shield. Her own daughter.

She turns the gun to point at her daughter's head. She presses it hard into the soft flesh of her temple.

Alice whimpers. "Mommy?"

The man is in awe as he watches the mother of this child, his child, move toward him.

"Drop the gun and take us through the woods the way you came. Back to the inn. Then give us a car. Or I swear to you, I will put a bullet in her head."

The man is wide-eyed as he lets these words reach into his soul, the way they do mine. They do not have anyplace else to go.

His hands tremble but he holds the gun steady. I watch Daisy's finger pull back the safety lever. I hear the click. She knows—I can feel it—she knows he won't fire that shotgun. He will stand there in a perpetual state of human conflict, wanting her dead, but afraid of hitting his daughter. Afraid she will pull the trigger first. He will do exactly what she tells him now. And then she will be free.

I am there again, five years ago, turning the corner on my street. The corner just before our driveway. I am worried that something is wrong. I can feel the anger that will come when I find out nothing is—that it was just Nicole being a teenager. Both hands on the wheel, both eyes on the road. Thoughts on what I might find inside my house.

I feel my feet move. I feel a heavy rock in my hands. I feel eyes turn.

But I am there five years ago. Turning the corner, seeing the flash of something. What is it? What could have suddenly come into the road, into the path of my car?

I hear a crack. And a scream. My hands ache.

I am back there. My foot on the brakes, my hands turning the wheel. Hard enough. All of it is hard enough. I turn to see Annie safe on the other side.

I feel arms grabbing my legs. Little arms squeezing tight.

I look down and see Alice crying with relief. *Not Annie. Alice.*

I look down and see Daisy unconscious at my feet. The rock still in my hands.

The man runs toward us now.

We hear the sirens stop and voices call from the driveway.

"Here!" the man yells back. "We're down here!"

Alice cries harder. I let the rock fall and I lean down to pick her up in my arms. She wraps her entire being around my body and I hold her tight.

"It's all right," I say.

Nicole comes now, out from the woods. She sees me and I see her. And I am floating in an ocean of love.

Just devastating, blissful love.

"It's all right," I say again.

And I think to myself, that maybe it is.

56

Seven months later

t was not easy to make the turn down Hastings Pass.

Nic had insisted on driving. She knew the way, she said. But that wasn't the reason. That turn, this road, everything about this town had become a monster under her bed. The flashes came in nightmares. They came in daydreams as she ran, stopping her in her tracks. Stealing her breath. A flash of the inn, or the fence, or the woods.

She needed to face it. To look under the bed and see that there was nothing there. That it was just a town, and the people who had terrorized them were now dead or in prison.

Her mother held on to her shoulder as they drove past the Gas n' Go.

"Are you okay?" she asked, though her eyes were on the gas station—the place where all of this started.

Jared Reyes had followed Daisy Hollander to Hastings after that summer in Woodstock. He'd been working in the kitchen—one of a string of odd jobs he'd taken after leaving the force in Worcester.

Then he'd found work in Hastings providing security for the company that owned the property behind the inn—the investors who had wanted to build a mental-health facility but were shut down by town protests. They owned the Gas n' Go as well. Reyes monitored the security cameras at the station and looked after the property and buildings that had once been part of Ross Pharma. He used these positions to find his marks and run his cons, even after Watkins took him under his wing.

Nic smiled, nodded. "I'm okay," she said to her mother. Though she had a knot in her stomach as they drove over the wave of hills, past the neglected cornfields on both sides. But it was different this time. The air was warm. The sun was shining. Green leaves covered the trees as they entered the town.

Mrs. Urbansky met them at the door of the station. She pulled Nic into her arms, then did the same with her mother.

"Oh!" she said. "What a sight for sore eyes!"

Chief Watkins appeared from the back office. He looked at them, her mother mostly, with gratitude. Molly Clarke had saved his life that day.

"Don't they look wonderful!" Mrs. Urbansky commented.

Nic managed a new smile. She hadn't thought about how they looked. Not one way or another. Her mother had let her hair go back to its natural chestnut brown. She'd cut it short as well, and changed her wardrobe. She wore skirts and loose tops and pretty much whatever she felt comfortable in. It was the way she'd dressed before Annie died. It was as though she was reclaiming herself, one small piece at a time.

And Nic, she thought she looked just the same. She was still running. Hadn't changed her hair or her clothing. Those things hadn't felt important to her. Her father had told her that her face had light. He stopped from saying the word that should have followed—*again, your face has light again.* But Nic knew what he meant.

Watkins led them to his office where they sat down across from his desk. Nic had a new flash now—back to that first day she'd returned to Hastings. His uniform with the short sleeves. The patches on his chest. The blue tie.

But today was not about finding her mother. Today was about resolution.

"You were very kind to come," he said.

This was not their only stop. Her mother had a second meeting less than hour from now.

"It's good," her mother said. "Necessary, I think."

Watkins tilted his head as though he wasn't quite sure of any of that. But now that they were here, he seemed willing to do what he could to fill them in on the progress with the case.

"Have you read her statement?" Watkins asked.

Daisy Hollander had pleaded guilty to manslaughter for the murder of Jared Reyes. But that was all. She had a hearing later that month and had submitted a statement to the court as part of her campaign for a lighter sentence.

"Does anyone believe her lies?" Nic asked. "What she said about it being self-defense?"

Daisy's story had been carefully crafted. Reyes had followed her to Hastings after that summer camp. He'd been obsessed with her, even though she didn't even remember him.

That's what she said in her statement—though other girls from the camp, women now, had started to come forward with statements of their own, statements about Daisy and Reyes being together the entire summer. About Daisy sneaking out of their cabin at night to meet him.

Daisy denied all of this.

According to her, Reyes followed her to Hastings and stalked her. She said she told no one because she was scared. She swore she was in love with Roger Booth and that she planned to stay with him and marry him, but Reyes wouldn't have it. He kidnapped her and kept her a prisoner in that house for ten years. She was finally able to escape and had been in hiding, terrified because Reyes was a cop. She came back that day to try to save Alice.

She killed Reyes in a moment of terror—rage and terror that was produced from years of abuse and captivity. They were comparing it to battered spouse syndrome. It may not have been self-defense in that moment, but justified by the culmination of years as a captive.

Watkins thought carefully before giving an answer to the question. Did anyone believe her story?

"It's complicated," he said. "Of all the people who have been coming forward now, saying what Reyes did to them with his cons—not one of them identified Daisy. She was very careful to stay behind the scenes. They found his beat-up truck behind the house—no prints belonging to Daisy. And the things all of you saw in the woods that day—the things you heard her confess about being Reyes's partner in crime, not his prisoner—she has experts willing to testify that she was saying those things to take back control, or manipulate him. Years of captivity had messed with her mind."

Nic knew all about the experts and their case studies—women who had been abused and battered and held captive who didn't do or say the things that would be expected under the circumstances. Daisy had suffered abuse in her home as a child. And then Reyes had imprisoned her. They had come close to pleading diminished capacity—insanity—as a result.

Still, it was more than just the words Daisy had spoken in those woods.

"What about the note?" Nic asked now. "To Booth—and the texts to her sister?"

"She claims Reyes made her write them. Look—it fits. He forged that note he left at the casino, in the room he charged to your mother's credit card. He proved himself to be pretty adept at planning a kidnapping and covering his tracks."

Nic was far from satisfied. It was just now that she was feeling the extent of her anger at how things had unfolded in the aftermath of finding her mother.

She started rattling off the loose ends.

"And what about her sister—Veronica? Forensics found Daisy's prints and hair all over the house . . . and I saw that jacket at her house the very same day."

Watkins had more excuses.

"But they don't know how old they are, and Daisy explained the jacket—said she stopped to see her sister for the first time that morning . . . on her way to rescue her daughter."

Nic continued.

"But the witnesses who saw her over the years—free as a bird! In three different states! She was coming and going as she pleased this whole time! And she had the app for those cameras on her phone. Why would Reyes give her access unless she was his full accomplice? There are so many pieces that paint a different picture!"

Then, a new voice—

"Nicole," her mother said. The voice was calm, resolved. "You're forgetting about Alice."

Nic hung her head. *Alice.*

The reason Reyes had targeted her mother—the girl who needed a mother.

Alice had been granted visits with Daisy Hollander. The social workers thought it would be good for her, to help put what had happened in those woods into some sort of context. After those visits, Alice had told the prosecutor a string of facts that backed up everything Daisy Hollander said. They were all lies. She spoke about the grate with the bars and the back room and the boarded-up window—all the things that had happened to Molly Clarke, Alice said had happened to her real mother—to Daisy Hollander.

"I still don't understand why they believe her," Nic said.

Watkins answered. "Again—this comes down to the discretion of the prosecutor. How can anyone ever prove that he didn't do the same things to Daisy that he did to your mother?"

The truth was, they couldn't. Those witnesses who saw her in different towns may have been mistaken about the woman they saw. The girls from the camp may have been jealous, or remembering things wrong. And Veronica would never turn on her sister. Daisy had likely been supporting her for years with money from the cons.

All Nic had was what she'd seen and heard in those woods. Not just the words, but the way Daisy had said them. And her laughter. Daisy Hollander had been willing to kill her own daughter that day. There was no chance she had been Reyes's victim.

"Well—that's where we are," Watkins said. "She will get time. She will pay for the murder. Maybe not what she deserves, but not nothing."

Then a pause, a sigh. And—

"There is something else, and I was waiting until today so I could tell you in person."

"What?" Nic asked. "What else could there be?"

Watkins slid a folder in front of them. Nic opened it. There were three photos—one was from a security camera at the casino. The second was of a hole, dug in the ground, on some kind of construction site. The third, a copy of a partial, handwritten note.

Watkins explained. "Daisy's lawyers hired an investigator. They went back through the footage at the casino and found that—the picture of that man at the registration counter. See the man with the baseball cap? The flannel shirt? That's Reyes. Those items of clothing were found in the house."

"So they can prove it was Reyes who charged the room to my mother's card?" Nic asked.

"And not Daisy—that's the point. Reyes acting alone."

"And this second photo—the hole in the ground?" her mother asked.

Now a long pause as Watkins steadied himself. "Some workers found it and contacted the state troopers. It's a hole near an abandoned building on Laguna Road. A hole big enough for a body. Daisy's lawyers claim that Reyes dug it so he could kill her and bury her body. They found a shovel at Reyes's house. The soil matched."

No, Nic thought. That's not what it was for, and the three of them in that room knew it. Daisy had been long gone. Reyes had dug that hole to bury her mother after he got his hands on Nic.

She heard her mother draw a long breath, but it stopped short and left her chest. She had just seen her own grave.

"And this one," Watkins said, "this note was in the house. In the basement where they found his research—papers and recordings and pictures. It looks like he was starting to forge a note—does this mean anything to you?"

Nic looked at the first two lines. "That's my handwriting," she said. She read the words out loud. "'I'm so sorry, Daddy and Evan. I just can't live knowing what I've done to Annie and now Mom. I have thought about the bridge for a long time.'"

"Nic?" her mother stared at her now. "Did you write that?"

"No, but I said those things to him. I told him how I felt guilty about the day Annie died, and about the things I said to you that morning."

"What about this bridge?" Watkins asked.

Nic hesitated. She didn't want to say these things in front of her mother. She said them anyway. "I told him how I sometimes thought about jumping from the bridge downtown—he asked me if I had ever told anyone else, and I told him that I had. That I'd told the counselor."

Watkins nodded, leaned forward. "He was planning to stage your suicide. Plant this note somewhere. Maybe leave your purse on the bridge."

"And no one would wonder why my body wasn't found because of the currents."

"He was going to keep you there. In that house."

Her mother took her hand and held it tight.

"I think we know enough. I think that's enough. Thank you, Charles," her mother said. She was smiling politely, even as a shiver ran through her body.

Nic shoved the pictures back into the folder and slid it toward Watkins.

"Is that everything?" Nic asked him.

Watkins nodded. "For now." He took a breath, let it out. Placed his palms on the desk.

"Do you still want to go, Molly? To see her?"

They drove the short distance to the Hastings Inn.

Nic parked. Turned off the ignition. Chief Watkins's truck was right behind them.

"Are you coming in with me?" her mother asked.

"I can't, Mom. I can't look at that girl."

Her mother nodded.

"I don't get it," Nic said. She couldn't hold back. "Why don't you hate her? After what she did to you in that house, and how she's lying now to help her mother?"

There was a long pause, and then, suddenly, a relenting that washed over her mother's entire body. Her eyes were looking out at the diner, and the little girl whose face was now pressed up against the large glass window.

"She's just a child, Nicole."

Nic leaned over and rested her head on her mother's shoulder.

"You don't know, do you?" Nic asked her.

Her mother kissed Nic's forehead. "What don't I know?"

"What a great mother you are."

Seven months later

kiss my daughter on the forehead. I smile and watch her leave me. She walks across the street to a bar—not for a drink, but to meet a man. A nice man for a change. And I don't just hope there will be more nice men. I know there will be.

I leave the car and walk into the diner. Chief Watkins walks right behind me.

I have never been here before. My only memory is driving past it that night. The night of the storm.

Inside, they are waiting for us. Roger Booth. The social worker who's been looking in on the family.

And Alice.

Oh, how I have dreamed of this day. How I have dreaded this day. I have had nightmares about Alice, her hands petting my skin. Her fake tears. Her faces. And I have longed for her. For the child in her.

She has no ambivalence toward me. I see that now, as she jumps down from the bench of the booth and runs into my arms. I hold her tight. I kiss her forehead, the way I kissed Nicole moments before.

I don't know what I feel. I don't think I will know for a long time.

I walk to the booth. Everyone stands to greet me warmly. Roger is grateful because I found his daughter and saved her life. Chief Watkins is grateful because I didn't leave him to die like a dog in the street. I could have taken his car and driven us away from there. But I stayed, and now they say that he lived because I stopped the bleeding.

I stopped the bleeding. That is something, I suppose.

Somehow I do not feel worthy of their gratitude.

We sit down, tears in all of our eyes, as we talk of the resolutions that have occurred. Alice has started school with other children and she is doing nicely. She is ahead in every level and that is something that those twisted people gave her.

Still, I wonder what remains.

"How have you been?" I ask.

Alice has Happy Face. "Great!" she says. "I love my new school and my new friends. And it turns out I don't have any allergies, except to cats, but I can have dogs. And I can go outside anytime I want."

I smile. "That's wonderful news."

We are all so happy for this little girl who is doing so well.

This little girl who made me drink milk but then set me free.

This little girl who watched her mother shoot the man who raised her, then felt her press that same gun into her head.

This little girl who has now lied for her.

That little girl.

We eat French fries and drink soda. The social worker leads us in a productive discussion about life and moving forward. She told me when I agreed to come that it was important for Alice to see that I was all right. That I was living a normal life now. That I needed to be a role model since we shared a similar experience in that house, even if I was only there for two weeks.

"I started working again," I say. This is true. I have started tutoring students in science and I hope I can eventually go back to teaching.

"And my son is almost done with his junior year. I can't believe how fast time flies!"

It has killed us to keep him at that school. It is that school that links us to this town. It was Evan's choice to stay.

But when we go, we take the long way. And each time I see him, I remind him that nothing he could ever do would make me leave him. Not ever. Because he is enough. He is more than enough. He is everything. He and Nicole.

I will never speak of that moment in the storm, when my legs carried me away from them. When I walked away.

I am here now. We are here now.

We. That is a word I have been using more lately. John and I drive together when we bring Evan to school. He's been taking days off from work to come with me. He doesn't want to lose me again. How strange that it took this horrific experience for him to know this, and for me to believe it.

I feel it more every day since I was saved—my love for John tiptoeing across that invisible line. It has not been a watershed. But it is no longer impossible. I feel it. He feels it.

He doesn't close his eyes until I am lying next to him in our bed. And, sometimes, I will curl up close beside him.

And Nicole—the changes in her have been more pronounced. She will start college next fall. She has been coming with me to my grief support sessions. Yes, she mocks everyone the second we leave, the things they say and even the way they say them, always in a neutral tone. She calls them emotional robots. She says it makes her want to scream out into the room that they are all *full of shit*. Maybe she's right. But she still comes. And sometimes we have dinner after.

Sometimes we talk about the woods in Hastings. Sometimes we talk about what she should study next year, or what classes I might teach. Sometimes we even laugh, though tears often follow.

I don't mind her tears. I don't mind my own.

Do I owe this to Jared Reyes? To the horrible things he did to our family? He took me, yes. But he took me to care for a child who was not even his own. He took me to care for her when her own mother left without a second thought. A mother who put a gun to her head. I see them sometimes before I can catch them— images of Reyes and Alice. The way he carried her through the rain. The way he made her laugh. The way she looked at him like any child looks at a parent who loves her.

And then I feel his body pinning me to the kitchen floor. His strong hands dragging me to the dark room. His hot breath in my face when he tells me about Nicole. He was going to kill me and take her.

And now, here is my family, healing. And here is Alice, surviving.

There are so many shades of gray that sometimes I feel life is one long, beautiful, cloudy day.

The conversation lingers and now begins to die. The social worker turns to Alice and says, "Do you want to give her the present now?"

Alice nods. Coy Face is here and it sends a shiver down my spine.

Shades of gray.

She is just a child.

She reaches down into her lap and sets on the table two plastic dolls.

I feel my stomach turn. I feel a violent urge to vomit.

She takes the doll that she calls Suzannah, and she hands it to me.

"I want you to have this so you will never forget me."

Now come her tears. Real tears. And I feel my own start to well.

I force my hand across the table and take the doll. I swear to God it burns my skin, but I take it anyway.

I take it and I straighten its hair.

Acknowledgments

If anyone could find a way to escape from a caged room to save her child, it would be my mother, Terrilynne Kempf Boling. The lessons she taught us about never, *ever*, accepting defeat were in my head in each of Molly Clarke's chapters, and behind every courageous thing I have ever done. I am grateful for the tenacity of mind and spirit she often employed to get us out of scrapes when we were growing up, and which now reside within us all. Thanks, Mom.

There are never enough words to express my deep appreciation for my agent, Wendy Sherman. Thank you for the unwavering, never-ending, 24/7 and 365 dedication to fostering my career and providing both sound counsel and brilliant guidance. And to Michelle Weiner and Olivia Blaustein at CAA and Jenny Meyer, thank you for always finding new homes for my work.

To the team at St. Martin's Press, thank you for championing this book from the very start. Specifically, to my editor, Jennifer Enderlin, for encouraging me to lean in to the emotional and psychological aspects of this story while safeguarding the twists and turns. To Lisa Senz, Katie Bassel, Brant Janeway, Erica Martirano, Jordan Hanley, Naureen Nashid, and Sallie Lotz for your creative and tireless efforts in sales, public relations, and marketing. And to Olga Grlic, for nailing the cover!

To my sister, Jennifer Walker, and the team at Walker Drawas—thank you for jump-starting my online presence with sheer cunning and impeccable style.

To Kathleen Carter, thank you for taking me on with this book and working your magic to spread the word.

As always, I relied on experts for advice with the more technical aspects of the book, from apple-seed poisoning to grief psychology. Thank you to Detective Christy F. Girard and Dr. Felicia Rozek.

Thanks also to Callie Dietrick for her great notes, Pamela Peterson for listening to every idea and reading the same chapters over and over, and Carol Fitzgerald at BookReporter.com for my gorgeous website and for always being in my corner.

To my ever-expanding family—you fill my life with joy and stuff to write about. To "the council"—thank you for the great company, cosmos, and soul-lifting laughter. To my lifelong friends—thank you for holding my history and helping me remember what matters most.

Writing a book about the bond between a mother and her children was an incredibly emotional journey for me. Along the way came the breathtaking recognition of the depth of love I have for my own sons and the vulnerability that love creates. I did my best to honor the power of these relationships while writing *Don't Look for Me*. Thank you Andrew, Ben, and Christopher for being such incredible young men, and for being on this journey with me.

CREDITS

Orion Fiction would like to thank everyone at Orion who worked on the publication of *Don't Look For Me* in the UK.

Editorial
Francesca Pathak
Lucy Frederick

Audio
Paul Stark
Amber Bates

Design
Debbie Holmes
Joanna Ridley
Nick May

Editorial Management
Charlie Panayiotou
Jane Hughes
Alice Davis

Production
Hannah Cox

Marketing
Tanjiah Islam

Publicity
Alainna Hadjigeorgiou

Finance
Jasdip Nandra
Afeera Ahmed
Elizabeth Beaumont
Sue Baker

Contracts
Anne Goddard
Paul Bulos
Jake Alderson

Sales
Jen Wilson
Esther Waters
Victoria Laws
Rachael Hum
Ellie Kyrke-Smith
Frances Doyle
Georgina Cutler

Operations
Jo Jacobs
Sharon Willis
Lisa Pryde
Lucy Brem